I0673115

Seven Miles from Destiny

Julia Scott

Copyright © 2018 by Julia Scott

All rights reserved.

No part of this book may be reproduced in any form or by any
electronic or mechanical means including information storage
and retrieval systems, without permission in writing from the
author. The only exception is by a reviewer, who may quote
short excerpts in a review.

This book is a work of fiction. Names, characters, places, and
incidents are the product of the author's imagination or are used
fictitiously. Any resemblance to actual events, locales, or
persons, living or dead, is coincidental.

Julia Scott
Visit my web page at juliascottbooks.com

Printed in the United States of America

ISBN-13: 978-1-7322333-0-0

ópeego publishing

This book is dedicated to Kelli, who makes everything possible. And to Walter, Kimmy, Julie, Bryan, and Jordan. You make life wonderful, wild, whimsical, and worth living!

CHAPTER 1

"Not baseball," groaned Addie as she watched Heather flip through TV channels from the couch in the living room. Addie scooped the thick icy margarita mixture from her blender into two giant glasses rimmed with salt.

"I just want to get a score," Heather said watching the game unfold.

Addie Butterfield walked out of her kitchen carrying the enormous drinks and had to step over her small dog, Mel, who was curled up on a pillow. "I hate to be the bearer of bad news, but he's out at second," she said sitting beside her friend.

"What are you talking about," asked Heather not taking her eyes off the screen.

"He's going to try to stretch a single into a double and be out at second."

The two women watched as the batter smashed a deep ball to the corner in left field. The ball careened off the wall and spun into the dirt completely fooling the outfielder. The first-base coach motioned the hitter to take second, but before he made it halfway there, the outfielder scooped up the ball and threw a frozen rope toward the infield. The second baseman one-hopped the throw and tagged the runner out at second.

Staring at the TV, Addie frowned. It was yet another example of the complete and utter uselessness of what should be a pretty remarkable gift. Heather looked at her and shook her head "How do you do that?" she asked throwing her hands up.

Addie raised her glass to her lips trying to hide her irritation. It was a question she'd been asking herself for almost 20 years.

"Just dumb luck, I guess," she said finally and shrugged. Addie had an unusual ability to know things before they happened. And while that sounded wonderful, it usually involved pretty mundane events. Knowing that a squirrel is about to run in front of your car or who the killer is just moments after the opening credits in the latest murder blockbuster was interesting, but not terribly useful. After all, it wasn't like she could summon a vision on command. They came when they came, simple as that.

"Well, next time you're feeling lucky, try it on something helpful. Like picking the winning lottery numbers." Heather said reaching for the glass Addie handed her.

"If I could do that, it would have happened by now,

trust me. Besides, what would I do then?"

"You could always give up teaching to live the rich and glamorous life. Imagine having more than thirty minutes to eat lunch," Heather said batting her eyelashes playfully.

Addie laughed. "You know I could never do that. I'd miss those little balls of hormones we call students. Besides, after I split my winnings with you, there might not be enough to retire on."

Addie smiled at Heather who muted the sound on the TV and sat back on the sofa. She always had a good time when she got together with Heather, and tonight was no exception. They had been teaching middle school together for the past six years. Heather was older than Addie by about seven years and was her best friend at the school.

"Speaking of teaching," Heather said turning her attention back to Addie, "I heard Josh Tanner telling Chris Sanchez that you yelled 'shut up' at Kimberly Nixon today. True, or vicious rumor?"

Addie rolled her eyes and took a sip of her drink. "I didn't say it to her," she said defensively. "Kimberly was reading her poem to the class, and my sainted mother took that opportunity to pop into my head and give me sage advice. I was politely asking her to please quiet down."

"Didn't anyone ever tell you that yelling at your mother, even when she's just in your head, is a sin?" Heather found it charming and a bit eccentric that Addie often had conversations with her mother in her head. "So, what was Mom saying this time?"

"She told me to just get on with my life and not worry about Bradley," Addie said with a sigh.

"Did you guys have a fight? I knew something was up because you've been kinda mopey lately, but I didn't want to pry," she said waiting for Addie to give her all the juicy details. Heather had been divorced for five years, and Addie knew she fancied herself as something of an expert in the flaws of men.

"Yes, we had a fight. It started with him not being a supportive boyfriend and ended with him sleeping with my roommate."

"What? Bradley is sleeping with Clara?" asked Heather, sitting up and pointing wide-eyed toward the cheating roommate's bedroom. "Did you kick her out?" she asked.

"They had already moved her stuff into his apartment before I even found out," answered Addie and downed a huge gulp of her drink, which gave her an immediate ice cream headache.

"When did this happen?" Heather asked her brow creased with concern.

"A couple of weeks ago," Addie said pinching the bridge of her nose to relieve the frozen pain.

"What an asshole. Make that two assholes!" snapped Heather.

"No argument here," said Addie as she stirred her slushy drink with a straw.

Heather patted Addie's hand comfortingly. "I'm so sorry."

"No biggie," Addie said unconvincingly and stood up. "I'm going to throw together a few nibbles for us.

Go ahead and watch your game."

"Can I help?" Heather offered as she unmuted the TV.

"I got it; it's nothing fancy," she said over her shoulder as Mel jumped up from his pillow and followed her into the kitchen. Addie leaned down to scratch him under his chin. "You going to help me, big guy?"

Mel was a small wire terrier that Addie had rescued from the pound. She had named him after Herman Melville when he took a liking to a stuffed white dolphin she had on her bed. It wasn't a whale, but Mel loved that toy and searched for it every day.

Addie pulled a large bowl out of a cabinet and frowned as she grabbed ingredients from the fridge. So much for psychic intuition, she thought irritably dumping a can of Rotel into the bowl with such force that it splattered on the counter. She could tell when a cat was about to sneeze, but she couldn't see a cheating boyfriend? Over the years, Addie tried to convince herself that she had just made up the whole "psychic" thing. But then she would call a pick six in football just moments before it happened. And she wasn't even that into sports!

Addie had never told anyone about her "special gift." Not even her family, none of whom seemed to have been anointed with psychic vision fairy dust. It was both miraculous and annoying. And, occasionally, it was life altering.

When she was about 15, Addie had a dream about her future. When she woke, she knew she had seen images of the life she would live. She was going to move to Texas where she would graduate from college and become a teacher. She would meet her husband there, and Addie knew all kinds of things about him. He was born in Texas, rode a white horse, was over six feet tall, had a master's degree, was a pretty good cook, and spoke a foreign language. And even though she couldn't tell what language he spoke, she knew it wasn't Spanish, which seemed weird because she assumed everyone spoke Spanish in Texas.

To a teenager from Connecticut, it had seemed completely outlandish. She wasn't even sure she wanted to get married. And she wanted to be an artist, not a teacher. Even so, she had written it all down and kept it hidden in her jewelry box. It was still there today, and Addie secretly checked each man she dated against her husband-to-be checklist. She had never met a man who met all of the criteria, and she was beginning to think she never would.

"No!" screeched Heather from the living room. "How do you miss that? Even I could have made that play!"

Addie smiled from the kitchen. "You OK in there?"

All she heard in return was frustrated grumbling, so she let it go.

Bradley had been a close match, Addie thought as she stirred the bowl of queso dip before shoving it back into the microwave. He was over six-feet tall, was an attorney—she figured law degree was the same thing as master's degree—and was from Texas. He had done some horseback riding when he was a kid. Addie had seen a picture of him on a pinto pony that had a large patch of white across it's middle. But he only spoke English and couldn't boil water. In a fit of desperation, she suggested they take French lessons and cooking classes, but he had refused.

A couple of weeks ago, she discovered that he was cheating on her with her roommate, so they broke up.

Another break up. Addie had dated a lot of men looking for her future husband and was growing ever frustrated by his lack of appearance. On more than one occasion, usually after a post-breakup margarita outing, she reread the list written in her teenage scribbling. She would tell herself just to throw it out, burn it, rip it to shreds. But she never did. She couldn't. Because she knew it was all true. Now, she wondered if that list would keep her from ever finding happiness.

So, at 27, she was living in Texas, had graduated from UNT in Denton, taught middle school English, and had just broken up with yet another man who failed to measure up to her adolescent psychic dream vision list. With a sigh, she piled food onto a tray and headed out to join Heather.

"Here we are," said Addie placing a large plate of appetizers between them. Glancing at the TV, she asked, "How's the game."

Heather picked up the remote and clicked off the set. "That should tell you how it's going," she said reaching for a jalapeño popper.

Still lost in thought, Addie sat on the wing chair across from the sofa and dunked a tostada chip into the bowl of queso.

Watching her, Heather leaned forward and said, "You OK?"

"I just don't know what I'm going to do now. Everything in my life suddenly seems magnified somehow. I feel like I'm running out of time."

"For?"

"Everything! To find a partner. To figure out what I really want to do. To make sense out of my life."

"You're only 27, silly. You have your whole life in front of you. You're young. You're gorgeous. What are you worried about?" Heath asked sipping her drink.

"My sister is only a year and a half older than me. She has a home, a career, a husband, kids. I don't have any of that."

"What do you mean? You have a career. You're an English teacher, and a great one at that."

"No I'm not! I had a student start a poem in class today with the phrase 'there once was a woman from Venus' before I could stop him. That's not a good teacher. I'm not good at anything—especially relationships."

"That's because you look at them all wrong. You're still waiting for your true love to ride up on a white stallion and whisk you away to his castle where you'll be fabulously rich and live happily ever after."

"Is that so much to ask?" Addie asked reaching for another chip.

"Well let's see how it's working so far. You followed your white knight from Connecticut to Denton to go to the University of North Texas, and he left you for his music career—he was an asshole, by the way. You dated that German guy, Gunther, for his big brain, and he left you to go work at a think tank in Switzerland—another asshole. You dated Stan because he made you laugh, and you dated Frank because he was a great dancer, but they both left you for each other! Now Bradley left you for your roommate."

"Is there a point coming anytime soon?" Addie tried but failed to keep the edge out of her voice.

"My point is, you've had many successful relationships. It's just they've been successful for other people." Heather giggled and reached for another popper, then leaned over and punched Addie's arm jokingly. "Learn from your mistakes and move on. Change your expectations. Look for something different. Don't keep hanging your hopes on the white horse. It doesn't exist!"

Addie sat for a second before adding, "For your information, I didn't really 'date' Stan or Frank; we were just friends."

"I think this is a perfect chance for you to just explore your options," Heather said between bites.

"I am so very tired of exploring my options," Addie said resting her elbows on her knees. "You know, I wanted to be an artist when I was younger. Like Mom. I tried too but I just wasn't any good. Then I wanted to be a writer. I even wrote a book—well started a book. I want to be a wife and lover. And mother. Maybe I should just accept the fact that true love is an illusion and settle for the first decent guy who comes along, and if that doesn't work out I'll trade him in for another model. That's what everyone else seems to do.

Why not me?"

Heather raised her drink and said, "That's the spirit! The best way to get over a man is to get under another one."

Addie shook her head and raised her glass with a smile.

CHAPTER 2

S everal hours later after the two women had finished off the pitcher of margaritas, Addie walked Mel to the mailboxes at the front of her enormous apartment complex. The night was clear with a whisper of a warm wind that flowed across her face and bare arms. She felt relaxed and ready for a good night's sleep, something she had not experienced in several weeks.

Addie could hear random voices coming from the pool area and saw the blue glow of televisions in the windows of several apartments. She passed one door that was open, and several college students were swaying to the beat of some sort of rap song as one young man in shorts and a muscle t-shirt kept punching the air while trying to "sing" what Addie assumed were the lyrics.

I really need to move, she thought. Addie had

decided to stay in the same apartment after college graduation because it was close to her teaching job and the rent was reasonable. Besides, she had always thought it was only temporary. She wanted to find a husband, buy a house, and make the "big" move instead of several small ones from one apartment to another. But here she was years later walking to the mailbox in an apartment complex that she had outgrown, alone and depressed.

The overhead light near the mailboxes was burned out, but Addie could see her box in the moonlight. She was just about to insert the key when she spotted what looked like an insect near the keyhole. Instinctively, she jumped back several steps, her heart beating so loudly she was afraid it might drown out the music, which was now a rock song from the '70s. Mel looked up at her and cocked his head. Even though no one was around to see her, Addie felt foolish. She'd had a mortal fear of bees since she was a child. Her parents had moved into a new house when she was about nine, and the first thing Addie did was rush to the swing set in the backyard. Her love of that swing, and the entire backyard for that matter was short lived when a huge yellow jacket nest fell on top of her head. Her father had rushed to her aid quickly, but she was stung several times. The incident had scarred her ever since, and now, here she was, frozen in fear over what may or may not be a bee near her mailbox.

Finally, the insect flew off into the darkness, and Addie could see its soft yellow-green glow against the night sky. It's a firefly, she thought, her knees almost collapsing under the weight of her relief. She watched the tiny flashing light and wondered where it had come from. She stared until she could no longer see the glowing light, then turned to get the mail. Tasty food and cold margaritas had her craving the soft comfort of bed.

Mel was still staring at her, and she grinned. "You would have saved me from the big bad firefly, wouldn't you?" She cooed the words at him, and he wagged his tail happily. "Come on, mutt. Let's get back."

Addie walked into the bedroom and kicked off her utilitarian brown flats. She pulled the light pink polo shirt over her head and peeled off her khaki pants leaving them crumpled on the floor of her room. She had what most people would consider a slim athletic build, which to her just meant her breasts were too small. Peering at herself in the bathroom mirror, she grimaced. Strands of white-blonde hair had escaped her pony tail and now hung haphazardly about her face. She pulled the lime-green band from behind her head and let her hair fall loosely in soft waves around her face and shoulders. Usually, she kept it much longer, but she had impulsively cut it to just below shoulder length about a month ago. She was getting used to it and even enjoyed the fullness of her shorter hair.

Looking at her reflection now, she found the face staring back at her almost disturbingly unfamiliar. They were her round, glossy blue eyes outlined by long black lashes, but there was no life behind them. And the smile that she had used to win more than her fair share of arguments over the years was missing.

Taking a deep, ragged breath, she turned away from the mirror to wash her face and pull a short nightshirt over her head. Addie fixed herself a tall glass of water, took an aspirin to ward off any morning headaches, and settled into bed to sort the mail. Mel jumped up and curled into a ball at her side.

A hand-addressed envelope dropped from the stack she was about to toss into the garbage, and Addie looked at the return address to see who sent it. "Woodrow Dudley, Attorney at Law," Addie read aloud, "in Destiny, Texas." It's probably just an ad to get me to create a will or a living trust or whatever attorneys charge people to do, she thought. But something about the writing on the envelope and the fact that it was from someone out in West Texas made her open it.

Inside was a short note written in the same handwriting that was on the envelope.

Dear Ms. Butterfield;

I am the legal representative for Stella Pennington and am writing to inform you that she named you the executor of her estate in her last will and testament. I have been unable to locate a telephone number for you and would appreciate it if you would please contact my office at your earliest convenience.

Thank you for your assistance in this matter.

Sincerely;
Woody Dudley
Attorney at Law

Aunt Stella? Aunt Stella named her to be the executor of her estate? Addie had not seen nor had any contact with Stella Pennington for about 20 years. She couldn't even remember what the woman looked like. And she was her executor? What exactly is an executor? Too tired to think about it, Addie decided it would wait until morning when, at the very least, she might have a clearer head. She turned out the light, laid her head on the pillow, and fell sound asleep with mail scattered around her like leaves on a forest floor.

Saturday morning came sooner than a cranky Addie would have liked. Although the aspirin she took before bed probably helped, she woke with a dull pounding in her head. She sat up slowly and closed her eyes against the insultingly cheerful midmorning sun that was blasting through her window. So much for having a clearer head in the morning, she thought wincing grumpily. She stood up to make her way to the kitchen, her unruly hair swirling about her head.

"What are you looking at?" she grumbled at Mel as she made her way to the kitchen.

After preparing a piece of wheat toast and coffee and revisiting the aspirin bottle, Addie shuffled back to the bedroom and sat on the bed. She picked up the envelope from the attorney and reread the letter while sipping her coffee. Since she hadn't talked to her mother in a couple of weeks—at least not outside of her own head—Addie decided to call her and see if she could shed some light on the Stella mystery.

"Addie, darling, how are you doing?"

"I'm great Mom. How are you and Dad?"

"You know, we're getting by just fine. Your father is working on a new symphony, so he's been spending hours in his studio. Oh, and he's been asked to guest conduct in Vermont, so we'll be going in late September. I'm insanely busy at the college. The new gallery will be opening in about a month, and there's still so much to do. We're hardly ever home lately; you're lucky you caught me. I was just about to run out to check on a few pieces we'll have on loan from the Robinson Collection."

Addie sat quietly and waited for her mother to hand the conversation back to her. She had learned over the years that it was best to let her mother talk about whatever was going on and not ask any questions unless she could devote at least an hour to the call. Addie loved her mother, truly she did, but sometimes their chats left her feeling a bit deflated. It's not that she was overly negative or directly critical, but the thinly veiled digs at her single lifestyle were tiring.

"By the way, Janet called just yesterday," her mother continued. This was Addie's cue to jump in.

"Really? How's she doing?" Janet was Addie's older sister, the "good" daughter who had an interesting career as a photographer, a husband who made a very comfortable living as a financial consultant, and two adorable children. She and Addie had always gotten along well as kids, and it was easy for Addie to admire her sister's life, even if she was a tiny bit jealous of it.

"Well, she's fabulous as always. They were here last

weekend and brought the grandbabies. They're growing up so fast! We all had a wonderful time together—I wish you could have been here too. That would have made it perfect."

There it was, a little dig about living all the way across the country. Although it was almost too subtle to notice, Addie felt a small twinge in her heart nonetheless. She let it go and said, "I'm sorry I missed it, but I'm calling for a reason. I got a letter from a lawyer in Destiny, and apparently, Aunt Stella passed away."

"Oh really, that is sad news. She was a nice woman and especially fond of you. I don't think we ever told you that you were named Addison because she helped deliver you when you were born. Her middle name was Addison."

"You're kidding? I thought I was named after a great grandmother or something."

"No, she was there when you were born, and your father and I were swept up in appreciation. You were almost born in the car that night. Thank God we found her when we did."

"Wow, that's amazing. Is that why we went to see her when I was eight?"

"You remember that? You had such a great time running around her ranch. After you were born there at her house, she felt a real connection to you. I think the name had something to do with it. And she didn't have any children of her own. I guess living alone all those years, somehow, she felt you were part of her family—the family she didn't have in life."

"I'm supposed to call this lawyer and help settle her estate."

"She named you her executor? That's a great honor, and it brings you two full circle—she helped bring you into this world, and you'll help send her out.

"But Mom, I don't know anything about being an executor. I mean, what am I supposed to do?"

"Honey, the lawyer will handle all of the legal stuff and can tell you what needs to be done. If you've got the time this summer, you ought to do this. I know it would mean a lot to her, and besides I'm sure you won't have any other travel plans."

Dig number two delivered. Take time to help an old woman—ignore your mom.

"I guess I will take care of it then. Thanks for the advice—I know I can always count on you for practical advice. I love you mom. Give dad a big hug and kiss from me."

Addie hung up the phone and laid back against her pillows. She knew she should have told her mom about Bradley but her head was hurting and she would still be broken up with him the next time they talked.

"Aunt Stella and Destiny, Texas. The adventure begins!" Addie rolled over and pulled the covers over her head.

CHAPTER 3

nderson was sitting in a large cushioned wicker chair on his front porch with his border collie Festus. Both were staring down the quarter-mile drive that led to his home, a sprawling one-story house that sat toward the front of his expansive ranch. It had a definite Texas flair with its white-stone exterior, chunky cedar beams, and enormous metal star that hung proudly on the front face. He had lived there since he was a child, and now that both his parents were gone, he and his second wife, Cora, whom he made sure was away on this particular day, called it home.

He took another puff on his cigar and then froze when he noticed the dust cloud made by a line of heavily armored black Range Rovers coming up the dirt drive. Festus stood and growled at the approaching parade. Usually, he was left free to roam the property, but today he was restrained by a leash that kept him confined to the porch.

Anderson knew who was coming. The short phone call he had received on his business phone yesterday said simply, "We need to talk. I'll arrive tomorrow at noon."

Yes, he knew who it was.

Anderson was accustomed to being the one in charge. Judge, rancher, former town mayor, and major land owner had been part of his story for the past forty years, making him one of, if not the, most powerful men in Destiny, Texas, and the surrounding areas. Nothing about this surprise visit made him comfortable, and Anderson was accustomed to being comfortable.

Even though he knew he was a big fish in a somewhat smallish pond, he enjoyed the power and prestige his life had brought him. But the line of cars coming up the drive changed all that. Even a big fish can be eaten by an even bigger fish.

He knew who was about to make this rare house call, and it was a very big fish indeed.

Anderson's mouth was dry as he stood stiffly to meet the arriving vehicles. About 20 armed men poured from the cars creating a security perimeter around the middle vehicle. A stocky, fifty-year-old man with a short but full mustache climbed out confidently and dusted off his pants as an assistant closed the car door behind him. The man was dressed in a well-tailored dark navy suit, crisp white shirt, and a green and red striped tie. He paused and adjusted his sunglasses before walking toward the house.

Anderson had good reason for being nervous. Dario Chavez was a notoriously dangerous man with whom Anderson had a long-term, but until now, distant relationship. Dario's nickname was "Muerte Ruidosa" or "Noisy Death," because of his reputation for making loud, gratuitous examples of his enemies.

"Dario, what a nice surprise," said Anderson walking down the porch steps and extending his hand. Festus barked loudly and strained at his leash. "Please come on in. I've got cold beers for everyone inside the house."

Chavez stood motionless sending a very clear message that this was not a social call. Anderson withdrew his hand awkwardly and tried again. "Would you like to come in where it's cooler?"

Festus continued to bark and growl, and Anderson turned to admonish the dog and hopefully quiet him down.

"He does not seem to obey you," said Chavez evenly. A flurry of shots rang out just behind Anderson's head. A high-pitched yelp and moan followed in quick succession, and Anderson jerked watching Festus fall in a bloody heap, his life force oozing across the porch boards. The dog's eyes stared hollowly at Anderson.

"Perhaps that will help."

With his ears still ringing, Anderson turned back to see the barrel of a nine-millimeter Beretta pointed at his face. "Let's go inside unless you wish to die on your front porch." Chavez walked past Anderson and the lifeless dog and motioned toward his men. Four of them escorted Anderson into the house while the remaining men took up guard around the grounds.

This was only the second time Anderson had met anyone from the Chavez family in person. The first was more than thirty years before when Dario's father had approached him about a business arrangement. Anderson had been a new judge at the time, and the relationship was simple and extremely lucrative. Judge Anderson looked the other way while the Chavez family operated a drug smuggling operation through West Texas. Over the years, their enterprise had grown and was now a major drug and human trafficking empire. Anderson had done what he could to keep the actual town of Destiny out of harm's way, but that was becoming harder to do now that Dario was running the business.

Today, the Chavez syndicate had an increasingly violent reputation. The judge knew that Dario's conversations usually ended badly for whomever he visited—often much worse than a slain dog. And, Anderson knew why he was here, and that had him worried.

The group entered the living room and casually sat down on the enormous leather sofas like they were just finishing a Sunday after-church fried-chicken social luncheon. The room was spacious with expensive but tasteful décor and solid wood flooring. But no one was here to admire the furnishings.

Anderson sat stiffly trying desperately to think, but fear choked his brain. One of Chavez's men returned from the kitchen with a couple of beers and placed them in front of the two men as Chavez spoke.

"Anderson, I am here in person out of respect for your position in the community and your history with my father. You have been a very reliable partner for many years, and you have profited from your relationship with my family," he reached for his beer while Anderson sat without moving.

"I must express my disappointment that when we asked you to secure the property known as the Destiny Ranch, you failed to do so. I understand the owner has recently died. My family is insistent that you obtain the property immediately." Chavez spoke casually as though he were asking a neighbor if he could borrow his lawn mower. But there was nothing casual about this conversation, and Anderson knew it.

"I tried to get the owner to sell me the place, but she refused," said the Judge immediately regretting the comment.

"You cannot handle an old woman?" Chavez chuckled, and his men joined him. "What kind of man are you? No, no, Anderson. It was a simple task and something you should have completed a long time ago. You do understand we are not asking you to do this but rather telling you that this will be done. You do know the difference, yes?"

"Yes, I understand," said Anderson dryly.

"Our family is making a move into food production. You know, tomatoes, peppers, onions— that sort of thing. And we are building very large greenhouses. We need the water on that property for the plants to grow. No property, no water, no greenhouses, no food. Do you see the problem?"

Anderson looked at him carefully, not sure how to reply. "You want to grow vegetables? Why would you want to do such a thing?" Realizing his question was a mistake, Anderson sat quietly holding his breath.

Chavez smiled under his mustache, but his eyes remained fixed on Anderson. "Why do you speak to me as if I am your gardener?" He said the words softly.

Anderson hurried to correct his blunder. "Dario, I meant no—"

Chavez held his hand out to silence him. "I'm sure you meant no disrespect. Let me explain. We want the water, and you will get it for us. This is a very remote location and an excellent place to grow all kinds of vegetation. So, you see, we require that you secure the property for us. We thought you understood that when we make a request, we expect it to be fulfilled."

Anderson understood completely. Thirty years of bribes and overturned convictions were catching up with him. How could this have happened?

"Dario, I have been faithful to your family for years. I've done everything you've asked. But growing drugs, manufacturing them right here, it's dangerous for our town. If you give me a little time, I know I can find you a secluded location out at Richards Reservoir. It's only 50 miles or so from here—"

A bullet flew past Anderson's face and into the wall behind him with a loud crack. Chavez lowered the gun.

He stood and moved toward Anderson. "I don't give a flying fuck what you think about our plans, and

I am not asking for your business advice. We own you. The only reason you've got a pot to piss in is because my father had a soft spot for you. I'm not my father, and I won't tolerate any further delays. We've buried more than 100 bodies in your backyard. The only reason you are still walking around is because you do your job and keep your mouth shut. Once you stop doing your job..." Chavez pressed the gun directly on Anderson's temple, the heat from the barrel singeing his flesh.

"We put you in a position to produce. We paid you well, and we even let you have a taste of our businesses in the area. Public water won't work for us. We want the Destiny Ranch. You'll do what I ask, or I will be forced to find someone who will. And that will require us to tie up loose ends—like you, your wife, and son." Chavez had raised his voice and now glared directly at Anderson.

"They don't know anything about my business," said Anderson with wide eyes, his voice cracking.

"That may be true, but we're not the kind of organization to take that chance. We'll burn down your house with you and your family in it. If I have to come back here, I'll cut off your wife's head and fuck her dead corpse while you and your son watch. Then I'll burn you alive, and the last images of your sad pathetic life will be watching everyone you love die."

Chavez stood up and downed the rest of his beer. He set the empty bottle politely on the coffee table.

"You have three weeks to buy the property or you and your family are dead."

Chavez walked out the front door, and his men followed him.

Anderson watched them from his front window and only walked out to the porch when the dust from the SUVs had settled. He looked down at his dog in disbelief. The urge to put his head in his hands and weep was almost overwhelming, but he knew he couldn't afford to waste time.

Before taking care of his beloved dog, he strode inside and picked up the phone.

"Manuel, I need you up at the house." Anderson ended the call and dialed another number.

"Law office," said a voice on the other end.

"Woody Dudley, please." Anderson waited for less than half a minute before he heard the familiar voice.

"Anderson, how nice to hear from you. What can I do for you?"

"Well now, I hate to do this so soon after her death, but I'd like to extend an offer to buy the Destiny Ranch from whoever will be handling that. I know I've spoken to you about this before with Stella, but I've had a bit of a change in my plans. I'm prepared to sweeten my offer significantly."

CHAPTER 4

It was early evening before Addie made it into Destiny. She squinted at a green road sign and followed its helpful arrow instructing her to exit the highway and then turn right. With a small sigh of relief, she tugged her sunglasses off her face and massaged her temples. After driving for hours heading directly into a giant fireball, she was all too happy to head in any other direction.

"The sun indeed sets in the west!" she mumbled to herself.

When Addie had spoken to Mr. Dudley on the phone, he seemed excited that she had agreed to handle the estate and was insistent that she come out to Destiny to take care of Stella's affairs in person.

"It's really the best way," he had assured her in a voice that was both robust and soft-spoken at the same time. "These things always go more quickly and smoothly when people can talk face-to-face about what needs to be done."

Addie had agreed easily since school would be out in a week and she had the time to take a trip. It might be like a small vacation, she had told herself. But now that she was almost there, Addie was thinking perhaps she should have gotten more information before she agreed to drive for seven hours with little more than sketchy maps printed off the Internet and some hand-written directions. She wasn't even sure where she would spend the night.

Mel, who had been curled up in his crate sleeping peacefully the entire trip, stood up and stretched as the car slowed and turned the corner. "We're getting close, boy," Addie turned around to check on him, and he answered her with a high-pitched bark, his way of requesting a potty break. "Not just yet, sweetie," she said turning back to the road. "I just have to make sure I know where I am first."

Her surroundings were becoming somewhat less rural, which Addie took as a good sign that she was headed in the generally correct direction. How hard could it be really? She found the hand-written directions she had scribbled on the back of one of the maps during her phone conversation with Mr. Dudley. She was supposed to turn off the interstate onto FM 1226, pass Tony's Texaco and then turn left on Main St. Was she on FM 1226? She hadn't seen a sign, but that didn't mean it hadn't been there. She let out a frustrated sigh and tried to pay closer attention. Glancing again at the directions, she saw she had written "10 miles" off to the side, but now she couldn't remember why she had thought it was important enough to write down.

"Addie, Addie, Addie," she scolded herself with a groan. Following maps and directions had never been her forte and she silently hoped she had not gotten herself lost out here in the middle of nowhere. She passed an abandoned metal building on her right and saw what looked like a gas station up in the distance. Hoping it was the elusive Tony's station, she drove on with purpose completely missing the breathtaking splash of color the sun painted across the desert landscape. Instead, she let out a small "yes!" when she saw the landmark she had been seeking. Main Street was easy to spot on the left, and after she turned, it wasn't but a few minutes before she found herself at the town square.

It was just after six, so she had a little bit of time before she was supposed to meet the attorney. She drove around the square in search of his office so she would know where she was supposed to meet him. Addie had always loved the town square in Denton and spent many nights and weekends poking through shops, having a drink with friends, or listening to live music in front of the courthouse. It gave the city a quaint small-town feel that she loved. Now, driving around the Destiny square, she had the same sense of calm and quiet. She passed a couple of antique shops, several offices of local lawyers and businessmen, and an appliance store that was closed up for the day. A stunning courthouse that resembled a stately southern manor with reddish brick, shiny white trim, and a grand staircase leading up the front of the building stood proudly in the middle of the square. The entire scene was picturesque and peaceful, and Addie could feel some of the tension in her shoulders begin to ebb.

It had been a long trip, and she was dying to get out of the car and stretch as much as Mel. On the corner, she saw a little diner called The Hushpuppy Café. "Perfect," she said aloud remembering the advice her father had told her on one of their family trips. "When you're in a small town, go to the restaurant on the town square. It's where most of the locals eat, and the food is usually great."

She parked near a patch of grass and let Mel take care of his business. She was careful to scoop up after him even though she had the feeling that folks around here would find her big city behavior more comical than conscientious. She filled Mel's little water bowl, and the dog drank thirstily. Then she gave him a chew bone, rolled down the windows, and tucked him back in his crate before going into the restaurant.

The Hushpuppy was a typical diner with photos on the wall of the famous and semi-famous celebrities who had eaten there. Newspaper clippings of local events and history; pictures of the local high school football teams and cheerleaders; and the obligatory family photo of the owner, his wife, and favorite hunting dog, peppered the walls. It looked like the café had been a corner drug store years before because the wood floors were old and uneven and a large counter and old glass freezer stood against the back wall.

A sign near the front door told customers to "please seat yourself," so Addie slid into a small booth near the front. Looking around, she saw that only a few of the tables and booths were occupied, mostly with elderly couples. One table held a family with two young children and a baby who was sleeping peacefully in a baby carrier perched on a chair next to the mother who ate with one hand and rocked the baby with the other.

Everyone seemed to have stopped at the same time to turn and watch her. She felt like a new student who had joined school in the middle of the year. Feeling her cheeks warm slightly, she unfolded one of the menus stuck between a ketchup bottle and salt and pepper shakers and decided to order a Dr. Pepper and a plate of nachos figuring this place would know how to do both of them well enough.

Addie looked up again when she heard a brisk clicking on the wooden floors and saw a young woman approaching her with a glass of ice water and a straw. The girl was wearing blue jeans and a red T-shirt that had The Hushpuppy logo on it, but instead of the comfortable shoes you would expect a busy waitress to wear, she had on pointy-toed red pumps with about three-inch heels. An apron cinched around her tiny waist revealed an exceptionally thin frame, which was offset by abundant breasts that were straining against the shirt and peeking out the top.

Addie was not sure she had ever seen so much make-up on one face before. Although the fake eyelashes seemed enormous, they still did not quite conceal the blue eye shadow sparkling behind them.

Her huge eyes were offset by a wide mouth that was painted fire-engine red, and her brown hair was pulled back into a massive ponytail that had Addie wondering how she could hold her head up. She was probably in her mid-20's, but her exaggerated features made it hard for Addie to guess her exact age.

"What'll you have honey?" she asked with great enthusiasm, setting the water in front of Addie.

"I think I'll just have a Dr. Pepper and a plate of nachos," answered Addie.

"Hhmm," the waitress hesitated and pursed her lips with concern. She placed a hand on the table and leaned forward as though about to share a secret. "I think that might be a mistake. You see Junior went out to Overton this afternoon, and TJ is handlin' the cookin'. All that poor boy knows how to cook is hamburgers. If you order nachos, he might have a stroke or somethin'."

Addie continued to stare at the woman who had yet to blink but had now straightened up and pulled her order book from her apron and removed a pink pen from her ponytail.

"Ummm," was all Addie could seem to utter.

"I'm just trying to tell you that I would suggest you order a burger unless you want to leave hungry. If dumb was dirt, 'ol TJ would cover about an acre." She looked at Addie as though there was nothing wrong with telling a customer what to order. "By the way my name is Marsha, and it's nice to meet you, Addison Butterfield."

"How do you know my name?" asked Addie too

stunned to be angry.

"Well, I saw you drive up in that German doodlebug, and everyone in town is expecting you today," said Marsha. "But I'd have to say that name badge danglin' out of your purse was my best clue."

Addie reached for her purse and hastily stuffed her school ID back in. "What do you mean everyone is expecting me?"

"Oh, you're pretty big news around here. It's not every day that one of our town founders dies, and when she did everyone started looking to see who would come to claim her. I guess that'll be you," Marsha stated matter-of-factly. "It's a small town, and everyone knows just about everything—especially the important stuff like you."

"Is that right? I didn't know anyone was expecting me. Actually, you probably knew my godmother better than me. I haven't seen her for about 20 years now," responded Addie a bit flustered by both the familiar tone and complete lack of discretion of someone she had just met. Folding the menu she continued, "I guess I'll have a hamburger then."

"Great choice! I'll put that right in for you. And by the way, I'm sorry about your godmother, "Marsha patted her hand. "She was a really sweet lady. We're all going to miss her." Then she turned and clacked her way back to the kitchen.

Wonderful, Addie thought, the whole town is expecting me. She wondered how many of the people in the diner had come to the same conclusion about her as Marsha had. She suddenly felt like a prize pig at the state fair and hoped desperately that her business in town would conclude quickly so she could leave and never be seen again.

Addie got up from her table still stiff from the long drive and wandered over to the glass freezer in the back of the diner. It was full of an odd assortment of items. There was what appeared to be an albino squirrel sitting next to a baseball signed by Tom Landry. A picture of several WWI soldiers sitting under a tree was propped up next to an old military style canteen. There were a couple of pistols, a rifle, and a basketball that read "State Champions 1964."

Marsha walked up while Addie was looking at the strange collection.

"What's all this?" she asked.

"Oh don't even bother with this junk. Some of that stuff is just made up. Like that baseball. Tom Landry was a high school kid about 15 years ago, and Junior thought it was funny to have him sign a ball. And that squirrel is just a tube sock with some string and cotton on it. The whole thing is a mess, but Junior loves it, and he keeps dreamin' up new things to add to it. He thinks it'll be fun for tourists, like we ever get any around here."

"I don't know some of it is interesting. Like that jar of bull farts," Addie said with a smile.

"Oh dear, that's real. Don't never open that," joked Marsha before bursting into laughter. She handed Addie an icy-cold glass of Dr. Pepper with a straw sticking out the top of it. "Here, you start with this, and I'll be back in a minute with your burger."

She sat down and wondered about Marsha and her life. Small towns had always fascinated Addie, and she couldn't image what it would be like to live in a place that was hundreds of miles from the conveniences she took for granted. What would it be like to go to the store and buy the jar of spaghetti sauce they sell instead of driving to three different strip malls to find the brand that had sun-dried tomatoes, roasted red peppers, and sweet basil? Would she find it relaxing or restricting?

Her thoughts were interrupted by Marsha returning with an enormous hamburger and a generous serving of thick-cut steak fries on a platter. She set the plate in front of Addie and slid into the seat across from her.

"So, tell me all about Dallas. I heard you were from Dallas, and I'd just love to go there sometime. I hate to say it, but I've never been more'n a hundred miles from this booth."

"Well, I'm not really from Dallas. I live in Denton, which is about 40 miles north. And I grew up in Connecticut. But I've been to Dallas many times, and I like it a lot," Addie replied as she squirted ketchup onto her plate. "My name is Addie by the way."

"Nice to meet you, Addie, I'm Marsha. Marsha Brady. And before you say it...yes, it's like the TV show. My mother loved The Brady Bunch and swore she would name her oldest daughter Marsha. Just my luck she married a man named Brady."

Addie stared at her to judge whether she was joking, but Marsha's straightforward tone made her think she was telling the truth. Besides, who would make up something like that?

"That's amazing!" Addie finally replied. She picked up a French fry and gestured for Marsha to help herself.

"And that's not the half of it. My father promised his dying grandmother he would name his first daughter after her too. That was Grandma Dorcus, and it makes me Marsha Dorcus Brady!" Marsha shook her head and reached for one of Addie's fries.

Again, Addie found herself at a loss for words. "Well, I bet you never met anyone else with the same name," she finally said trying to sound comforting.

"True enough. What makes it even worse, if you can image anything worse, is that I have brothers named Greg, Peter, and Bobby. Now, little Bobby is a twin and they named the other twin Sam because it was a good Christian name and was also my daddy's brother's name. It was weeks later that Mama finally remembered that the butcher's name on The Brady Bunch is also Sam. From then on she thought it meant that Sam had some greater purpose in life, otherwise why would the Lord have guided her to name him Sam?" Marsha confided all of this matter-of-factly while Addie worked hard to look interested rather than dumbfounded.

"So, are you just getting to town?" Marsha continued grabbing another fry. "Have you been out to Stella's place yet?"

"I did just get to town. I was planning to head out to her place tonight," Addie picked up her burger and changed the subject, not wanting to talk about herself.

"Do you like living in Destiny?"

"I've been here so long I guess I'm just used to it. There ain't no good men, awful weather and the best thing to do here is …well there's nothing really to do around here. That's why I decided to be local color."

"Local color?" asked Addie.

"You know that one person in town everyone always talks about when they leave. I figured since I had the name for it I'd take the job too. I like being flamboyant," she said raising her arm with a flourish. Addie had to smile at this.

"I say ridiculous things like, 'Never kick a fresh turd on a hot day' and stuff like that. It started when I was a kid, and now I don't think I could stop if I wanted to. But I seem to use them more often that I probably should," explained Marsha. "It's like my daddy says, 'Lettin' the cat outta the bag is a whole mess easier'n puttin' it back in.'"

"I think I'm gunna cotton to you, Marsha Brady," Addie said in her best West Texas drawl.

"Me too Miss Butterfield, it's a pleasure to make your acquaintance," replied Marsha with perhaps the worst northern accent ever attempted in The Hushpuppy Café. With a smile, she returned to the kitchen, and Addie finished her amazingly tasty burger.

At least TJ can make a good burger, she thought as she wrapped the last few bites in a napkin for Mel.

Before she walked out, Addie left money for the check and a nice big tip for her first friend in Destiny.

CHAPTER 5

Addie left The Hushpuppy and took Mel for a short walk across the square to a small three-story skinny building with a free-hanging sign that read "Dudley Legal Services" written in old western looking letters. Mr. Dudley had insisted they meet before she went out to Stella's place, even though Addie told him she couldn't be there before early evening.

"Don't you worry about it," he assured her. "This was real important to Stella. I can stay late."

The law office was in the middle of the block and appeared to be only about half the size of the other nearby storefronts. The extremely small width gave the structure a very narrow appearance, more of a slice than a space. She turned the antique pewter handle on the heavy wooden door. A bell attached to the door frame jingled a friendly greeting as she and Mel entered the modest lobby. A hurricane lantern sitting on a table near the entrance was the only source of light, but it gave the tight space a coziness that was quite comforting. A tufted chair upholstered in a dark striped pattern, a brown leather love seat, and a small butler table that held an odd assortment of magazines were the only other furnishings in the tiny waiting area.

"Hello," called Addie, "is anyone here?" No reply was forthcoming, so she decided to try again. "HELLO!" she called a bit more forcefully, but still nothing. There was another wooden door at the back of the narrow room, and Addie knocked on it several times. Again, no answer.

For a minute, she wondered if she had gotten the day and time wrong, but the fact that the door was open and a light was on made her think maybe Mr. Dudley had just stepped out for a minute. Deciding to wait, she took a seat on the sofa and called Mel, who lay down next to her feet on the green floral area rug having sniffed every inch of the room to the limit of his leash.

She reached for one of the dusty magazines stacked on the table and read "National Geographic July 1973."

"It's older than I am!" She laughed out loud, and Mel sat up to stare at her. She was flipping through the yellowed pages still smiling when the back-interior door burst open, startling both Addie and Mel, who jumped up with an anxious bark. A portly, red-headed man filled the doorway, his smile hidden behind a great bushy mustache.

"Didn't mean to startle you. I'm Woody Dudley, and you must be Ms. Butterfield," he said stretching out a thick hand in greeting. "Sorry I'm late. I was upstairs in the file room and didn't hear you come in."

Addie's smile was friendly as she took his hand. "Not a problem. Please, call me Addie."

"Only if you call me Woody," he said hitching up his baggy brown slacks. His short-sleeved dress shirt was a bit rumpled showing signs of a long day, and Addie thought she spotted what appeared to be a small mustard stain on his striped tie. "And who's this little fella?" he asked reaching down to scratch Mel's head.

"This is Mel. Short for Melville. I named him after Herman Melville," Addie told him wondering why she threw out that detail.

"How clever. And does he chase after whales?" Woody was now scratching Mel's belly while the little dog all but purred in satisfaction.

"Actually, he has a stuffed whale – well, dolphin really. It was mine, but he claimed it for himself when he was a puppy, so…" Addie stood up wondering how Mr. Dudley would feel about having a dog in his office. "I hope you don't mind me bringing him in. I didn't want to leave him in the car."

"Of course, of course. Not a problem," Woody said as he motioned her into the back. He led her down a narrow hallway and into a room on the right as he continued to chatter away.

"I completely understand about people and their pets. I once wrote a will for a woman's cat." Addie looked at him skeptically as she entered the room, and he continued. "It's true. Of course, I didn't charge her. She was a friend of the family, so I couldn't really refuse. You come across some strange stuff being a lawyer."

The room was obviously his office and a well-used office at that. A row of bookcases monopolized one wall of the room. Each shelf was completely stuffed full of books, leather-bound briefs, and three-ring binders. A massive ornate wooden desk stood proudly in front of the bookcases facing the door. A pile of folders and papers nearly a foot high were stacked on one side of it, while a green desk lamp, pen and pencil holder, and laptop computer took up the remaining space.

"Did you have a good trip?" Woody asked following Addie through the door.

"It was fine, but I got a bit tired driving into the sun all day."

"If you live out here long enough you get used to it. That's about all we have—a big, bright sun—all day, everyday. I swear, God must have come to Destiny one day, and that's when he invented sunglasses!" Woody chuckled and put his hands on one of the two overstuffed chairs that sat opposite his desk. "Here, have yourself a seat," he said moving to sit behind the desk.

Addie kept Mel on a tight leash, not wanting him to soil something valuable. The room was about ten times larger than the lobby, and everything in it appeared to be an antique of some sort. A gun case full of ancient-looking rifles hung on a wall, and an enormous map that was equally old and framed in elaborate gold-leaf took up most of the wall next to the door. The atmosphere was easy and friendly, just like the man behind the desk, and Addie could feel some of her earlier apprehension begin to fade away.

"This building is quite unique," Addie remarked thinking how small it looked from outside and how spacious it now felt.

"I know what you're thinkin'—tiny entrance, narrow hall, small West Texas town, country bumpkin lawyer."

"No, no, no. Not at all," Addie said quickly. Her eyes widened in shock and embarrassment but relaxed when she saw the teasing grin beneath the heavy mustache.

"That's all right. I think you'll find Destiny has more than meets the eye sometimes. I own the entire block. The ice cream parlor, the antique shop, the music store, they all rent space from me. And when Sally Parker— she runs the general store next door to me—when she needed extra room for her inventory, I chopped this space in half. Works out well; I didn't really need all that space for my practice anyway. I keep that lobby area the same as it was when Daddy had his practice here. It helps me remember that there's more to life than work. He died right here in this room."

Woody seemed to think nothing of telling a client that she was sitting in a room in which a man had died. Were all of the people in Destiny so open with their thoughts?

"I'm sorry," Addie said softly.

"It was several years ago. I'm just sorry you have to deal with Stella's estate. She was a magnificent woman—one of the truly great people in this world. We are really going to miss her. I know you said you weren't close when we spoke on the phone, but let me tell you, she adored you. She spoke of you often."

"She did?" Addie was surprised that she had so impacted the life of a woman she had really only met once as a child.

"Oh, yes," he continued. "As part of her will, I have been instructed to give you this letter. I don't know what's inside, but she told me it would be all you need to get going on settling her estate."

Woody handed a sealed large envelope to Addie. "Should I open it here?"

"Please do. I've wondered what's inside it for 20 years now."

Addie tore open the flap of the brown envelope and unhooked the brass clasp. She pulled out a hand-written letter, a key, and what appeared to be a map from inside.

She looked at the letter. The handwriting was smooth and elegant with a uniform slant to the words, and it appeared to have been written with a steady hand. As an English teacher, she was pleasantly impressed. Addie read the letter silently:

Dearest Addie;

I know this must be quite a shock to you. Not only am I writing to you from beyond the grave, but a virtual stranger has named you to be the executor of my estate. Mr. Dudley will help you with all the details regarding my affairs and will take care of anything you might need while staying in Destiny.

I have enclosed a map of the grounds at the Destiny Ranch and a key to my house. I don't usually keep it locked, but since I am not there to open the door for you, I thought this might come in handy.

I have left a gift for you in the nightstand next to my bed. I won't provide greater detail, but it is something you might find useful while trying to decide what to do with my things. I died with no children and no family. The only connection I have to this world is you, and I am confident you will do the right thing by me.

And remember, I will be watching.

All my dearest love;
Aunt Stella

Addie stared at the letter for a moment, then looked up at Woody. "You've had this for 20 years?"

"Yes, I've had it locked in my safe all that time."

Addie handed the letter to Woody so he could read it for himself. She shivered slightly at the thought of a woman writing about her own death in such an unemotional manner. The fact that she had not seen the need to change anything in the envelope for so many years was a bit eerie.

"She wants you to stay at the house this evening," Woody said as he finished reading the letter.

"I guess so." That had been Addie's plan until she read the letter. Now, she wasn't so sure.

"Oh, I know so. She gave me a note to attach to her

will, and it instructed me to make sure you stayed at her house your first night in town." Woody grinned as though he was proud of the fact that he could carry out Stella's directions. "She marched to the beat of her own drummer," he added with a chuckle.

"Well…" Again, Addie felt slightly hesitant, but she had to admit she was also curious. What had Stella left for her?

Sensing that she was about to agree, Woody continued. "I've made arrangements for all the utilities to remain on for your stay. After you've had a chance to look the place over, let's get together, and I can talk you through the whole probate process. Here's my card," Woody said handing her one of his cream-colored business cards. Addie was surprised to see both a cell phone number and e-mail address listed.

"Should I call you on Monday?"

"If you want to wait until Monday, that's fine, but I'm happy to meet you anytime between now and then if you prefer. I'm in church until 11:00 on Sunday, but any other time is fine."

Again, there was that West Texas charm. "Thank you so much for your help." Addie stretched out her hand and Woody clasped it robustly. "I'll call you as soon as I see what I've gotten myself into!"

Addie and Mel stood at the same time, and Woody followed them back down the hallway.

"The ranch is real easy to find. It's about seven miles south of town on Highway 62. You can't miss it." Woody held the door for Addie. "Good luck, and call me if you need anything."

"I will," she assured him and turned to lead Mel
back to the car.

CHAPTER 6

—⋆—

The drive to the Destiny Ranch took less time than Addie expected. Woody was right; it was easy to spot. The entrance was marked by an oversized gate with the letters "D" on one side and "R" on the other. After crossing the cattle guard, Addie followed a long dirt road, which she assumed would lead her to the main house. She was glad she was able to make it to the ranch before the sun went down, thinking it could be a bit spooky at night.

Addie had not put Mel in his crate, and now the little dog stood on his hind legs straining to poke his nose out the open back window and sample the fascinating new smells of the country.

Driving slowly over the uneven road, Addie was struck by the feeling that no one had lived there for a very long time. Overgrown vegetation was beginning to trespass onto the road, and she passed a small utility shed that seemed to be crumbling under the weight of bulky vines and thick shrubbery. Up ahead, she saw several structures and what appeared to be the main house. From a distance, the three-story farmhouse was completely charming with wrap-around porches on the first two floors and green shutters that contrasted nicely against the white house. As she drove closer, however, the charm began to fade as she noticed that most of the paint was peeling and a part of the first-floor porch railing was completely missing. A few of the shutters hung loose and slanted, like crooked teeth in an otherwise nice smile.

"Not exactly what I remember," she said to Mel, who was now barking his enthusiasm for his new surroundings.

She had only visited the ranch once a very long time ago, and her memories were more than a little fuzzy. Addie recalled wide open spaces with horses and cattle gently grazing in the sunshine, and she remembered Stella's laugh as they played together near the pond.

Childhood memories were like that. In the light of adulthood, giants became people, oceans became ponds, and unfortunately, mountains became mole hills.

What faced Addie now was about 2,000 acres of overgrown landscape. In addition to the main house, there was a massive barn and several smaller buildings. There were no signs of people, domesticated animals, or civilization. Addie had the feeling she was visiting an archeological dig—a graveyard of lost hopes and broken spirits.

"What have I gotten myself into?" wondered Addie as she pulled the car up near the house. She got out and stretched in the still-bright sun before opening the door for Mel, who sprang from the back seat and set out to explore, nose to the ground.

"Don't run off," she commanded as Mel turned a corner around the car and headed into some tall grass.

The initial shock was beginning to sink in. This place will have to be sold, Addie thought. But who would buy something like this? It's in the middle of nowhere, the buildings are falling apart... Oh my God! This is going to take all summer to complete!

"*Relax, darling*," said the voice of her mother. "*It will sort itself out. Just take it all in and enjoy the experience.*" Usually, Addie was annoyed by her mother's voice in her head, but right now, when she was surrounded by the unfamiliar, she found it comforting.

"Thanks, Mom," she said aloud and looked up at the spectacular painting made by the sun as it began to dip toward the horizon. She had never seen such a vast expanse of sky, and the effect was both breathtaking and calming.

After a few moments, Addie looked around and realized she couldn't hear Mel any longer. "Mel, Mel, come here buddy," she called to the wind, but there was no response.

She started off in the general direction she had last seen him go and had not gone more than three steps when Mel ran up, tail wagging and mouth open with rapid pants. She could tell he liked the new place— quite a step up for an apartment dog.

Addie was about to head into the house when a large ornate bronze windmill caught her eye. It stood out in the dense pastureland, and she wondered how she had missed it when she drove up. It was exquisite. The windmill stood about 12 feet high, with large metal blades at the top that were spinning in the wind. About two feet from the top, a series of vertical blades revolved around the center column, which was shaped like the trunk of a tree. Each of these "blades" was in the shape of a different child, and when they revolved it gave the appearance of children chasing one another around a tree.

It's absolutely amazing, thought Addie as she took in all the intricacies of the artwork and complexities of the design. It belonged in a museum, but here it stood in the middle of a field. Who had designed such a wonderful piece of moving art?

After a few moments, she returned to the car and took out her luggage. Calling for Mel to follow her, she walked up the creaking steps onto the porch, which held several dusty chairs and a badly weather-beaten oval run. A huge swing suspended on the south end of the porch offered a view of the grounds that would have inspired even old master painters.

Addie opened the torn and split screen door and gasped. She was standing in front of the most beautiful leaded glass door she had ever seen. Addie felt small standing in front of the massive door, and at 5 feet 7 inches, she didn't often feel short. The rectangular beveled glass enclosure held elaborate iron scrollwork with a five-point star in the center. The door itself was a rich dark wood with a solid wrought-iron knob. On either side of the door were two engraved wood panels. Reaching out her hand to touch the intricately carved wood, Addie realized in awe that they depicted scenes of the seasons, two seasons on each panel. Winter was a starry night with children throwing snowballs. A fall scene showed people gathering at a large Thanksgiving table. Summer was a pond with kids swinging out over the water, and spring was a beautiful meadow with butterflies and blooming wildflowers. Each carving told a story, and the craftsmanship was stunning.

More to Destiny than meets the eye Woody had said. Pushing the key into the lock, Addie wondered what she might find inside.

Mel ran past Addie anxious to explore the house. The entryway was open all the way to the third story, and rows of stained glass windows provided a rainbow of colorful light. A staircase with a stunning wrought-iron banister led up to each floor, which had a balcony that overlooked the entry.

A gigantic chandelier hung from the third-floor ceiling in the entryway. At least, Addie thought it was a chandelier. It was made of some sort of metal and was oddly shaped, almost like a nest. The structure seemed to fill the entire space in front of the stairs, but it didn't seem to have any light bulbs. Addie flipped nearby switches, and nothing happened. Maybe it's just another piece of art, she thought turning her attention to the rooms in front of her.

A living room immediately to the left of the entry was overflowing with hand-crafted furniture. Every inch of the walls was covered with art—water colors, oils, photographs, collages, mosaics. Some were of professional quality, while others had the look of a child's hand, but all were displayed with equal pride.

Addie put her suitcase on the floor and began to explore. She walked to the old Steinway piano and struck a few white keys, only to find the instrument horribly out of tune. An ancient television set with rabbit ear antennae sat atop a beautiful antique wood cabinet. No satellite TV this trip. An old dusty record player was stuffed in a corner next to a bookcase that held what had to be hundreds of old records. Albums by the Beatles and Elvis were mixed in with the music of Tchaikovsky, Willie Nelson, and Louis Armstrong.

She wandered toward the back of the house and passed a small powder room that had peeling turquoise wallpaper before reaching the kitchen, which was remarkably spacious and well equipped. There were two double ovens and three stovetops as well as a wonderful deep farmhouse sink. Addie peered into the pantry that was the size of a large walk-in closet and saw well-stocked shelves that held a variety of food items as well as an assortment of kitchen appliances.

The countertops were made of some sort of natural-looking stone with a clean, shiny finish, and there seemed to be miles of them. The walls were a sunny yellow, and handmade tiles painted in a multitude of bright colors filled the backsplash behind the counters. Each was a delicate piece of art. A larger tile positioned directly behind the sink featured some type of flying insect and the phrase: "Find home, love, and life in the darkness."

"How sweet, I can think about bugs while doing the dishes." But even as Addie muttered the words, she had to admit that this kitchen would do many restaurants proud.

She opened the door off the kitchen and walked out onto a very large patio set up for Al fresco dining. An enormous stone table at least a foot thick and about 30 feet long was surrounded by a couple of dozen chairs in various states of decay. Much of the tabletop was hidden by a thick covering of dry branches and leaves. A three-foot brick wall enclosed the entire space with entryways on either end. Tall painted ceramic pots and metal bronze sculptures were placed haphazardly around the space.

Addie went back inside and continued to the den area, which again was cluttered and stuffed with furniture and bookcases that overflowed with art. This room was dedicated mainly to photography and books. There were framed photographs showing the history of the Destiny Ranch on every wall. Addie peered into them hoping to get a glimpse of Stella, but the faces were of strangers.

Adjacent to the den was the master bedroom, the last room on the floor. This space was orderly and well kept—a distinct change from the rest of the house. Addie knew instantly that it had been Stella's bedroom.

There were several exquisite paintings on the walls, and two life-sized statues of nude figures stood in corners of the room as if to keep her company. The furniture appeared to be hand crafted by a master woodworker. Stella's four-poster bed had a massive headboard that nearly touched the ten-foot ceiling. It featured carvings of song birds sitting among branches in a sprawling tree. The detail was amazing, and Addie almost expected a bird to fly off as she moved closer for a better look at it. The bed posts were nearly a foot in diameter and were carved to look like trees. A canopy of ivy connected them in a forest of sweeping beauty. In any other room the bed would seem congested, even tacky, but here it was stately and elegant. The ceiling was painted a brilliant blue with wisps of white clouds providing the perfect finishing touch to this enchanted woodland setting. Addie let her fingers move across the highly polished wood and wondered how she could not have a memory of such a striking room.

Across from the bed, a very tall bookcase featured a collection of art, but unlike the pieces in other parts of the house, these were dusted and displayed proudly, as if they had been hand-picked for Stella's enjoyment. A fichus tree in a beautiful ceramic pot filled the corner next to the expansive window that was framed with heavy silk drapes.

Addie sat on the edge of the bed, suddenly tired after such a long, eventful day. Her calmness was interrupted with a loud bark from Mel and a crash coming from upstairs.

CHAPTER 7

Addie froze listening to Mel's barking. She should have been terrified. After all, the house was huge, and she had no idea what might be lurking inside. There could be somebody up there; maybe squatters were living in the house. But, somehow, she knew that wasn't the case. She didn't know why Mel was barking, but she knew it wasn't dangerous. Still, maybe this wasn't the time to place all of her faith in what may or may not be a psychic feeling.

Looking around the room, she picked up a sturdy metal candlestick. Mel continued to bark, but she could hear little else. Addie rushed up the first flight of stairs and then peered into the darkened hallway, clutching the candlestick tightly, in search of Mel. She heard his frantic barking on the third floor, so she ran up the second flight taking the stairs two at a time. Addie found a light switch and saw Mel yapping at a closed door as if to say, "This way! It's in here!"

"What is it, boy?" Addie asked in a surprisingly calm voice. She put her ear next to the door but couldn't hear anything over Mel's incessant barking. She turned the knob slowly and cracked the door slightly prepared to slam it shut if some wild animal or intruder tried to pounce. Since nothing like that happened, she opened the door wider. Mel forced his way into the room and growled at a dark gray cat atop a highboy dresser. The distressed feline was hissing its disapproval at the little dog with back arched and fangs gleaming. Mel jumped up hysterically but had little chance of reaching anything but the second drawer. Addie stepped closer and saw a litter of new kittens squirming inside a drawer that was half open.

She spied several bowls of water and food in a corner of the nearly empty room and a litter box inside an open closet. Obviously, the cats were guests of Stella's. She also noticed that the window was cracked open allowing the cat to come and go as needed.

"OK, Mel. I think we can leave mama and her kiddos alone now," Addie said after refilling all of the bowls.

She closed the door behind her and carried the wiggling dog down the stairs, deciding against further ventures into the rest of the house this evening. Instead, she opted to get settled for the night. After a quick trip to the car and kitchen, she had Mel's food and water bowls filled, and the dog was happily eating a snack in Stella's room.

"I'm glad you're here with me tonight, big guy," Addie joked with the dog scratching behind his ears. It was true. The house was huge, and she felt much more at ease having a watch dog with her, even a diminutive one.

Addie looked at Stella's bed with a frown and bit her lower lip like a student who had been called on to answer a really difficult question. Since this seemed to be the only room in the house that was fit for habitation, sleeping here seemed to be the only answer. She rummaged around in a nearby closet and was relieved to find a clean set of sheets.

Addie made one last trip to the car for the cooler she had brought. It had been a last-minute decision that she was now greatly pleased she had made. Wine and cheese seemed the perfect way to relax before her first night in a strange house.

After dressing for bed, leaving her clothes scattered across the unpacked suitcase, she opened the bottle of wine and splashed some into a crystal goblet she found in the kitchen. Slicing off a hunk of gouda cheese, Addie sat back against the pillows letting the bed envelope her suddenly exhausted body. She could feel the stress begin to ease, as though it were melting from every muscle, and she closed her eyes enjoying the serenity that seemed to wash over her. She opened them again when Mel jumped up on the bed to see her, covering her face with kisses.

"I feel exactly the same way," she said pressing her face next to his.

Addie sat up and reached for her wineglass,

admiring the art on the bookcase. These must have been Stella's favorite things. Each piece probably had some wonderful story behind it that had personal meaning for her. How sad that it's all lost now.

She took a sip and looked at the two life-size statues that stood in opposite corners of the room. One was of a woman and the other a man, and both were fully formed nudes. Their arms were outstretched slightly as if they were reaching out to one another. She wondered if she would wake in the middle of the night scared out of her wits by the huge figures. Who would keep something like that in their bedroom?

Daylight was nearly done, and Addie turned on a lamp on the bedside table casting the room in a soft yellow glow. Denton seemed a long, long way off from where she was now, as though she had been transported to a different time. It was going to be a big job going through all of Stella's things, and she wondered how long she would need to stay in Destiny. Her initial thought that a week should be more than enough time to get someone's affairs in order now seemed laughable.

Addie enjoyed another sip of wine and wondered what kind of person Stella had been. She knew some of the surface details—Stella had been a founding member of the town, and she had started a sort of colony for artists. But what kind of person does that? Addie knew that she was accidentally born here when her parents were driving by and that she had visited here when she was eight years old. But she knew virtually nothing else. Why had she been selected as the executor of her estate?

Addie reached for her purse and pulled out Stella's letter.

"*I have left a gift for you in the nightstand next to my bed.*"

Setting her wine glass on top of the nightstand, Addie opened the drawer only to find it empty. That's odd, she thought. The table next to her bed overflowed with books, lotions, nail files, batteries, flashlights, and numerous other trinkets. Stella's nightstand was completely empty. Addie looked around the room to see if she was looking in the right place, but it was the only piece that could be described as a nightstand.

Not ready to give up so easily, Addie pulled the entire drawer from the table and turned it over. She saw a couple of thumb tabs on the bottom, and when she twisted them, the entire bottom of the drawer dropped out revealing a hidden compartment below. In it was a leather-bound book tied by a yellow ribbon with a tag attached that read "For Addie."

Addie picked up the book and wasn't sure whether she should laugh or cry. It was all so "007." A book concealed in a secret compartment. Feeling a bit silly, she shook the book like a Christmas present, half expecting to hear the rattling of gold doubloons or some other hidden treasure.

Addie untied the ribbon and opened the book. A folded piece of notebook paper was sticking out from the pages. She opened it and saw that it was yet another letter addressed to her. Unlike the previous letter, the handwriting in this note was faint and written by a shaky hand.

My Dearest Addie;

This is the journal I have kept since you were born here at the ranch. I don't know if anyone ever told you, but you were born in my bedroom right in my bed. My time is ending soon, and it is my hope that you will care for my things and be patient with the failings of an old woman.

As the years have gone by I'm afraid I was not able to keep the house and grounds to any decent standard, but it's a good home and an inspirational place.

I hope you will feel that energy while you are here.

I have faith in you.

Love forever;

Aunt Stella

Addie stared at the note for about a minute before reaching for her wine. The paper was not yellowed at all, so the letter was probably written fairly recently. I can't believe I was born in this bed, she thought. What a nice entrance I made to this world.

Feeling a bit overwhelmed, she took another long sip of wine and carefully opened the diary.

June 29, 1983

A child was born tonight in Destiny. It was as if an angel had descended upon our land. She is the first child ever born here and a reminder that as great as man's art and creation can be— nothing compares to His.

There is something about this child that has touched my soul. I felt it before her parents even arrived last night. She was born out of place, into a dark stormy world, and I fear she may have a difficult time. However, the greatest creative work usually comes from suffering, and I know this child has the gift. I saw the light in her eyes the moment she was born.

I see dark days ahead for the people living here, and this child may just be the spark of light we need. I see this child as hope.

I will keep this journal along with my thoughts and impressions to help guide her when it is time for her to know. While it is certainly possible that she may never see these pages, I feel in my heart that she will. I hope it provides direction and a bit of comfort to understand that she is destined for more than she may realize.

June 30, 1983

I just found out that the Butterfields are naming the child Addison after my middle name. I told them it was the first time I had ever delivered a baby, but I was proud of the job and was so honored.

At 57 I know I won't ever have children of my own, but I think Addie and I have more in common than anyone will ever know or suspect. I see her as the child I never had. And so, my dear Addison, I write this book for you. And when it is time, you will read it.

July 4, 1983

You left today to return to your home in Connecticut, and I already miss you. Addie, my little one, where to begin? I guess I should let you know a little about where you were born. I am part of a group of free-thinking artisans who founded The Destiny Ranch. We all have lived here making and selling art and living off the fruits of the land for the past 30 years.

At the ranch, each person contributes to and shares in

everything. Our doors are always open. People come and go as the mood strikes. They stay and create; then they leave when it is their time to go.

We currently have 43 musicians, painters, sculptors, and writers most of whom have been with us five years or longer. We enjoy music and companionship as a community. I know that love is the path, and I am not meant to be a part of the hate-filled world of most of society. Here there is no animosity, jealousy or greed. I am proud of our historic past and hold out hope that our efforts will ring down throughout time.

All great societies are measured by their art. The Greeks and Romans, Egyptians and Mayans, all were judged by the art and literature they created. The paintings, sculptures, plays and other prose, pottery, and even their architecture are gifts they leave for those who come behind them as symbols of their lives, loves, and passions.

We set out to generate and accumulate the most beautiful art possible and only offer pieces for sale when we need money for goods. It was a community philosophy and something we have always abided by. Everyone stays at the ranch for free, and they either contribute by working for the community with their labor or by adding to our growing body of artistic accomplishments.

I daresay we have the greatest store of art riches to be found in any "hippy" commune in the world. I always hated being called hippies. Society has a way of labeling things they don't understand.

I am not much of an artist myself but I aide the community in any way that I can. I took a job in town, and for the last eight years, I have been an English teacher and school librarian. We use my paycheck to purchase art supplies and other things we can't make or grow here on the ranch.

I know that if you are reading this you have many questions, and I hope to provide some answers as we move forward together. While it may seem very strange to read a book written to you from beyond the grave, imagine how unworldly it is to try to write one!

I don't know what condition the ranch will be in by the time this finds its way into your hands. I am worried that things are going in the wrong direction and that we may have already seen our finest hours. Although I am fearful that we may be in for a slow and painful decline, I hold onto the belief that our work can and will make a difference in the world.

That is the most important thing for you to remember—I believe everyone can do good and make a positive difference in the world.

Addie took another sip of her wine. She couldn't remember the sound of Stella's voice exactly, but as she read the pages, it was as if she could hear her. The voice of a woman—strong and vigorous and full of life— seemed to be reading the journal to her.

July 20, 1983

We had quite a light show tonight! Every evening, we all gather on the patio for a sundown dinner. It gives us a chance to mingle and talk about the day or whatever moves us. Often, they turn into late night affairs, such as the one we had this evening. To our delight, we were treated to the most beautiful display of flickering light against the night sky by a swarm of fireflies. It was absolutely mesmerizing, and we all sat in silent wonder admiring the artistic dance of lights provided by nature.

Fireflies provide the spark of light that leads to love in the darkness. It's from a folktale my mama used to tell me, but it is so true. Watching the flicker of lights, I felt the love of this community wash over me. I am truly blessed.

   August 23, 1983

   I tried my hand at poetry again. I read my work to the community during sundown dinner. They were respectful and unimpressed. I'm the grand old lady around here and they never try to hurt my feelings but my art…oh my art. What a pity that someone who loves something so much is so utterly incapable of completing even the smallest task.

   What comes so easily to others is an impossibility for me. I know I should be grateful for the gifts I have been given, but it hurts to yearn for something I will never have.

Addie put the journal down as she thought about her own failed attempts to be an artist. Growing up, she had been surrounded by art. Her mother was an accomplished sculptor, her father played five instruments and wrote beautiful music, and her sister created gorgeous art with her camera. Addie had always felt she was such a disappointment to her talented family. She knew they loved her, of course, but she had grown up feeling she was never quite good enough. She lifted her glass in a silent toast to the statue of Stella. "I feel your pain," she said as she downed some more wine and continued to read.

   October 13, 1983

   I can't believe it's been so long since my last entry! The start of the school year is always full of energy, and we've had a very prolific period at the ranch as well. Juan Carlo joined us late last year, and he has been a real boost to our spirits and productivity. He makes the most interesting pottery, and he has been teaching his techniques to others here. The atmosphere has been lively and dynamic since his arrival.

We hung Dylan's fixture in the entryway today. I'm so excited; he's been working on it since last summer when we had such a flurry of fireflies. He said it inspired him. But I'm not going to tell you any more about it. That will be my surprise for you, Addie!

The next several entries were upbeat and enthusiastic, and Stella spoke about several art pieces that Addie thought she had seen earlier. It seemed as though she were reading a novel about people from a different time and place all working and creating together in harmony. Could the ranch really have been that idyllic? Addie had her answer in the next few entries.

February 26, 1984

There are happenings in town that I want you to know about. I take great interest in the town and its direction. I do not sit on the board, as that would not be the best use of my time, but I do attend every meeting. Since I am a town founder, they are very gracious and include me in most major decisions. I do not discuss these things with the artists at the ranch. I see it as my job to stay abreast of town business and not impede the creative process with minutiae.

You see, a greedy scheme is underway to rob the town of a beautiful future. But I refuse to get caught up in other peoples' avaricious intentions. I know what Destiny is. I founded it! Who should know better its direction and purpose than someone who originated it?

Our land here in Destiny is, as I've been told, "strategic." All some people can think about is growth and wealth. And I understand that to an extent, I truly do. The town must be able to sustain itself and the people who call it home. But to turn it into something it is not and was never meant to be is dangerous.

They think of me as a foolish old woman. And perhaps I am. But I have a vision. I came here when it was nothing and helped build it into a thriving, organic community that is flowing with ideas and intellect. All they think about is cattle, profits, growth, and greed!

Oh my, I'm getting carried away. I'll have to explain more later when I've regained my composure. But know this. Not everyone in Destiny can be trusted as I so foolishly thought they could be.

March 15, 1984

I attended the town council meeting tonight. The whole agenda was devoted to debate on the rail line expansion. It seems that most people are in favor of reserving city land for a future rail yard and switching station. They do not see the need for an amphitheater as I had proposed last year. I have been lobbying with these people for ten months, and I thought they understood my proposition. I thought they were excited by the prospect of expanding our performing arts. They seemed enthusiastic about the idea of a cultural showground that would elevate our artistic endeavors. I even told them we could hold rodeos and western themed plays that would attract attention from around the state, maybe even around the world.

No, they were completely dazzled by His Lordship's plan for more trains. More trade, more jobs, more money, more, more, more! This is land, mind you, that I donated to the city 15 years ago. They seem to have forgotten that and were not too pleased when I brought it up. But it didn't matter. It seems I have been overruled.

But overruled or not, I will not give up our dream. The town may grow, and commercialism, God help us, may choke the life out of the town eventually. But it will not suffocate the Destiny Ranch. And that cannot and will not be overruled!!

"Goodness," Addie said out loud sitting straighter in the bed. "My, my. You do have fire, Aunt Stella. Good for you." She was completely engrossed in the tale of Destiny unfolding before her. She read several more entries that were mainly about day-to-day happenings at the ranch. Then, the tone of her writing took a turn.

December 1, 1984

We are coming to the end of another year on the ranch. Our numbers have dwindled to fewer than three dozen. Everyone who remains is producing amazing art. The entire house and grounds are filled with lasting beauty. But I am worried that people are leaving, and new arrivals seem to have stopped. As long as people come and go, we'll be fine, but once they stop arriving our community is threatened. I am not sure how to turn the tide.

The next several entries read much as the last, and each included the name of a cherished member who had decided to move on. She also read an entry on her birthday. Stella had baked a cake, and everyone sang to Addie. It was sweet and touching to read how much of

an impact she'd had on this woman she could barely
remember.

September 13, 1985

*We are down to only 29 people now. Luke and Starlight left
today because one of his pieces was featured in a New York
gallery exhibition and sold for a princely sum. He is perhaps the
most talented sculptor we have had here. I have dozens of his
pieces in the house including a life size pair he did of Ven, my
old beau, and me.*

*Over the years, Luke has grown tired of living our Spartan
existence. He sees this as an opportunity to cash in on his talent.
There is no denying he will be quite successful elsewhere, but we
will miss his creative genius. He has been a close friend for 25
years.*

*We placed his windmill out in the field near the gate. He said
it was inspired by me and my constant chatter about children
being the future and by you, sweet Addie, as our community
symbol of hope.*

Addie raised her eyebrows and smiled with childlike
wonder. "I inspired a piece of art!" For some reason, it
pleased her a great deal. She made a mental note to get
a closer look at the windmill in the morning.

January 15, 1986

*Winter has been especially harsh. It has taken its toll on the
land and the people too. We lost another ten artists since Luke
left, and more than half of the houses now sit empty. We are at
the lowest levels since the ranch began.*

*But as long as I stay, the dream will never die. I had a
flashlight last night, and I see that others are coming. I know it*

will impact our community, but I can't see more than that.

Oh my! I guess I should explain my "flashlight." At least, that's what I call it.

It's difficult to explain, and I've never told anyone about it. It's just something I've always been able to do. I "see" things. Not all the time, and not often very clearly, but I have images that come to me. They are really just flashes of something. Like, when you are in a dark room with a flashlight. You can see what the light is shining on, but the rest is dark. I call it my flashlight. I had one the night you were born, and I know you have it too.

I hope I haven't scared you away! I'm not crazy, and I'm not psychic – at least not the way people think of psychics. I can't make it happen. Usually, it involves something mundane, like knowing when a quarterback is going to fumble a ball or that you are going to see someone you haven't seen in years. But occasionally I have stronger images like the one I had last night. I know new people are on their way to the Destiny Ranch. But I don't know who, when or why. It's often as frustrating as it is miraculous!

But that is the nature of "gifts" we can't understand. Perhaps that's why I've always loved fireflies. Like my flashlight, they show us the way. And they show up when we least expect it.

I desperately hope you understand this.

Addie snapped the book shut and stared straight ahead, trying to understand what she had just read. She had never known another person who had the same kind of prophetic feelings that she did. Of course, she knew some people claimed they could speak to the dead or see into the future. It's precisely because so many are skeptical of psychics that she'd never told anyone about her "visions" or whatever you want to call them. Stella called hers a flashlight, and that made perfect sense to Addie. It is like a flashlight in the dark. You can see something, but it is so out of context it's very difficult to understand what it means.

Addie recalled a time when she was 11, and her mother was driving her to a violin lesson. She told her mother to be careful because there was a car accident up ahead. Seeing nothing, her mother asked how she knew. Addie didn't have time to answer because the car ahead of them suddenly smashed into the car ahead of it. Her mother was barely able to stop before being hit.

That encounter had really startled Addie, but she was no less stunned now. What did it all mean, this flashlight? She wasn't even related to Stella. Why did they have this in common?

Addie reached over to scratch Mel behind the ears, suddenly feeling very alone. The little dog snuggled up to her, laying his head across her lap. She rubbed his head for a few minutes before picking up the journal. She wasn't entirely sure she was up for any more of Stella's astonishing revelations.

April 26, 1986

What a beautiful spring we are having. Three new people joined our community today. Luke sent them down from New York. They asked him about the most influential place he had ever worked and his reply, "The Destiny Ranch."

It is nice having younger people around. They bring so much drive and energy. I feel hopeful.

May 11, 1986

The newest arrivals left yesterday, and quite a few art pieces are missing. It appears they rented a truck and hauled everything they could load in the middle of the night. I am crushed. I knew these new arrivals would be impactful for our community; I just couldn't see how. Now I know.

I'm afraid we've been taken advantage of. I think they always intended to come here and steal. How sad but how typical too. Great works have been plundered throughout history.

We lost at least 50 paintings and several dozen sculptures. Initially, everyone wanted to call the police, but we decided that perhaps this is the way in which our works will become known and collected. We have never been about the money but rather the art.

As long as they find good homes, our mission is still valid. Still, the betrayal of our trust stings.

September 15, 1986

We suffered a mass exodus today. Fourteen of the remaining 19 left. They had been unhappy, and the creative energy has been low since the theft. It's me and just a handful of people now. It is becoming harder and harder to handle the ranch duties, feed ourselves, and create work at the same time. My job in town is used to buy more groceries and fewer art supplies. It's a bad sign.

October 28, 1986

Raffie and Gwen decided to pull out yesterday. We will miss them. We all gathered on the patio for a final meal together. I suggested they take some pieces with them to help defray their expenses. In true Destiny Ranch tradition, they declined. I cried myself to sleep last night.

December 20, 1986

I came home from school ready for the Christmas break to find the ranch empty. All I found was a note which read "Sorry" and signed by Carole, Felix and Juan. They had dropped hints for several weeks, but I refused to accept what was coming.

I am now alone. After 33 years of dreaming and believing in something better, I now stand at a crossroads. I never thought I would say it but thank God for my town job. I make a difference in the lives of children now, and even if I must change my method, the mission remains the same—make a difference for the future.

We started with 23 vibrant souls, and now it's down to one foolish old woman. What was I thinking? How can I do this to you?

Addie slowly closed the book. She wanted to know more, but not tonight. She had gone through too many emotions and wasn't sure she could process any additional information. She took a last sip of her wine and laid the book on the nightstand. Sinking into the soft comfort of the bed, she pulled the blankets up under her chin and felt Mel's small body close to hers. She hoped she wouldn't have any dreams tonight, at least, none that she would remember.

CHAPTER 8

—⊛—

A ddie woke with the light the next morning after a late night with Stella's journal. Rubbing her eyes so she could read the clock she saw it was only 6:23. She had a hint of a headache from the wine the previous night, but at least she would get a good start on the day.

With the whole day in front of her, Addie stared at the sky painted above her head and wondered what to do first. The grounds and rest of the house needed to be explored, of course, and she also needed to see if there was anything to eat here. As a thought hit her, she turned to Mel who was still snuggled on a pillow next to her and said, "I think I'll do laundry." Mel stood up and wagged his tail as if he thought that was a fabulous place to start.

Addie dressed quickly and gathered the sheets she had tossed aside last night. She also stripped off the clean sheets as they smelled a bit musty, reminding her of the summer when she was about nine years old. She made a fort with her sister out of a huge box full of old sheets. They spent hours tying linens and blankets together and hanging them around the garage. When they finished, they had a living room, two bedrooms and several escape tunnels that took over the entire two-car garage and wrapped around her father's old Pontiac. Her parents actually let them sleep out there for a couple of nights before making them take it apart and return to living inside the house. That was a great summer!

Shaking off her trip down memory lane, Addie returned to the task at hand. She remembered seeing an old washing machine in a covered area of the back patio.

"All I need is some soap, and I'll be sleeping in high cotton tonight!" As soon as the words came out of her mouth, she felt foolish and wondered if she was channeling her inner Marsha Brady. "Come on, boy," she said shaking her head with a smile.

In the pantry, Addie found soap and fabric softener along with several laundry baskets. She took a quick look at the shelves and saw neatly stacked canned vegetables, bags of pasta and dried beans, along with other staples like flour and sugar. On a shelf near the door sat a couple of loaves of molding bread. Crinkling her nose, she deposited them in a nearby trash can, and then looked up. I wonder how the trash works here? At home, she tossed it into a huge bin that was emptied by the city once a week. Did it work like that here?

"Make a list! Make a list of questions for Mr. Dudley. Do it now so you don't forget."

"Yes, mom," Addie said to the annoying voice in her head. What made it even more annoying was that Addie knew she was right. She pulled her planner from her purse and wrote, "Questions for Mr. Dudley" on a blank page and then scribbled "Number 1, how does trash collection work?"

That done, she decided to work on finding food before wrestling with the washing machine. She filled Mel's bowls and found a corner in the kitchen that could work as his feeding spot. Now it was her turn. An industrial looking coffee maker sat on the counter near the sink, and after locating filters and a can of coffee and fiddling with the machine for a bit, Addie soon had the comforting aroma of freshly brewed coffee filling the air. Suddenly ravenous herself, she decided not to brave the pantry just yet and instead went back to the bedroom and pulled a breakfast bar out of the cooler.

Addie ate her bar and sipped coffee while standing against the counter, not bothering to sit down. She and Mel finished at about the same time, and when Addie piled the sheets into a laundry basket, the dog followed her out onto the patio.

The washing machine appeared to be in working condition, but its avocado color and rust spots on the bottom edge revealed its age. After stuffing the sheets inside, Addie checked the settings and was about to change it to hot water, when she noticed that the machine was hooked up to a garden hose. "Cold water it is," she said thinking what a joy it must be to do laundry here in the winter. "Well, as long as it works today, that's all I really need." She turned the knob to the start position and was pleased when it rattled to life.

Addie called for Mel, and they headed back inside. Pouring a second cup of coffee, she decided to tour the rest of the house.

In the bright daylight, the art on the first floor was even more astonishing. Many of the pieces were museum quality. After reading Stella's journal, Addie thought about the people who had crafted the art and left it here to be enjoyed by others. Some of them might have gone on to become famous, which meant that some of the art could be worth quite a lot. Addie marveled at the idea that none of the artists who had lived here seemed even slightly motivated by money. Of course, she understood the idea of art for art's sake, but even with her parents, there was still some awareness of material worth.

The journal had Addie seeing a lot of things differently today. The tile above the kitchen sink, for example, was not just an insect, but a firefly. It was a symbol of hope, spiritual prosperity, and of finding your way in life. It was a beautiful metaphor for how Stella had lived her life.

She and Mel returned to the entryway to head upstairs, and her breath seemed to stop for a moment when she saw the dance of colors cascade down as the morning light streamed in through the stained-glass windows. The wall opposite the windows had been painted white and left blank—a canvas for the art that nature and man created together. Addie had the feeling that no matter how long she stayed, she may never uncover all the wonders of the Destiny Ranch.

She and Mel headed up to the second floor. It was really nothing more than a long hallway with doors on either side. Opening each one, she found four bedrooms and two bathrooms. In stark contrast to the first floor, each room was nearly empty. Most of the rooms held only a naked bed and a dresser making it look and feel like a college dormitory before students arrived. The rooms were modest in size, but larger than her own bedroom back home, and each had a double door that opened onto the second-floor porch.

Continuing up to the third floor, Addie found it similar to the second—four nearly empty bedrooms and one bathroom. This floor lacked the wrap-around porch of the second floor, but each room had an enormous picture window showcasing the undulating hills and mesas in the distance.

She decided to peek in on the kittens, but first picked Mel up and cradled him tightly so he wouldn't run in snarling and foaming at the mouth. When she opened the door, the mama cat seemed to fly to the top of the dresser and stood warily eyeing Addie and Mel with her back arched. At least she's not hissing at us, Addie thought and crept closer very slowly. Her cautious approach seemed to calm mama cat slightly, but when Mel suddenly barked and wiggled in Addie's arms, the cat reached out with her claws and caught Mel on the nose drawing blood.

"You asked for it mutt," Addie scolded him and

pulled a Kleenex out of her pocket to wipe his nose. "You'll live," she said and decided that was enough for today.

She closed the door and set Mel down, who whimpered a bit but was otherwise fine.

"You know, Mel, this won't be too awful. The house is nearly empty, except for the first floor. I bet it won't take as long as I was thinking."

With a somewhat lighter mood, she tried to open the last door at the end of the hall but found it was locked. Instinctively she felt along the top of the door frame and found a key that fit the lock. The door opened revealing a darkened space with a narrow staircase leading up.

Thinking it probably led to the attic, she climbed the tight steps grabbing the wooden railing tightly to guide her. At the top of the stairs she flipped a switch on a nearby ceiling beam, and about a dozen bulbs all flashed into brilliance illuminating a massive storage area that was filled to the top with... "More art," she sighed the words, and her heart literally seemed to sink a bit into her chest as she tried to take in the vast store of sculptures, books, and paintings. It looked like a storage vault for the Smithsonian.

Addie pushed through the sea of material, but there was simply too much to get a good look at anything clearly. Boxes were stacked up nearly six feet high in some places. There were numerous frames in all shapes and sizes scattered about while clay pottery and sculptures seemed to be tucked into every available space. It was a mess.

"My summer just got a whole lot harder," she said wearily pressing her hands to her temples.

She opened a nearby box and found it stuffed with kitchen gadgets, coat hangers, and other odds and ends. "OK, so it's not all art," she said picking up an old heart-shaped copper Jell-O mold with ducks on the front of it. "Some of it is probably just complete trash." She dropped the mold, and it fell with a clink back into the box. Addie rubbed her temples again before throwing her hands up and letting them fall limply at her sides. She turned off the lights and crept carefully back down the rickety steps.

Mel was waiting for her when she reached the bottom. He seemed to think it was safer staying near Addie than braving the room with the killer cats. He followed obediently behind her as she returned to the first floor to check on the laundry. She was just about to the kitchen when she heard a ringing sound from the patio. Mel bolted ahead of her to investigate the strange sound barking rapidly as if to say, "I'm on it! Don't worry!"

Addie giggled at the dog's courageousness and said, "It's OK, Mel. I think the sheets are done."

Grabbing a laundry basket, Addie headed out to the washing machine. She looked around curiously for the dryer. "Of course," she said with a heavy sigh as she spied four enormous clotheslines toward the back of the house. Addie could not remember a single time in her entire life that her mother had used an outdoor clothesline to dry clothes. It had always seemed like a bit of a lower-class activity to her, but here in this rustic setting on a warm, sunny day, it was perfectly natural.

She picked an area where the grass was not too high and started hanging sheets and comforters. Even though it was still morning, the sun was already bright, and the breeze was warm on her bare arms. "It won't take long before these are ready."

Local insects and other critters were buzzing and chirping in the yard and Addie waved her hand in front of her face as one of those inhabitants flew across her path. Mel had wandered off to explore the fields but came bounding back when he saw Addie heading toward the house. She poured a final cup of coffee and sat at the round kitchen table while Mel found a patch of sunlight on the tile floor that was perfect for a morning nap.

The attic made Addie question whether she was up to the challenge and responsibility of being Stella's executor. It was still more than a bit surreal to her that a few days ago she was in a middle school classroom and now she was virtually in the middle of nowhere with no idea about what she was doing or why. She had told herself that it might be an adventure and to be open minded, but heading out to West Texas on little more than a whim had already bumped her beyond her comfort zone.

"It's a challenge, sweetie. It could be fun. And you never know what may happen when you least expect it. Honestly, where's your sense of adventure?"

"Right where it always is, Mom – carefully folded, neatly pressed, and tucked away in the back of the drawer."

Trying her best to shake off her feelings of doubt, she glanced at the clock on the stove and saw it was only 8 o'clock. Since it was still too early to call Mr. Dudley, she decided to explore the ranch while the sheets were drying. Addie dashed to Stella's bedroom to exchange her flip flops for sturdier footwear, deciding that tennis shoes might give her a little more protection against whatever might be lurking in the overgrown grounds.

The Destiny Ranch consisted of about a dozen buildings of varying sizes situated between the main house and a large pond. Several smaller buildings were clustered together, and each of them seemed to be some sort of guest house or mini dormitory containing four bedrooms with small closets and a shared bathroom. Most of them were completely empty except for an occasional bed or dresser, and each room had a window air conditioner. Like everything else at the Destiny Ranch, the buildings were richly painted inside and out with a variety of scenes from abstracts to landscapes. It appeared that there had once been a pebbled walkway up to each of the entrances, but weeds and other foliage had long since concealed the paths.

Situated beyond the houses were several larger structures where it appeared people had worked. Addie pushed open the creaking wooden door of one of these buildings and found it filled with artisan tools and half-finished works. These larger buildings were obviously built for function, and some of them were little more than barns. One of them had been used for iron works and came complete with a forge. Additional blacksmithing tools were scattered across large wooden tables. An adjacent building was set up for ceramics with several pottery wheels, some of which were still caked with dry clay. Ceramic pots of all shapes and sizes littered one whole side of the room.

The other buildings were much like the first she had seen, open and functional. There were tools for just about any type of artistic endeavor Addie could think of. Spinning wheels, wood working equipment, painting easels, sewing machines, glass blowing rods, leather crafting supplies, and many other mystery tools filled these workshops. It was all so incredible. Addie closed her eyes and tried to image people living in the houses and working in the barns creating wondrous works of art. She could almost hear the clanking of metal and whirring of saw blades when her idyllic scene was interrupted by Mel's barking.

Addie turned to look in the direction she heard Mel and saw him jumping excitedly in some nearby tall grass. As she approached, she saw something about a foot taller than him. She couldn't tell what it was, but it was brightly colored. She could see bits of pink, bright green and yellow peeking through the grass.

"What did you find here?" she asked the barking dog whose tail was wagging wildly. She saw a small sculpture of a scene that looked like it was right out of Alice in Wonderland peeking through a patch of tall grass. Addie rocked it back and forth to dislodge it from its tangled nest of weeds. Finally, it began to move, and she was able to pull it free.

"How completely appropriate," she said in awe staring at the brilliantly colored miniature statue of Alice and the Mad Hatter standing in front of a giant toad stool. Other than some crusted dirt that was stubbornly clinging to the base, the piece appeared to be in perfect condition. Addie stared at the statue closely and stood very still. She suddenly had the distinct feeling that this figure was not alone. Bending down, she pushed large patches of tall grass and weeds aside. She could see several other brightly colored mounds resting in the twisted grass.

"Oh my," she gasped when she realized that she was in the middle of what must have once been an entire Wonderland garden. Addie looked around fully expecting a large talking rabbit to spring out. Laughing, she carefully returned Alice to her original resting place, deciding that uncovering Wonderland would have to wait for another time.

Pulling her cell phone from her pocket, she saw it was now past nine. Feeling she had waited long enough before disturbing Mr. Dudley on a Saturday morning, she returned to the house to set up an appointment to see him. She was both happy and surprised to see that her phone got reception at the ranch.

Mr. Dudley had suggested lunch at noon at The Hushpuppy. Wondering if that was the only restaurant in town, she had agreed nonetheless because at least she knew how to get there. Having a little time to kill, she decided to check on the drying sheets. It had only been an hour, but the morning was growing hotter and what had earlier been a morning breeze had begun to pick up speed.

The sheets were fluttering and flapping against the wind, and she had to pull with some force to get them down. She tried to fold the first sheet, but the wind was not cooperating. Looking more rolled than folded, the sheet was stuffed into the basket, and Addie decided she could fold them later.

She was about halfway through with the laundry when a gust of wind caught one of the sheets and blew it out of her hands. It quickly flew high into the air and caught another gust. Before Addie could react, the escaped linen was a good eight or nine steps away.

She set out in pursuit but between the tall grass and uneven footing she seemed unable to gain on the runaway sheet. Addie watched it soar into the air twisting in the wind eerily making ghostly shapes. Then, just as quickly as it had taken flight, it stopped abruptly caught on a fallen tree limb. Seeing her chance, Addie surged forward, but just as she was about to snag it, the wind whipped it free. She watched it sail gracefully over a nearby hill and disappear from sight.

She bent over with her hands on her knees. It was just a stupid old sheet, and she felt a bit foolish for running after it in the first place. She was about to turn and head back when she heard a low rumbling coming from the hillside. She froze in place instinctively, and her eyes widened in shock when she saw a man on horseback riding over the hill carrying the fugitive sheet like a white flag. She was still too shocked to do anything other than stare stupidly when the man pulled the horse to a stop about two feet in front of her.

"Yours?" he asked with a grin holding the sheet out to her.

She continued to stare, and his grin grew wider. He was wearing a straw cowboy hat, a stiffly pressed white western-style shirt, and dark blue jeans that covered boots made from some sort of animal. Neither he nor his magnificent white horse had a speck of dirt anywhere on them. Addie felt her cheeks begin to warm under his continued stare, and she stumbled forward.

"Oh, yes," she stammered finally, reaching for the sheet.

The man slid gracefully from the horse holding the sheet and walked toward her still smiling. She could see wisps of blonde hair from beneath his hat, and his smile was absolutely dazzling, but it was his deep blue eyes that seemed to render her incapable of normal thought. He was perhaps the most gorgeous man she had ever seen that wasn't on a movie screen.

Handing her the sheet, the man held out his hand. "I'm Cole. I live just beyond that hill over there. Our property backs up to the Destiny Ranch. I was just out for a morning ride and thought I'd come by and say hello." When Addie didn't move, he continued. "I heard you were due in last night."

Finally coming to her senses, Addie moved forward to shake his hand. He squeezed hers slightly before letting go, and she could feel a tingle run all the way down to her ankles. "I'm Addie Butterfield. It's very nice to meet you," she said managing to regain a bit of her composure.

"So, you're in from Denton, is that right?" Cole's smooth Texas drawl completed the picture of handsome cowboy and nearly had Addie swooning. He bent down toward her and continued, "They said you were pretty."

Addie tried to hide her reddening cheeks by brushing her hair with her arm and shifting the sheet. Sensing her discomfort, Cole quickly continued. "I'm sorry. I didn't mean to say people are talking about you. It's just that this is still a pretty small town and word gets around."

There was an uncomfortable pause, and Addie searched her brain frantically for something witty to say when Cole rescued her. "I'll drop by again later if that's OK. You might need some help moving something or maybe need some company for lunch." He flashed his smile again revealing straight white teeth. Addie smiled back, still a bit star struck.

"That would be great. I'm meeting Woody Dudley at The Hushpuppy for lunch in a few hours."

Cole climbed back onto his horse. "Well, I've been known to drop by The Hushpuppy from time to time myself. Maybe I'll see you there." He lifted his hat slightly and nodded at her. "It was great meeting you Addie," he said with a smile.

"Thanks for rescuing my sheet," was all she could think to say.

"Anytime," Cole said with a wave as he turned the horse. "See you around, neighbor."

"See you," Addie called out as she watched him ride

over the hill.

"See you? That's the best you can do?" Addie walked back to the house clutching the sheet while her mother's voice echoed in her head. *"A beautiful man rides up on a white horse and calls you pretty, and the best you've got is 'see you?'"*

"I know, I know," Addie said hanging her head. "I'm pathetic."

"And what's up with that lunch thing? When a man says he wants to have lunch with you, you don't tell him you're meeting another man!"

Addie kept playing and replaying the conversation in her head until she finished folding the sheets. She made the bed and even the fact that the linens smelled like a sunny meadow on a crisp summer day didn't console her. Since she still had a couple of hours before she was supposed to meet Mr. Dudley, she decided that a long soak in Stella's tub might help improve her mood. And she was right.

Sitting in the hot soapy water with her hair piled on top of her head gave her time to think more clearly. She was only one day into her adventure, and she had actually met a spectacular cowboy on a horse who wanted to take her to lunch. And, she reminded herself, he has already met two of the husband requirements since he rode a white horse and was at least six feet tall.

She giggled like a teenage girl on a first date at the thought of what Heather would say when she told her. The summer was definitely looking better by the minute.

CHAPTER 9

A ddie showed up at The Hushpuppy a little earlier than planned. She wondered if Marsha would be working today. Seeing a familiar face, no matter how outlandish, was just what she needed. She had her answer as soon as she walked in.

"Look at the tumbleweed that just blew in," Marsha said over her shoulder as Addie walked through the door. Addie couldn't help but smile as she watched the fragile waitress, who was obviously much stronger than she looked, expertly balance a tray piled with plates of food. Marsha was dressed in the same t-shirt and jeans as yesterday, but today's high-heeled shoes were electric blue. "You're a sight for sore eyes this sunny Saturday morning. Have yourself a seat honey. Junior's here so order anything you want. I'll get your drink in a blink." She flashed a wide red smile and clacked into the kitchen before Addie could even say hello.

Unlike the previous evening, nearly every seat in the restaurant was taken. Addie found a table near the kitchen thinking that might be the best place to chat with Marsha if time allowed before Mr. Dudley arrived. She tried to ignore the fact that most of the heads in the diner had turned in her direction when she walked in. She had left her hair down today and was thankful for the blonde shield it provided as she pretended she was not on display. She was beginning to regret her choice of bright pink shorts and white tank top that hugged her frame. Addie was not normally overly careful with her attire, but today she had dressed to impress a certain cowboy she hoped might stop by and had even applied a bit more make-up than usual to bring some color and shine to her cheeks and lips. Feeling self-conscious and a bit foolish, she quickly slipped into a chair and hid behind a menu.

Marsha was busy topping glasses of tea and delivering meals but when a break allowed she brought Addie a Dr. Pepper and sat down with her.

"So how was the first night in the big scary old house?" quizzed Marsha.

"It wasn't that scary, and I had a fine night's sleep. Besides, a bottle of wine makes both a great companion and sleeping pill."

"I prefer my 'companions' to have more muscles than corks," Marsha replied with a smile. "What'll you have?"

"I'm meeting Mr. Dudley for lunch, so I'll wait to order until he gets here."

"Okey dokey," said Marsha popping out of the

chair. "I better get back at it. I see old man Bennett is outta ice tea, and he gets as impatient as a kid on Christmas mornin' when his glass is empty."

With some time to kill Addie took the opportunity to people watch in the small-town café. There was a wide range of ages, but most were young men sporting dirty work clothes with hungry looks in their eyes like they had been working all morning and were ready for a hearty meal. Several of the men were wearing well-worn cowboy boots with actual spurs on them. The only time she had ever seen anyone wear spurs was at a country and western bar Heather had dragged her to, and they were purely decorative. The men here were working ranchers and spurs were simply a tool of the trade.

There were several groups of older men sitting in what Addie assumed was probably their "regular seats." She imagined they spent hours talking about old football games, complaining about their variety of health issues, and exchanging their favorite hunting stories.

After a few moments, Mr. Dudley walked in. He spotted Addie near the back and raised a hand in greeting but stopped at several tables along the way to shake hands and chat with a few of the patrons. But he excused himself quickly and made his way to Addie's table.

"There you are," he said as he neared her. "You probably don't realize it, but I usually sit over there." He pointed across the restaurant to the last window seat, which was vacant as if it had been left for him.

"Oh, I'm sorry Mr. Dudley," Addie said feeling a bit embarrassed but not sure why. "Would you like to move?"

"Heavens no, this is fine," he said sitting across from her. "Besides, I don't want to have to listen to Marsha tell us we're like a teeter tooter in an earthquake changing seats like that," he joked with a wide smile beneath his mustache. "And it's Woody, not Mr. Dudley."

"Sorry, old habit from school. You get used to calling everybody Mr. or Ms." Addie said and relaxed into her seat. Woody had an easy way about him that put her at ease.

"So how was your night?"

"It was very nice, actually. I slept well, and I found the 'gift' that Stella left."

"Really, what was it? A million dollars stuck in a fake bottom in a drawer?" He was joking of course, but Addie smiled conspiratorially and leaned forward.

"Well, you're half right," she said looking him, and he cocked his head waiting for her to continue. "I did find it underneath the drawer in her bedside table. But it wasn't money. It was her journal. She'd been keeping a journal for me ever since I was born out on the ranch."

"I didn't know you were born out there," replied an obviously surprised Woody.

"Yeah, my parents were driving through, and my mother went into labor early. Stella even helped with the delivery. By all accounts, it was a pretty remarkable thing." Addie couldn't help but feel a little pride in the fact she was a local girl—a thought that had not occurred to her before this very instant.

"I guess that makes you a Destinian, an original Lobo," said Woody nodding his head with approval.

"A what?"

"A Lobo, a wolf—it's the high school mascot," he explained as Marsha walked up and placed a tall glass of sweet tea in front of Woody.

"So, what do you think of my new friend, Woody?" Marsha asked taking the pen from her ponytail.

"I think she's great. I just found out she's a local girl, and no one even knew it. She was born out at Stella's place," Woody told Marsha as he reached for his tea. "Ain't that summpin'!" he said with a pronounced Texas twang poking fun at Marsha just a bit.

"Well shoot the antlers off a moose in summer!" Marsha exclaimed without missing a beat. "A local girl! And here I thought you were a big ole city slicker. I'm gonna have so much fun showing you all the sights and delights of your original hometown," her eyes sparkled beneath purple and blue eye shadow. "Now, what'll ya'll have?"

Woody waited for Addie to order first.

"I think I'll go with a chicken fried steak, mashed potatoes, fried okra, and a side salad," answered Addie without hesitation. The tiny breakfast had left a gnawing feeling in her stomach, and although she was not normally a heavy eater, chicken fried steak was one of her weaknesses, something she had discovered when she first moved to Texas. Some women might have been embarrassed to order such a big lunch in front of people they hardly knew, but Addie felt very comfortable with her newfound friends.

"My oh my. You're as empty as a cookie jar in a preschool, honey," Marsha said without looking up from her order book. "A number one comin' right up. What kind of dressing would you like?"

"How about oil and vinegar?" asked Addie.

"Eye-talian it is! And you sir?" Marsha said with a flirty look at Woody.

"The usual, please."

"Of course," Marsha said and shoved her pink pen into her ponytail. "Be right back with your salads."

Addie and Woody talked for nearly an hour before during and after the food came. They decided that he should start the probate immediately and Addie would work on getting together a rough inventory of the estate. She knew it was a big job, but now that she knew Cole was right next door she was excited about the prospect of spending hours side by side with him going through each of the treasures at the ranch. Of course, it was summer, and the attic would be hot, so he would have to take his shirt off, and his muscles would ripple as he worked and she would have to move closer to help and his masculine scent would...

"Sorry?" Addie could feel her cheeks begin to warm as she realized that Woody had asked her a question. "I'm so sorry, Woody. Can you repeat that?" She hoped he wouldn't notice the huskiness in her voice.

"No need to apologize. I was just asking if..." Woody's question was cut off as a group of five men came in laughing and slapping each other on the backs. They made quite a commotion, and several of the younger men in the restaurant called out greetings to the rather unruly group. They sat at a large round table in the middle of the restaurant that had recently been vacated by a family of six.

"Marsha, get your butt out here—heroes are hungry," one shouted. "And thirsty," called another.

"Hold your horses—I'll be right there," Marsha yelled from the kitchen. Addie and Woody watched as Marsha emerged from the back carrying a pitcher of iced tea and several glasses.

"You know what you need Marsha?" asked one of the men as she approached. "You need a man."

"Well when I see one I guess I'll reach out and grab him," retorted Marsha completely unbothered by their gruff behavior.

"Not unless I grab you first," said the man as he roguishly pulled her into his lap. "Travis Granger, you let me go. I've known you since you were just a little boy, and that's all you'll ever be to me—a boy!" Marsha wriggled to her feet, and the others at the table chuckled at their companion.

"Trav, I think you're losing your touch!" one of them said.

"You boys better behave yourselves. We have company," Marsha turned toward Addie and winked.

Addie and Woody had stopped conversing and were watching the playful display as were most of the other diners. It was clear from the amused looks on their faces that these men were well known and well liked in the town.

Travis turned in the direction Marsha was looking and seemed surprised to see a face he didn't know. His eyes locked with Addie's and with the ease of an athlete he rose to his feet and approached their table. He was wearing faded blue jeans and a plain white t-shirt that stretched across his chest and showed tan, muscular arms. His brown hair was cut short and neatly combed and was highlighted by too much time in the sun. Laugh lines at the edges of eyes that appeared both brown and green gave his tanned face a friendly appearance as though he spent much of his time enjoying life rather than worrying about the details. Watching him move toward her, she had the impression that he was quite comfortable with himself and was probably what other men would describe as a man's man.

"Excuse me, ma'am," he said smiling coolly, his eyes never leaving hers. "I would like to apologize for our rude behavior. You see, we've been practicing our firefighting skills all morning, and after we got the practice blaze put out, we decided to have a few cold ones, you know, to help us cool off. We didn't realize someone as sophisticated as yourself would be here enjoying the fine Hushpuppy cuisine." His smile widened as he extended his hand. "I'm Travis Granger."

Addie waited a moment before taking his hand and said, "It took you all morning to put out a practice fire?" She had on her best school-teacher-listening-to-another-outlandish-reason-why-a-student-had-not-turned-in-his-homework face. "I guess we'll pray for rain." With that, she let go of his hand, and his smile turned to a chuckle.

"Sit your butt down Granger," said Woody. "Can't you see I'm working here?"

"And what a lovely job it is." His eyes wandered leisurely and deliberately from her tennis shoes up her long tan legs pausing briefly at her breasts before meeting her eyes. Addie felt her mouth open slightly and she snapped it shut, embarrassed by her response to him. Travis grinned again, and the crinkles that appeared at the sides of his now mostly green eyes gave his face a handsome ruggedness that seemed to hypnotize her. She watched him turn and walk confidently back to his table, and she let out a breath she didn't know she had been holding. Irritated with herself, she turned her attention back to Woody, who was watching her with amusement.

"Ignore them, Ms. Butterfield. They represent our make-shift fire department, and Travis there is sort of the captain," explained Woody. "They do a good job but lately have taken to celebrating every successful training. In fact, training seems to be more of an excuse to have a few beers than it is to improve fire safety. But they provide a very valuable service, and we're proud of 'em, so we put up with their excess merriment once in a while," Woody said with a smile watching the firemen.

"That's OK, I don't mind. I live in a college town myself," said Addie. "I guess boys will be boys no matter where they are."

"Well put, my dear," said Woody. "I think we've covered enough for one meeting. I'll expect to see you Monday morning, and we'll get things rolling. Until then, please let me know if there is anything I can do for you." He hesitated a moment before continuing. "By the way, I spent some time out on the ranch myself back when I was younger."

"Did you?" Addie was a bit surprised that a commune full of artists would appeal to him.

"Well, I was young, and it was a different time. I didn't stay long." He hesitated a moment before continuing. "She was a great lady, that aunt of yours." Finally, he grinned and took her hand into both of his. "See you Monday." Addie watched him pause at the table of firefighters who all turned and laughed heartily at something he said before he left.

The door had not yet shut behind Woody when Marsha appeared at her table. "So, I've been dyin' to talk to you," she said as she plopped into Woody's chair. "What are you going to do now? Have you got any plans for the afternoon? Because, I get off in 20 minutes and the way I figure it, those cute firemen will be just about done by them. What'd you think?" Marsha asked staring at the table of men who had quieted considerably and were now hungrily feasting on bulky burgers and huge platefuls of steak fries. Without waiting for Addie's reply, Marsha continued. "I say we talk those guys into taking us to the lake for the afternoon."

"There's a lake around here?"

"Well, it's not exactly around here, but it's only

about an hour or so away. It's at the Richardson Reservoir, but there's a pier and a spot for swimming and having fun in the sun. Oh, say you'll come."

"Ummm," Addie said hesitantly. She didn't want to tell Marsha she had plans for getting some company of her own for the afternoon. But where was Cole anyway? Hadn't he hinted that he would be coming to the restaurant today? Addie looked across the table into Marsha's enormous hopeful eyes and wasn't sure what to say. "I really shouldn't," she started. "I have to start going through the house, and I haven't even seen all of the ranch yet."

"Oh poo!" squeaked Marsha. "You have all summer for that. Firemen are here now! I'd look too slutty going out there by myself – not that it wouldn't be fun. But you know what I mean. Pretty please? With sugary sprinklies on top?" Sensing Addie's hesitation, she quickly continued. "At least come talk to them with me. Then, you can say you're too busy when we all decide to go to the lake. How about it?"

"I guess I can talk to them," Addie agreed reluctantly.

"That's the spirit! Once they finish scarfing down their burgers, we'll make our move." Addie could almost hear Marsha squeal with delight as she returned to the kitchen.

Feeling a bit deflated that Cole had not shown up to dazzle her during lunch, Addie leaned back in her chair and listened to Patsy Cline wail about her aching heart. "I hear ya, sister."

Addie sighed and reached for her Dr. Pepper, but

her hand froze in midair when she saw Cole walk through the door followed by an older man. Cole quickly scanned the tables and smiled when he saw her, making his way to her table. The other man waved to a group of men seated near the front window, and he went over to greet them with hearty handshakes.

Watching Cole approach her table, Addie was once again struck by the sheer beauty of the man. He was wearing dark blue jeans that seemed to hug his thighs as he walked. A crisp blue and white striped shirt was tucked neatly into pants that were secured by a brown belt with a huge silver belt buckle. His shirt sleeves were rolled up casually, and she noticed he once again was wearing a pair of very expensive looking shiny boots. His blonde hair was close cut with wisps falling softly across his forehead giving him a boyish appeal.

"Ms. Butterfield, how nice to see you again." Cole reached out a hand in greeting, and when she raised hers, he lifted it gently to his lips. The sensation sent a physical shock pulsing down Addie's spine, and for the second time that day she had to remember to breath. Who knew this little town in West Texas would turn out to be a den of dazzling men? "How was your first night in Destiny?"

Addie urgently tried to calm herself and act as though she had a brain in her head, although it was nearly impossible while he still held her hand and was staring at her with those blue eyes. "Yes. I mean fine. I had a good night, thank you for asking." *Oh my God, get a grip!* She nearly screamed the words at herself while taking a deep breath. "And please, call me Addie. The only people who call me Ms. Butterfield are my students."

"You're a teacher!" Cole said and squeezed her hand affectionately. "I come from a long line of teachers. My mother and grandmother both taught elementary school, and even Daddy taught a couple of classes at the university. What do you teach?"

"Middle school English," she replied trying not to sound matronly.

"Uh oh. I better watch what I say. Grammar was never my strength."

Addie chuckled and began to relax. "Well, you'd never know it."

Their conversation was interrupted when the man who had come in with Cole joined them.

"This must be Ms. Butterfield," he said in a voice that was smooth and unmistakably Texan. He reached for her hand, but unlike Cole, he merely shook it gently but firmly.

"Addie, I'd like to introduce my father, Judge Anderson Wescott." Cole made the introduction casually, but Addie noticed that he stood a bit more stiffly when his father had joined them.

"It's very nice to meet you, Judge," said Addie not knowing the correct reply when meeting a court official.

Although she had never heard of him, she could tell he was a sort of local celebrity the way others in the restaurant reacted to his presence. He was nearly as tall as Cole with a thick head of graying hair. He was stockier than his son but not overweight.

"Call me Anderson, my dear. It's very nice to meet you as well."

"Please join me," said Addie gesturing to the other chairs.

As the two men moved around the table to sit, Cole said, "We just came by for a late lunch. I had hoped to be here earlier, but dear old Dad had to finish 18 holes instead of the nine I was planning."

Addie smoothed her hair and tried to keep from smiling at the thought of him trying to get here earlier. She actually had butterflies in her stomach. What is wrong with me? I've been with good looking guys before, and I didn't swoon in their presence! Something about this place—the mystery of the ranch, being beckoned by a woman from beyond the grave, the people she met who were like a cast of characters from a Broadway play—it all seemed so surreal. Addie wasn't quite sure what her part in all of it was. She felt like she had wandered into Brigadoon and would wake up one morning to find the entire town had disappeared into the mist.

"My son is quite a good golfer. I'm afraid I'm the one who needs practice," Anderson said breaking into Addie's thoughts.

She spotted Marsha out of the corner of her eye as she pretended to hang herself with an invisible rope. Addie felt a little guilty that Marsha's plans for the lake were now ruined.

"I understand you are here for Stella Pennington, sweet woman," continued Anderson. "She was a real pillar in our community, and it's a shame she's gone.

Were you very close?"

"No, actually, I had not seen her in about 20 years and only remember her from one visit I made when I was eight years old."

"That's just like her," laughed Anderson. "I never knew what was going through that woman's head. Why on earth she would have a virtual stranger deal with her estate is beyond me." He shook his head. Addie wasn't sure, but she felt as if Stella had just been insulted, and she didn't like it.

Sensing he had made her uncomfortable, Anderson added, "And that's what I loved most about her; that free spirit and unpredictable nature."

The words seemed empty somehow, and Cole carefully avoided eye contact with either his father or Addie. Was he embarrassed?

"So, I understand you are our neighbor now," Anderson continued. "How do you like the Destiny Ranch?"

Although Addie had just met the man, she thought she heard a tone in his voice when he said the word "ranch." It was the same feeling she got when her mother talked about her friends' daughters who were all getting "married" or when she told Addie that teaching was such a "noble" profession. He was saying all the right things, but something didn't ring true.

"It's fantastic," Addie said quickly trying to show great enthusiasm. "I've never seen a more enthralling place. I mean, who would have thought that such a vast treasure trove of artworks would be hiding in the pastures of West Texas? Some of the pieces are truly exquisite. Aunt Stella was quite a patron of artistic endeavors." Addie quickly took a sip of her water. Somehow, she felt she needed to defend Stella. She just hoped she didn't sound like a walking thesaurus.

Anderson leaned back in his chair watching her closely. Addie met his gaze with a small smile trying hard to calm her nerves. Luckily, Cole jumped in to help out.

"I know what you mean. I've never seen or even heard of a place to equal the Destiny Ranch. I always loved visiting Stella." Cole said with a small smile.

"I understand you are from Denton, is that right?" said Anderson not waiting for Addie to reply. "What do you do there? Is there a Mr. Butterfield?"

"I teach English," said Addie, again trying not to sound unimportant. Why did she always feel like she had to defend her chosen occupation? "And no, there is no Mr. Butterfield." Addie glanced at Cole who was looking directly at her.

"What a coincidence. Stella used to teach English as well, I think," said Anderson.

"Yes, she did Dad. I had her in school when I was in the 4th grade. I think she stopped teaching shortly after that. I'm not sure why. But she stayed on as the school librarian."

"We have great respect for teachers out here, Ms. Butterfield," said Anderson. "Cole's mother was a teacher and so was my mother. It's such a terrific occupation and much harder than it looks, as I'm sure you know. Cora really loved teaching, but she gave it up when Cole was born so she could stay home with him full time."

Addie started to relax at his change in tone. Perhaps she had imaged the insult in his voice earlier. He certainly seemed agreeable now.

Another waitress, older than Marsha and much more robust, came and set plates and drinks down for Cole and his father.

"Honey, are you still working on this?" she said with a pleasing drawl looking at Addie's plate of half-eaten food. Though Addie had come in practically starving, her appetite was easily curbed.

"I think I'm done. It was delicious, but I'm afraid my eyes were bigger than my stomach today." Addie smiled warmly at the woman as she cleared her plate away.

"Are you planning to stay with us very long?" asked Anderson. Again, not waiting for a reply, he continued. "Our founders' day festival will be held next weekend, and Stella was going to be one of our VIPs. We're celebrating our 60th year as an incorporated town." Addie could hear the pride in his voice. "Since Stella won't be joining us, perhaps you would do us the great honor of representing her?"

He smiled at her over his glass of iced tea as though he had just invited her to the White House.

"Goodness," was all she could get out. A VIP at a local festival. She had attended city banquets, commemorative celebrations, gallery openings, and other ceremonies where her parents were either chairing the event or being honored. But this would be the first time that she would be an honoree.

"I'm sure Cole would be happy to serve as your escort if you are uncomfortable attending alone," Anderson looked over at Cole who nodded in agreement.

"It would be my pleasure," said Cole sincerely, staring into Addie's eyes. "Oh, say you'll come. You may not know it yet, but my father is used to getting his way. You have no idea how 'persuasive' he can be." Addie chuckled at Cole's teasing tone.

"Well, if you're sure it would be acceptable to everyone. I mean, no one in this town even knows me." Even though Addie was dying to attend an event on the arm of Cole Wescott, she knew that small towns could be tough to navigate. Did she really want to be held up with the other founders of the town when she had only just arrived and didn't plan on staying?

"Since I'm on the board of organizers, I say it is perfectly fine. And Stella was well known. People will be curious about her relations and would enjoy meeting you. So, is it a date?"

"OK, sure. I mean, yes, I would love to attend. But I don't want to be a bother. I can attend alone if Cole has other plans." She looked over at him hesitantly, but he beamed back at her.

"We can't have that! I will escort you to the festival. It's settled." Cole patted her hand squeezing it slightly, and again Addie felt a physical spark that nearly made her jump.

She enjoyed chatting with Cole and his father while they ate their lunch. Anderson told her a bit about the history of Destiny and some of the challenges the town was now facing. Cole let his father do most of the talking, but he smiled at her often and asked her a few questions so she could join in the conversation. She was just beginning to truly unwind when their time was up.

"I'm sorry we have to eat and run, but we have business in White Spring," said Anderson pushing his chair back. "But I look forward to seeing you next weekend. Cole will let you know all of the details. It was a pleasure meeting you, Ms. Butterfield." With that, he turned and walked back toward the counter. He stopped briefly at the firemen's table and patted Travis on the back. The two shook hands, and Anderson waved a quick hello and goodbye to the group.

Addie saw that Cole was watching the interaction closely. When Anderson moved away, Travis and Cole exchanged a quick glance. Travis nodded his head slightly to acknowledge Cole, who stood and held Addie's chair while she rose.

"Thanks for a great afternoon, Addie." Cole leaned down to kiss her cheek and seemed to be very aware that Travis was still watching them. "I'll see you soon," he said with a smile.

"Yes, see ya," she said awkwardly. Addie watched Cole and his father leave, and she waved stiffly when Cole turned at the door and tipped his hat at her. Aware that several in the restaurant were staring at her, she dropped into her seat. Travis was still leaning back in his chair watching her. Feeling suddenly very self-conscious, Addie turned and looked away. To her relief, she saw Marsha hurrying toward her.

"That was a close one. I thought you might be stuck with them all afternoon and we'd miss our chance at the lake." Marsha, still hopeful for a fireman fling, looked over at their table.

"Hey Trav, you ready?" The others were standing and throwing money onto the table. Travis turned his attention back to his friends and stood. The group headed out the door, and Travis looked back at Addie one more time.

Marsha let out a loud sigh and slumped into a chair.

"I'm sorry, Marsha. I didn't mean to take so long."

"It's not your fault, girlfriend. Some things are just not meant to be." Marsha seemed to sweep away her disappointment with practiced ease. "A lot of my life is like water in the desert. You can see it clearly but by the time you get there, it's all dried up."

"It looks like it's just us then," Addie offered, trying to cheer her new friend.

"Hell, yeah! You and me. Who needs muscular, cute, heroic firemen anyway?"

"There you go," agreed Addie.

"So," said Marsha looking at Addie with a bit more intensity. "What kind of man do you see yourself with? Maybe a rich, really good-looking, golf-playing lawyer?"

"Cole is a lawyer?" Addie asked before realizing that her interest in Cole had been so obvious. She automatically went to her husband-to-be checklist. Law degree met the master's degree requirement, and her eyes literally sparkled with delight.

"Of course. His dad is the richest man in town, and Cole's a partner at Bailey, Simpson and Wescott. I'm sure he does real well for himself, but the old man is just not quite ready to stop wearin' the pants. Cole has had to put up with playin' second fiddle for a long time. I'd feel sorry for him, except he's rich, good lookin' and lives on the biggest ranch in the county. I should be so sorry." Marsha leaned forward before continuing. "And I could tell by the way he was eyein' you that he's more than a bit sweet on you."

"And how can you tell that?" Addie asked with what she hoped sounded like disinterest but was afraid sounded more like childish enthusiasm.

"Well, Cole has dated a bunch of women around here, and I have known him since we were kids. He's not seeing anyone now, and I see the way he looks at you. And, I couldn't help but overhear that he is taking you to Destiny Days next weekend. His father may have pimped him out, but he was a pretty eager beaver. Trust me, he likes you."

Addie felt as though she were back at school overhearing her students talking about a cute boy. It felt a little juvenile, but Marsha continued. "I wouldn't have been surprised if he wasn't going to ask you on his own. He's a pretty smooth talker and has a reputation for workin' the women fast and hard."

Addie was a bit flustered and opened her mouth to respond, but Marsha jumped in. "Now, don't go getting' yer hackles up. There's nothing wrong with fast and hard, if you know what I mean."

"Well, he's been a perfect gentleman around me,"

said Addie defensively.

"Yeah, he's the total package. A woman could get lost in those eyes for a long time before she realized her panties had fallen off!" Marsha laughed out loud at Addie's reddening face.

"You're awful Marsha Brady," said Addie chuckling. She lowered her voice covertly and added, "It's not like you weren't looking for a fireman with a big hose yourself."

Marsha threw herself back in her chair and laughed heartily. "Ms. Butterfield, I just know we're going to be the best of friends. You already know me so well."

CHAPTER 10

Addie found herself very relaxed in her new friend's company. "Come back to the ranch with me," she invited Marsha. "I really haven't explored much of it yet, and it would be great to have some company."

"Sounds fun," said Marsha untying her apron. "Just let me clock out, and I can follow you over."

The two women left The Hushpuppy in separate cars and drove out to the ranch. Addie noticed that the trip seemed shorter each time she drove it.

"Welcome to The Destiny Ranch," said Addie spreading her arms wide as Marsha climbed out of her truck.

Marsha lifted her enormous sunglasses and perched them on top of her head to have a better look. "Goodness. I really didn't know it was so big. I mean, I've seen it driving by, but it looks so much bigger up close." She shaded her eyes as she slowly spun around taking it all in. "It's fantastic," she said with a smile unwittingly echoing Addie's earlier description to Judge Wescott. "I mean, it's in a bit of a state now, but I'll bet it was quite something back in the day."

The two women climbed the weathered steps up to the front door, and the wobbly boards groaned in protest.

"Oh my," Marsha gasped when she saw the front door. "Will you look at this?" She leaned forward to get a closer look. For some reason, Addie was pleased that someone else saw the beauty in the rough exterior of the ranch.

A sudden explosion of high-pitched barking gave Marsha a start. Addie chuckled and pushed open the door for Mel who burst onto the porch barking and wagging his tail with excitement. Laughing, Marsha bent down to let the little dog smell her hand.

"I'm guessing he belongs to you," Marsha said scratching Mel behind the ears. "Well, aren't you just a little house shoe on steroids," she cooed at the dog who was beginning to settle down. When Marsha stood, he ran down the steps eager to take care of business.

"That's Mel. He gets a little wound up around new people, but he's never met a stranger."

"That's good because they don't get no stranger than me." Addie chuckled at Marsha's easy humor and led the way inside. She left the door open for Mel to join them when he was ready.

"I've never been in this house before," said Marsha

looking curiously into rooms that were darkened with shadows. "We used to park out on the highway and imagine all the scary things that went on inside. Even though we all loved Ms. P."

"Who?" asked Addie.

"Ms. P is what we called her at school. She was very old but nice as you could ever ask for. She really made a difference in my life, encouraging me and stuff."

"I didn't know her that well, but from what I know of her, that doesn't surprise me." Addie walked over to a few windows and opened the curtains throwing a bit of dust into the air.

Marsha coughed while waving her had in front of her face to clear the air. "You stayed here last night?"

"I know. It's a bit stuffy, but the bedroom is much brighter. I'm guessing that's where Stella spent most of her time toward the end."

Addie and Marsha poked through several rooms examining photographs and marveling at art pieces they liked. At the back of the house, Addie paused in front of the bedroom door.

"And here is the best room in the house," she said proudly as she flung open the double doors. She had left the air conditioner on, and the room was bright, cheerful, and refreshingly cool in stark contrast to the musty, hot rooms they had just seen. Addie turned to the bed and said, "Look at this," but Marsha said nothing. When Addie turned back, she saw her standing by the statue of Stella. She had tears in her eyes.

Addie walked over quickly and put her arm around

Marsha. "I'm sorry to be so blubbery," Marsha said, dabbing at her eyes. "But this was her. It looks just like she did when she was younger. I know she's gone, but it didn't really hit me until I saw this. She was so sweet."

The two sat on the bed for a couple of minutes and leaned their heads together while Addie rubbed Marsha's back. Marsha heaved a final sigh and looked up at Addie.

"Goodness, it's been awhile since I've done that." Marsha stood up and grabbed a tissue off the night stand.

"Why don't we have something to drink," suggested Addie.

"Good thinkin'! I'll have a Lone Star."

"Actually, all I have is Dr. Pepper," said Addie feeling silly for suggesting it when she didn't have much to offer. "But I still have a little wine left, and…"

Marsha interrupted her. "Dr. Pepper is fine."

They went to the kitchen and then decided to sit on the patio and enjoy the sun. The sky was a brilliant blue and the day was pretty mild for West Texas in June. Addie brought out a damp rag so they could wipe down two of the least dingy plastic chairs. Marsha entertained her with tales of Destiny and what she could remember of Stella.

Their drinks gone and the heat starting to rise, the two headed back in for some shade. As they did, Addie pointed to one of the buildings in the distance.

"You see that building? The large barn? It has a walk-in kiln. And that one has dozens of easels for painting. There is even a forge in one of them."

"Wow, I never really thought much about what they were all doing out here. We just joked about the naked orgies when I was growing up."

Suddenly realizing that afternoon was giving way to early evening, Marsha grabbed Addie's arm. "Come over to my place for dinner. It's getting' to be about that time, and it doesn't look like you have much here. I'll fix my famous gopher dogs."

Addie looked at her sideways and arched her brows. "I'm almost afraid to ask, but 'gopher dogs'?"

"Oh relax! It's really just chili dogs, but my dad used to say he could really 'go fer' a chili dog when I was growing up. We shortened it to gopher dogs. We ate them the night we buried him, and after thinking about Ms. P, I don't know…"

Addie squeezed Marsha's arm comfortingly. "I think Aunt Stella would want us to eat gopher dogs tonight. Let me get Mel settled, and then I'll follow you over to your place."

Addie pulled up behind Marsha at her apartment building. It had a rather institutional look except for the Mexican tile roofing, which was pretty but out of place against the brown and grey exterior. The entire complex consisted of two buildings with eight apartments each. It was drastically different from Addie's apartment community with several hundred units. There was no pool, no recreation room, and no beach volleyball pit where drunken undergraduates slapped at a ball with one hand while holding a

Budweiser in the other and listening to Jimmy Buffett croon about a carefree island life.

"Watch your step," cautioned Marsha pushing a tricycle out of the way. "The kids next door are always leaving stuff around all the time."

She led Addie to the second building and up a flight of stairs. They passed a dimly lit laundry room that held two washers and two dryers, one of which had a hand-written 'out of order' sign taped to the lid.

Addie followed Marsha into the apartment and was stunned by what she saw. The walls were filled with detailed mosaics depicting western landscapes, old churches, and beautiful sunsets.

"These are stunning," said Addie moving in for a closer look.

"Oh, thanks," said Marsha throwing her purse on the kitchen counter. "It's just something that I got into back when I was in school. I find I want to create stuff when I don't have a man in my life. And as you can see by how many I've got – there ain't been too many men."

"You did these?"

"Yep. I didn't have much money, so I decided to use all natural materials. I think the rocks around here are kind of pretty."

"They certainly are." Addie was admiring a particularly large image of a landscape. "How do you make them?"

"I cheat mostly. I go out and shoot a bunch of pictures around the area. It's mostly sunsets and scenery I like. Then I start looking for rocks that have the colors I need. See, I already have a bunch of different stones." She pointed to a group of gallon pickle jars in a corner near the kitchen. There must have been 30 jars, each containing a different colored rock. "I draw a rough outline that I want to fill in. I've always been pretty good at seeing something and then drawing it in pencil. I use a hammer to get the size rocks I need. Then it's glue, glorious glue."

"This is just fantastic. You could sell these. Have you ever tried?" Addie was excited to find that her new friend was so talented. Was everyone in this town a frustrated artist?

"Who would I sell them to around here? Besides, art is for art's sake. That's what Ms. P always said. She was the one person who encouraged me and got me started," Marsha's lips curved into a small smile, but her eyes were clouded with emotion. "She gave me my first canvas and glue. I think that's why I got so upset at her place today. I knew it was full of art, but I never went out there because I figured it would be full of real art. I'm just a fake."

"You're not a fake," Addie said emphatically. "I've been around artists my whole life, and your work is amazing. I'm sure Stella would be proud."

"I know. I started crying today when I saw she had a small mosaic I had given to her on the shelf in her room."

"The cactus," nodded Addie now seeing the similarity to the other works in Marsha's apartment.

"Yeah, I did it when I was 12. It's not very good, but I gave it to Stella as a thank you for helping me. I couldn't believe she still had it."

The two sat on the sofa silently for a minute before Marsha slapped both of her hands on her legs and stood.

"How about them gopher dogs?"

"Can't wait," Addie smiled at her.

"We have all kinds of crazy names for food at my house," Marsha said trying to lighten the mood. "One of my favorites is 'rawhide.' It's fried round steak with gravy, rice, and pea salad. My parents used to eat that meal while watching the TV show – you know, with Clint Eastwood?"

"I've heard of it," said Addie wondering how a person so packed with personality could be hidden in such a desolate place.

"I'm sure it won't take long before you and I have our own special meal. Wait, I know. Foot long hot dogs could be called Firemen's Delight!"

"Ha ha," Addie replied. Marsha put a pot on to boil, and the two sat again.

"Enough about food. Tell me what it was like to grow up in Destiny."

"Well, it's all I've known so I can't really compare it to anything. Football is big. Most of the men around here are more likely to forget their wives' names than the score of the 1996 playoff final. It was 17-14 by the way, and we lost. Damn those White Springers!

"We live a simple life here, I suppose. The major sport for women is gettin' married. I'm 24, and my mom thinks I'm an old maid."

"Girls get married in the city too, you know. I'm 27

and single. And my parents just love that," Addie said sarcastically looking away.

"Parents! Thank God they weren't too stupid to have us!" Marsha tossed the idea out like a beach ball to be played with. "Mine are dumber than a box of hair. What about yours?"

Not exactly sure how to respond, Marsha said tentatively, "Not the sharpest knife in the cutlery cupboard?"

"Cutlery cupboard! Girl, we're gonna have to fix that Yankee thing you got goin' on. As we say around here, that dog just won't hunt!" Marsha laughed heartily, and Addie smiled.

"OK, I like my parents. I just wish they were happy with me the way I am."

"I know what you mean. The Hushpuppy is a great place to work. I know everyone in town, for the most part. I get to eat for free. And, if an eligible man comes to town I can get my hooks in him before anyone else. Why don't my mama get that?"

"Not the shiniest penny in the roll?" offered Addie.

"Better," said Marsha with a nod heading back into the kitchen.

"What can I do to help?"

"You can grab us a couple of Buds from the fridge," Marsha said putting hotdogs in the boiling water. "The secret to a great gopher dog is to toast your buns so the bread stays nice and fresh. Oops, that's a family secret. Now don't go tellin' no one, you hear?"

"I'll take it to my grave," said Addie holding up her right hand. She watched Marsha dice an onion expertly and then pull condiments out of her refrigerator.

"And the other secret is to use good chili. Not that stuff from the grocery store shelf. My mama makes this. She usually makes a big batch of it once a month and then cans it, so we all have jars of chili in the pantry."

"Looks great."

A couple of minutes later, the two were enjoying a treat of chili dogs, Budweiser, and Fritos. To Addie's surprise, she liked gopher dogs more than she expected.

"How's the nightlife around here?" Addie asked between bites.

"Nightlife? Oh honey, you are from the city. The nightlife around here is coyotes, coons, and darkness. There's a roadhouse or two for dancing, but our drive-in's been closed for about five years. I heard we're getting a new movie theater, but that won't be ready until the fall. When it's not football season, the town sort of lives for our festivals, like Destiny Days next weekend. Then, it's music, food, games, stuff like that. If you're lucky, you might get asked to dance by a good lookin' cowboy." She peered at Addie for dramatic effect. "And I feel like you're gonna get lucky."

Addie just shrugged her shoulders. "Judge Wescott asked his son to escort me to the festival, that's all. It's not exactly a hot date."

"I don't know. I've heard all about escorts."

She ignored Marsha's crude barb. "OK then, what can you tell me about Cole?" she asked trying not to sound like a teenager in heat.

"You already know he's good looking. And you know he's rich. You know he's a partner in a law firm and the son of a judge. And, he was the captain of the football team. Need I say more? He's quite the eligible bachelor."

"And you said he's single, so he's not seeing anyone?"

"Yes, he's single. And I get the feeling he sees anyone he wants. Of course, he's way out of my league. I don't know if it's his breeding or what, but he has never really given me a second look. He's nice, don't get me wrong, and he's not snobby like his dad can be. I don't really know much more about him. He dates, but apparently, nothing has been too serious." Marsha paused trying to find the right words.

"What?" asked Addie sensing Marsha had something else to say.

"Well, it's just strange that he's never settled down. I mean, a guy like that with his pedigree should have a trophy wife on his arm, don't you think?"

"Maybe he's a gentleman."

"Yeah, maybe. Now, if it's heat you're after—"

Addie held up her hand. "Don't tell me. I could go for a fireman, right?"

"Hey, those guys are the salt of the earth. I've known them a long time, and every one of them is a great guy. You could do worse."

"Oh, I'm sure Travis Granger is quite the gentleman. Did you hear what he said after he pulled you onto his lap?"

"No, what?"

"Well, he was kind of an ass. And then he came over to our table making a scene in front of the whole restaurant."

"That really doesn't sound like Travis. Come to think of it he was pretty grabby today. I don't remember him ever laying a hand on me except when we were dancing. Maybe something's bothering him," Marsha paused and tilted her head to look at Addie. "Maybe you were bothering him."

"Me?" Addie asked skeptically placing a hand on her chest. "What did I do to him? I only just met him."

"I know, but I saw the way he was eyeing you," Marsha said squinting her eyes at Addie.

"And how was that?"

"Like a bear just wakin' up after a long winter—hungry."

Addie rolled her eyes dismissively. "He looked well fed enough to me."

"I don't know," Marsha persisted. "Like I said, I've known Travis for years, and something about you threw him off." When Addie didn't respond, she continued. "Come on; you had to have felt it. I thought the whole room might burst into flames at the heat you two were throwing off."

"I really have no idea what you're talking about," Addie said crossing her arms and looking the other way. Marsha stared at her without saying a word, and finally Addie looked back at her. "What?" she huffed.

"Nothing," said Marsha evenly. "Nothing at all."

Addie felt a little ridiculous for her juvenile reaction. "Sorry," she said looking like a child who'd been caught taking one too many cookies from the plate.

Marsha shrugged. "Nothing to apologize for."

Wanting to start fresh, Addie asked, "So, how long have you lived here, in this apartment?"

"I've lived here a couple of years. My mama still lives in a mobile home park just down the road, and I wanted to be near her in case she needs help with anything. She's not that old, but you know. Let's just say we're close, and I don't want to get too far away."

"I understand completely. I moved to Denton to follow a boy to college. My parents approved of him, so they approved of the move. But when he was no longer in the picture, they just figured I would move back home. My mother would love it if I moved back to Connecticut, married a well-to-do son of a friend of the family, and bought a house down the street where I could give them grandchildren by the handful."

"Yeah, parents always want what they think is best for you. I just wish they approved of what I want."

"And what do you want?" asked Addie.

"I eventually want a husband and family. But just like when I go to a shoe store, I want to try a few on before I make up my mind. Who buys the first pair they see?"

"I have the opposite problem," said Addie with a sigh. "I get hooked up with some guy because ... I don't know," she hesitated not wanting to tell Marsha the ridiculous tale of her husband checklist. "Well, just because. And then as soon as the relationship gets going, I realize it's not meant to be, and I start looking for a way out." It wasn't exactly untrue. Even with

Bradley, the fact that he was sleeping with her roommate turned out to be a convenient excuse to move on.

Marsha broke into her thoughts. "At least with shoes you can keep the receipt and trade them in for a refund!"

"I heard that. As I get older, I worry that I won't find the right guy. I don't have as much time to try them on—if you know what I mean. I just want Mr. Right."

"I'll settle for Mr. Right Now! At least you've got that to look forward to this weekend." Marsha paused before continuing. "I hope you know that Judge Wescott didn't just drop by the Puppy and run into you."

"What do you mean," Addie asked with a frown.

"That man has a plan for everything. You're pretty big news around here, and I'm sure he is just trying to size you up. I was kidding about Cole and the whole 'escort' thing, but I'll bet the judge wants you close by so he can know what's going on."

"I'm sure you're just over thinking this," said Addie. It couldn't be possible that she was that important to anyone around here.

"That's the first time I've been accused of that! Usually I get the opposite reaction," admitted Marsha with a snort. "Maybe you're right, but I'd be careful. He might just want to buy the land, but he might have his eye on the art. I don't know, but I know he's probably up to something. Old Judge Wescott is very well respected around here, but there are whispers about shady deals and arm twisting that stick to him."

"What about Cole?" asked Addie.

"Oh no, Cole is Cole. He's better at golf than anyone, and I guess he's a pretty good lawyer. But as far as I know he never cheats. At least, I've never heard anything like that about him."

The more Addie heard about her white-horse-riding cowboy attorney, the more interested she was. And while she was having a good time with Marsha, there was a chance said cowboy could drop by the ranch tonight. Addie wanted to make sure she was there if he did.

"Well, darlin'," she said in her best West Texas drawl. "Your gopher dogs are a big hit with me." She stood to take her plate to the kitchen. "But I better get back. I'm worried about leaving Mel in the house for too long by himself."

Marsha followed her to the kitchen. "Oh, so you're the eat and run kinda girl. Or, is it the fact that Cole mentioned he might drop by tonight?"

"He did not," protested Addie, but then caught herself. "OK, you don't miss much do you? There is a slight chance he could come by this evening, and I kind of wanted to talk with him without his father around. Is that so awful?"

"Horny as an alley pole cat."

"Not at all! It would just be kind of rude for him to drop by and me not be there to greet him, that's all," Addie explained weakly, but couldn't keep her smile from betraying her. "Besides, it frees you up to start a fire and wait for a date."

Marsha smirked, and Addie offered to help with the dishes before she left.

"Naw, you go on and git outta here. I'll knock out the dishes and then set my couch ablaze," Marsha said with an evil smile.

"Marsha, Marsha, Marsha!"

Addie was heading out the door when Marsha called out, "Don't kiss on the first date and make good choices!"

"Thanks for having me," Addie waved.

"Any time darlin'! We'll catch up later, and you can give me all the juicy details!"

CHAPTER 11

After taking a wrong turn, Addie found the road back to the ranch. There was nothing she wanted to listen to on the radio, so she switched it off, which gave her plenty of time to think about her situation. Being here, in this place full of seemingly endless creativity, reminded her of being back home surrounded by her family.

She remembered her mother consoling her when she had failed at yet another artistic endeavor. "Don't worry so much about it darling. It will come to you. Whatever this life calls you to do; it will come to you. Be patient."

Funny how she remembered that now. It seemed that most of her memories centered around feeling somewhat inept and her parents being impatient with her choices. That one memory of her crying in her mother's arms while she gently stroked Addie's hair now filled her mind. She could hear her mother's soft, soothing voice, feel the gentleness of her touch. Addie breathed a heavy sigh. How she could use that comfort now when, once again, she felt out of place and unbearably ordinary.

Addie turned down the long driveway to the ranch when she saw Cole in the distance climbing into a white truck parked in front of Stella's farmhouse. Addie pressed the accelerator throwing dust up behind her. "Oh, no you don't. You're not getting away."

Cole spotted her racing down the drive and turned off the engine. Addie pulled up alongside him and rolled her window down.

"Howdy stranger. Were you looking for someone?" Addie said with a flirtiness of which Heather would most definitely approve.

"As a matter of fact, I was," said Cole sliding out of his truck. "But I think I must have scared the fur off whatever is barking at me behind that door."

"Yes, I have the most ferocious watchdog on the planet," said Addie climbing the steps to open the door for Mel. "Better brace yourself."

Mel erupted from the door and made a beeline for Cole, who was laughing with amusement. "Would you look at that," Cole took a step back instinctively as though he was afraid he might step on him.

"This is Mel," said Addie reaching down to scoop up the wiggling dog. "What he lacks in any actual protective skills he more than makes up for with loving intent." She put her face close to his and, he smothered her with kisses. Then she let him loose to run down the steps and sniff the bushes. Addie was growing more comfortable letting Mel explore on his own as he didn't stray far and always came back in just a few minutes.

"Would you like to come in?" asked Addie self-consciously tucking hair that had escaped her loose pony tail back behind her ears. She hoped she didn't look a mess, though she knew she probably did. Once again, Cole didn't have a hair out of place.

"Sure," he said easily and followed her up the stairs. "I've not been inside this house for a while. I bet it's been a couple of years since I've been here. Stella grew rather reclusive toward the end. But she was always so kind to me," said Cole holding the door open for Addie. "I miss her."

Addie threw a couple of light switches to chase away the early evening shadows. "I've got cold Dr. Peppers in the kitchen if you're thirsty."

"Sounds perfect." Cole followed her down the hallway. "This a great house. It's pretty run down now, but it's got good bones, you know? Solid," he said stomping a boot lightly on the wood floor. "They don't build them like this anymore." He took a swallow of the drink Addie handed him and continued. "It's the second most amazing thing I've seen since I arrived."

Addie met his eyes and grinned at him. "Is that so?" she said casually and hoped he couldn't hear her heart thumping in her chest.

"Yes ma'am," he said touching his hand to his hat. She laughed at his overly smooth cowboy act.

"It was nice meeting your father today," she said

trying to sound conversational. "I can definitely see the resemblance. What's it like being the son of a judge?" She sat at the kitchen table and motioned for him to join her.

"It's OK, I guess. Daddy is Daddy. He can be difficult sometimes. And I'm sorry about the festival thing this weekend. That's one of the reasons I stopped by. To give you a chance to back out if you want."

"Why would I do that? It was nice of him to invite me to be a part of it. And having a friendly face next to me will make it a lot easier." She looked at him over her can. "You are a friendly face, aren't you?"

Cole laughed out loud at this. "Of course I am. What else would you think?"

"I don't know," she said, feeling flirty again. "I've heard about you cowboy types. A girl has to be careful."

"I promise to be a gentleman," said Cole with his right hand over his heart. "But I think you'll have fun. We may not have a lot going on in this small town, but we love our festivals. We have a very active charity group, the Destiny Benefit League, and they love to plan parties. This is one of our biggest. And I didn't have a date, so I'm happy to be of service."

"So, no wife or girlfriend?" asked Addie.

"Nope," Cole smiled when he said it. "I'm afraid no one wants me these days."

"How sad," said Addie shaking her head. "I'm in the same spot. No husband, no boyfriend. Just me alone in this big scary house."

"Sounds awful. Maybe we should do something

about that," he said leaning toward Addie. "Got any ideas?"

"Just one," she said with a slight smile as he pulled her chair closer to him. He put his hand on Addie's shoulder and squeezed slightly. He was about to reach behind her head when they both jerked suddenly as Mel roared into the room barking and jumping. Both Addie and Cole smiled at being interrupted.

"Mel," scolded Cole teasingly. "Your timing is incredible, buddy."

Addie laughed and motioned for Mel to hop into her lap. "Well, I guess I do have someone in my life," she said scratching him behind the ears. "I just forgot for a moment." The mood was clearly broken. "Would you like to hold him?"

"I don't know. He looks pretty comfortable where he is." Cole reached over and tickled Mel under the chin. "I envy you, little guy."

"Would you like to see the grounds?" she asked. "I think we have a little light left."

"Sounds great," said Cole. He stood to hold the back of her chair.

"A gentleman indeed," said Addie smiling up at him. She couldn't remember the last time a man held her chair for her unless he was being paid.

Cole and Addie strolled around the property using the walkways, which were now mostly covered with weeds, as their guide. They chatted easily about Destiny and what Cole remembered about the ranch. He pointed to a fence line far into the distance showing her where the back of their property started.

"Wescott Ranch has about 60,000 acres and has been in our family for at least four generations. Daddy has never really done much of the ranching work himself, but he takes a keen interest in managing it. Since he took it over about 35 years ago, it has nearly doubled in size, and he's always looking for ways to expand." Cole sounded proud of his father's accomplishments.

"And what about you?" asked Addie. "Are you going to be head honcho one of these days?"

Cole stared off into the distance and didn't answer right away.

"Well, I guess that's the plan. But Daddy isn't going to retire anytime soon. You saw him. He's got miles to go before he starts slowing down."

Addie watched Cole closely. Was he relieved or disappointed? She couldn't tell.

"What's it like living in Denton?" he asked her.

"Oh, I don't know. I'm close enough to Dallas and Fort Worth for just about anything I want. But Denton still has a small-town feel to it. Not like Destiny. But we have a few festivals and concerts on the square, that kind of stuff. I moved there from Connecticut to go to college and then just never left."

"Sounds great. I love Dallas. I go out there a couple of times a year for work. That area has a lot of great golf." He looked at her smiling.

"Yes, I heard you were quite the golfer." She smiled back.

"Around here, anyway. Do you play?"

"My uncle tried to teach me once. He lined me up

with a club and a ball and gave me a list of about 29 things to do. I was thinking so hard, I couldn't move. When I finally did swing, I missed the ball completely. I decided then and there that golf was not the game for me, and I've never tried since."

"Maybe you just need the right teacher."

"Hmmm. Maybe. But I warn you, I may be a complete lost cause."

"I've cracked tougher cases than you, Ms. Butterfield."

"I bet you have." He chuckled, and then she continued. "Do you like living here? I mean, you haven't always been in Destiny. Where did you go to college?"

"I got my undergrad at Texas A&M and then went to law school at SMU in Dallas, so I've had a taste of city life. I worked for a couple of years in Dallas right out of law school, but Daddy really wanted me to work for his firm here."

"And do you always do what Daddy wants?"

"Not always," he said a bit defensively, but he looked over at Addie and grinned. "Usually, but not always."

"I understand about family. I guess that's why I haven't gone back home. I mean, there's really nothing keeping me in Denton, but the thought of going back and living near my parents who I constantly seem to disappoint..." She left it hanging. "I do miss them, don't get me wrong. But I don't think I could go back to live. Besides, I like Texas." But as she said it, she wondered if it was true. Since she was young, she knew she would live in Texas. Pondering whether or not she would like it had never really occurred to her. Until now, Addie realized she had not stopped to consider how much of her life seemed to be preplanned.

"Living near family has its challenges," Cole acknowledged. "My mother was the real reason I came back. Daddy's always been hard on her, so I guess I came back to make things easier for her. She's his second wife, and..." This time it was Cole who paused as though he just realized he was taking it further than he meant to. "Well, I'm glad to be back. Especially since I got a chance to meet you."

Cole led the way down a small game trail to the large tree-line pond.

"I remember coming here when I was a kid," she said. "And, if I remember right, there was a rope swing, just over..." Her eyes lit up when she saw it across the pond. "There it is!" The wood was rotted, and it dangled limply on a frayed piece of rope.

Spotting it, Cole said, "I don't think we'll be using that any time soon."

"Guess not."

Addie saw a turtle's head break the surface of the water for an instant before it dipped back down. The whole pond glistened as it reflected the reddish orange setting sun.

"It's so beautiful here." She stood for a minute admiring the spectacular scenery, and Cole moved to stand in front of her. The setting sunlight made his already dazzling smile glow as if he was posed for a toothpaste commercial. Addie would have laughed, but he took both of her hands in his and pulled her close.

The kiss was soft and slow and tender. It took Addie only a second to recover from her surprise before she leaned into him. She breathed deeply and for a moment was almost overwhelmed by a swirl of sensations, the wind tugging softly on her hair and sweeping across her face, the scent of the man mingling sensually with nature, the gentle flutter of the leaves and the faint rush of air as they breathed in unison.

After a minute, Cole pulled back and smiled slowly into her opening eyes. "I hope I didn't take you by surprise. The moment seemed right."

"Thank goodness Mel is back at the house," Addie said with a sultry smile. He pulled her into his arms hugging her gently against his chest. She was at least half a head shorter than Cole and felt totally safe and comfortable in his embrace.

"It's getting pretty dark," he said, and his voice was soft and low. "Maybe we should head back while we can still see the path." Though part of her wanted to stay and see where the moment would lead, she knew he was right.

"Good girl. He won't respect you if you come on too fast," said the all-too-familiar voice in her head. Talk about a mood killer!

Cole led Addie back up the narrow trail, but when they were in the open, they walked side-by-side, and he held her hand back to the house. They didn't talk but enjoyed the nocturnal sounds and the violet sky that heralded the night.

Back at the patio, Cole held the door for Addie.

"Well, it's getting late," he said moving to the front door. "And, unfortunately, I have some work to do tomorrow."

"You have to work on Sunday? So much for laid back country life," Addie replied feeling a bit deflated that he had to work.

"Not as a rule, but I have a pretty big case. We're coordinating with our office in Houston, and I need to go over some depositions. But next weekend, I'm all yours." He leaned down to give her a goodbye kiss and smiled sweetly. As he was walking to his truck, he turned around. "And I'm not working all day. Who knows, I may have time to stop by, you know, just to check on things. Since we're neighbors and all." She could hear the teasing in his voice, and she smiled and waved.

"Night neighbor!"

She watched him climb into his truck and back out. Addie waved one last time before closing the door.

CHAPTER 12

Addie leaned against the door and closed her eyes. Mel was sitting in the hallway watching her with his head cocked to one side. She laughed and threw her hands wide.

"What a day, Mel!" The little dog scrambled to his feet and ran to her. Addie lifted him up and twirled with him while he licked her face. "Can you believe this place? I know I can't! But sometimes, you just have to go with the flow, know what I mean?"

She stopped twirling and looked up at the fixture in the entryway. For the life of her, she could not figure out what it was. She didn't see light bulbs, and if it was a decorative sculpture, then she simply didn't understand it. Stella had said it was a surprise for her, so it probably did something, but what that was she could only guess.

"I wonder if we should go check on our feline friends," she said to Mel heading up the stairs. "I think if you just stand guard in the hallway, all should be well."

They still had plenty of food, and she refilled the water bowl, then headed back downstairs. When she got to the bottom of the stairs, she realized she had left the hallway light on. Searching for a switch downstairs that would turn it off, she flicked several near the entryway and was relieved when one of them was successful. At the same time, Addie heard a faint buzzing sound and was afraid something might be wrong with the electrical system.

"Please don't burst into flames," she pleaded with the house and could feel a knot growing in the pit of her stomach.

Suddenly, in the darkness above, she saw a flicker of glowing light that quickly faded a dim green before disappearing. She saw another, then another, and realized that the sculpture above her head was rapidly growing into a swarm of fireflies that danced in the darkness. It was mesmerizing. After about a minute, there was enough of the pale light to cast a soft glow in the entry. She had no idea how it worked, but the effect was magical. There were hundreds of lights, and Addie stared at them as though in a trance. She watched as several lights seemed to leave the nest and fly down the hallway. She had never noticed the small wires along the hall, but now, here they were, lighting her way to the kitchen.

"That's why I didn't see them before. They only

work when all the lights are off," she said softly. Now she remembered the words from Stella's journal. "Fireflies lead to love in the darkness."

Still staring up into the flickering lights above, she said, "Stella, you are one amazing woman."

She switched on an overhead light in the kitchen before turning off the firefly lights. Grabbing the opened bottle of wine from the fridge and a wine glass from the cupboard, she made her way to the bedroom. The room was cool, and she filled Stella's clawfoot tub with steaming hot water. She lit several candles around the tub and slipped in for a soak. Mel sat peacefully on the cool tile floor watching the candlelight glimmer on the ceiling.

The combination of the wine and hot sudsy bath had Addie sighing with contentment. She honestly could not think of a more memorable day. On her fourteenth birthday, she found out that she made first chair in the school orchestra. Her parents were so happy for her. They took the whole family out for dinner at Addie's favorite Chinese restaurant, and she got her first CD player as a gift. That was a pretty good day, but nothing like today.

Addie squished bubbles between her fingers and wondered if every day in Destiny would be so eventful. "I hope not, or I might not survive!"

Even the voice in her head was approving. "*Things are looking up dear. I told you to be patient.*"

"Here's to you, Mom," Addie said and drained her glass.

She climbed out of the tub too tired to do anything

except comb her hair, pull a nightgown over her head, and slide into Stella's enormous bed. Mel soon followed, and the two snuggled happily.

Although she was tired, she reached for Stella's journal anxious to know more about this intriguing little hamlet where all the women are strong and all the men are good-looking. She giggled thinking about the line from *Lake Wobegon*. It certainly fit here.

She propped herself up against the pillows and opened the journal.

June 29, 1991

I called your parents today and invited you to the ranch. They said the timing was perfect, and they would arrive in a week or so. You just turned eight, and I wonder how you look now that you are growing up.

The past five years have been difficult. I have continued to work in town. I had to give up the classroom instruction, but I continue to run the library. Destiny has grown quite a bit. I bet they have 5,000 people now. It is remarkable, but once the artisans were gone from around here and I spent more time working in town, the community began to open up for me.

I still live at the ranch, which seems closer to town every day. I have continued to try to make a difference, but art education ranks pretty low around here. Thank God we have a library in town or the whole place would be nothing but football!

I have had an occasional traveler or two stay with me and work from time to time, but nothing to build a community around.

July 9, 1991

Your parents arrived with you today. It was so great to see how much you had grown. I also got to meet your sister. What a sweet pair the two of you make.

Your parents were both disappointed that the ranch had faded. They are great supporters of the arts, and I could tell they felt a sense of loss. I showed them around the grounds—the empty buildings still shout for someone to fill them. Ideas, like the land, are just waiting for discovery.

I wanted them to stay at the ranch, but your father wanted to stay in town—except for you! They are letting you stay with me tonight. We had a very nice lunch after which you and I headed out to Lake Addie—as you just recently named it. We even got a visit from a neighbor boy who heard you were staying with me. He taught you to fish and how to skip stones.

Actually, the pond is the reason we are in this particular location. When we came out here in the 50's our natural spring-fed pond was the only permanent surface water for more than 50 miles. My daddy purchased this land for the water. It was too isolated back then, so my family never lived here. But when he was gone and left the land to me, it seemed like the perfect place to launch our dream. The barn and several of the outbuildings were already here, and that gave us our start.

"Lake Addie," she said softly. "I had my first kiss from Cole at Lake Addie. How perfect."

July 10, 1991

My heart is filled with joy at seeing you again. Your smile and laugh fill this house and grounds like I haven't heard for a long time. We spent the evening catching fireflies and putting them in jars. I told you the story my mama told me about fireflies. Do you remember it?

'Long ago, a young fawn was lost in the woods. Separated from her mother, she became very scared as darkness fell upon the forest. The night sounds terrified the little fawn, and she began to whimper when she heard wolves howling in the distance. Too frightened to move, she looked up into the tall trees hoping beyond hope that her mother would find her soon.

'Suddenly, a small flicker of light appeared in front of her. She watched as it faded into the night. Then another light appeared, and another, and another. These flashes of light were the woodland fireflies. These magical insects are the sparks of light that lead to love in the darkness. Soon, there were hundreds of fireflies swarming in front of the terrified fawn, their flashing light showing the way through the forest. Stepping carefully, she followed the flickering light until she was once again reunited with her mother and the herd, where she was loved and safe.'

Don't worry, my Addie. When you need to find your way, when you feel you are lost or need direction, look for the fireflies. They will lead you where you need to go, where you will find love and happiness.

July 12, 1991
It was time for you to leave today. I gave you a small ceramic fish and a big hug. I fear I may never see you again. I watched as your family car pulled out of the ranch and headed away. The ranch has been essentially empty for four years now, but it never felt lonely until seeing you leave. I cried for hours after you left.

July 13, 1991

I went to town today and made up my final will. Woody Dudley was a former member of our community who longed, as a young man, to be a writer. He gave up his dream and turned to the law instead. I've told him many times that his creative defenses help people as much as a well written book. He just laughed at me like I was crazy, but he always gave me free legal help in spite of my off-the-wall thoughts. He is a good friend, and I am so glad he returned to Destiny. You can always trust him to help you when you need it.

Addie read through a few more pages of entries. Most of them were short with quick details about her day, and there was an entry each year on Addie's birthday. Toward the end of the journal, the time between entries lengthened, and it was becoming difficult to piece together a cohesive story. Then a particular entry caught her eye.

August 11, 1995

NAFTA is finally coming to Destiny. The Free Trade A-GREEDment is going to change our town forever. It was announced that several companies are building a distribution center in Destiny, now that the railyard has expanded. Texas Mart and Union Foods along with a few others are putting together a major point of entry from Mexico. People expect manufacturing, distribution, and transportation to combine and completely alter the financial landscape of opportunity around here. Locals think we will grow from a quaint 5,000 to more than 60,000 residents eventually. I feel ill.

None of this would even be here if it weren't for a bunch of hippies who believed they could make a difference. How ironic that we shunned wealth and money and our efforts are spawning huge industry.

June 29, 2001

You turned 18 today. A young woman. I got a card from your mother recently that said you were thinking about going to the University of North Texas to study music—wow! You're an artist. I'm so proud of you.

Addie lowered the book for a moment. Had her mother really told Stella that she was going to study music? Was she too embarrassed that Addie had decided to pursue a degree in education instead of the arts? Addie hoped it was just a misunderstanding on Stella's part, but deep inside she doubted it was. She knew her parents were proud of her and that they loved her. Still, it hurt to find out they may have harbored misgivings about her intended life plan. With a sigh, Addie read on.

April 26, 2001

I am 75 years young today. I hardly ever go upstairs in the house because of a dodgy hip, and the ranch grounds are getting worse by the day. I do have some of my former students come by periodically to help with chores and such, and that's a big help. My needs are few, but even so, times have been difficult. I almost made a call to Conrad but decided it was not needed.

I have spent my life serving the community, and now I find that I am dependent on others for all kinds of life's essentials. I still drive and try to get to the library several times a week. The children bring me such joy and energy. I feel younger after a day of reading stories to preschoolers.

June 12, 2006

I got another offer to buy the ranch today. Honestly, how many times is that man going to try to take what's mine before he understands that I am NEVER going to sell to him. He may be a fancy judge with a fancy ranch and lots of fancy money, but my answer is still no. I know it is not the right thing to do. I don't really know if it's a "flashlight" or just common sense. But I cannot sell my land to him.

Did she mean Judge Wescott? She couldn't image there were too many judges around here that owned a ranch. Judge Wescott wanted to buy the Destiny Ranch? But why was Stella so sure it was the wrong thing to do? She was getting older. Selling might have been a sensible thing to do. Addie wished she had written more about it.

February 26 2006

I have decided to close the journal and put it where you can find it. My handwriting and eyesight are becoming problematic. And I don't know how much longer I have before I leave this world. It is important to me to be prepared for your arrival because I was not ready the first time you dropped by.

I want to tell you that you still bring joy to my heart. To this day, you are the only child ever born here. During my most difficult times, I could think of you and it would brighten my mood. Please remember me fondly, and take care of my things.

I love you my child.

Aunt Stella

Addie closed the book and held it against her chest. She felt a closeness to this woman that went far beyond any bonds of duty. She was family. Aunt Stella was her family, and she would take care of her possessions as carefully as if they were her own.

Satisfied with her decision, she turned out the light and slid into a deep, much needed sleep.

CHAPTER 13

Monday morning started a little later than usual for Addie. She lay in bed stretching her arms and legs, which were quite sore from a strenuous day of moving boxes in the attic yesterday. She had thought about calling Marsha to help, but then decided she would rather spend the first day working by herself and getting acquainted with everything. The attic was unbearably hot and dusty, so she had taken frequent breaks to cool off and rehydrate.

It was during one of those breaks that Cole had stopped by with sandwiches and iced tea. Although she was excited to see him, she was horribly embarrassed by her disheveled, sweaty appearance. She made an excuse to duck into the bedroom to quickly brush her hair and towel off, but she knew she was no match for his casual but always pulled-together look. Did the man ever sweat? He lived in West Texas for goodness sake. He rode a horse. Surely he got dirty sometime! Thinking of it now had Addie groaning over the awkward encounter. Fortunately, Cole hadn't seemed to notice. He stayed for about an hour and then said he had to get back to work. And he kissed her sweetly before going.

Addie smiled at the direction her summer was taking. She might have lounged in bed even longer, savoring every delicious memory of her time with Cole, if not for Mel's incessant whining.

"OK, OK," she told the impatient pup. "But I hope you know you're totally ruining my morning with your constant neediness."

He barked back at her when she finally climbed out of bed and ran ahead of her to the patio door nearly jumping off the floor with excitement. After she let Mel outside, Addie stood in the kitchen massaging the back of her arm. Then she bent over and rubbed the backs of her legs.

"How can I be this out of shape?" she said out loud. "Coffee. Coffee will save me."

She turned to put on a pot of coffee when she heard a motor at the back of the house. Peering out the kitchen window, she saw a man on a tractor mowing part of Stella's land. It looked like it might be Travis. She thought about going out to see what he was doing, but that would require her to pull on clothes and actually move. She didn't feel capable of doing either at the moment.

Addie grabbed a cup of coffee and decided to skip her usual breakfast bar. She was typically a pretty light eater, and since being in Destiny, she noticed that the meals were more substantial than she normally ate. She still had over an hour to get ready for her meeting with Mr. Dudley, but at the rate she was moving, she would need every minute of it.

After she had bathed and dressed, she felt much more refreshed. She looked outside, but Travis was gone. Too bad, she thought. I would have liked to thank him for helping out.

She pulled up to Mr. Dudley's office a bit early, so she decided to pop into The Hushpuppy for another cup of coffee even though she knew Marsha wouldn't be there. Hesitating at the door, she wondered how she knew that. Had Marsha told her? No, somehow she knew that Marsha was supposed to be there but wasn't. And when she opened the door, she was greeted by a large, somewhat overwrought man trying to wait tables.

"Just find yourself a seat, ma'am," he said to Addie from across the room. "I'll be with you in a sec."

The café was reasonably full for a Monday morning, mostly business men and ranchers along with a few moms who were trying to keep wiggly kids from being too fussy. She squeezed into a small table near the curio cabinet.

"What'll you have," asked the man who had appeared at her table after delivering a pile of plates to several booths.

"Just coffee today, thanks," said Addie. "Is Marsha working?"

"Supposed ta be, but she got herself stuck out in a creek bed looking for some damned old rocks or something. She called and said she was 'stuck tighter 'n snot on a hot oven door' whatever that means." With that, he lumbered back to the kitchen to do some cooking.

I'm guessing that was Junior, thought Addie digging into her purse for her cell phone. The fact that Marsha was supposed to be there and wasn't, and that she knew it ahead of time had her worried. She had an uneasy feeling, although she figured if Marsha was talking like that then things probably weren't dire.

"Hey, you," said Marsha on the other end.

"I heard you had a little trouble this morning. Are you OK?"

"I'm fine. Old man Harris came along and helped me out. I'm on my way to work now. How'd you know I was stuck?"

"I'm at The Hushpuppy now. I'm just about to meet with Mr. Dudley."

"Well, you'll probably miss me. But come by later if you can."

Junior delivered Addie's coffee, and she sipped it absently still thinking about Marsha. She hadn't had a vision, or "flashlight," about people she knew since she was young. In the past several years her psychic episodes had been frustratingly dull. Come to think of it, she thought, this was the first flashlight she'd had since coming to Destiny. But maybe she'd just been too busy to notice them.

Not sure what to make of it all, she scanned her messages while waiting for her appointment with Woody. Her mother wanted to know how things were going. Heather was dying to know more details about her cowboy. There were a couple of work notices about technology and summer office hours. Her school was doing a book study on *The Primal Teacher*, so she would need to stop by and pick up her copy. Nothing too urgent, she decided. And a good thing, because she needed to head over to Mr. Dudley's office.

Sitting across from Woody, with his free and easy manner and cozy office, it was easy to think she had known him for years.

"I hope you're enjoying your stay in Destiny," he said rifling through his desk drawer.

"Very much," she smiled at him. "From what I've seen, it's a great place, and I've met quite a few people already."

"Yeah, that's Destiny. We have a lot of friendly folks here. So, you haven't changed your mind about being the executor of Stella's estate?"

"Absolutely not," said Addie with certainty. "I'm ready to go."

"OK, then. We have a few forms for you. I highlighted the places where you need to sign. And I'll need a copy of your driver's license."

The two worked on paperwork for several minutes, and then Woody made copies of everything for Addie. Despite the somewhat cluttered office, he was very organized and efficient. The teacher in her was pleased.

"Now then," said Woody pulling a long envelope off a nearby stack of papers. "That takes care of the formalities. But there are a few more things we need to go over. First, you should know that I'm handling this case pro bono. Stella was very important to me, to my life, and it's my way of paying her back for everything she's done for me over the years."

"How kind," said Addie.

"Next, I want you to expect that there will be interested parties in her house and land, maybe even some of the art. The Destiny Ranch holds historic value in this part of the country, and I've already been approached by Judge Wescott saying he wants to buy the place. He made a very generous offer." He looked at her curiously but continued without giving her a chance to reply.

"And finally, I have a copy of the will for you," he said pulling it out of the envelope. "You'll find that you are essentially the sole beneficiary of her estate. There is one other individual named, and he gets to pick one item from the estate as long as it's not the house or the grounds. I told you; Stella marched to her own beat."

Addie sat in silence for a moment with her mouth open. It had never occurred to her that she would be named in the will.

"You mean, the house, the art, the land, all of it belongs to me?" she asked slowly trying to understand how this had happened.

"Yup, it's all yours. Except for the one item selected by the other party."

Addie was still staring straight ahead and hadn't blinked since he told her.

"Didn't you know it all went to you?"

"I had no idea. I haven't had any contact with Stella since I was eight years old."

"What do you mean?" asked Woody.

"My family visited the ranch when I was eight. It was a wonderful trip. Stella and I did all kinds of stuff together. But that was the last time I had seen or heard from her, except for a yearly birthday card."

"You're kidding?" Woody seemed a bit surprised. "The way she carried on about you I thought she was in touch." He chuckled after thinking about it. "But this is just the kind of thing should would do."

"Mr. Dudley. Woody." Addie caught herself and looked up at him with wide eyes. "I don't even know how Stella died. At first, I didn't ask because I didn't want to seem pushy. Then after a while, I didn't want to seem stupid. I don't know how she died, I don't know where she was buried, or even if she was buried. I didn't know she had left me everything." She spoke in rapid succession as if she were a student trying to explain why she was tardy to class.

"Oh my... I had no idea," stammered Woody. "Let me fill in some gaps for you then. She passed away about three weeks ago on a flight to Dallas. We assumed she was going to visit you, so I guess we assumed you knew how she died. She actually died on the plane as it was getting ready to land."

"Stella," Addie whispered the words and went suddenly pale. It was Stella who had died on the plane the night she and Bradley broke up. She remembered it vividly. Bradly had been late getting to her apartment because traffic from the DFW airport was backed up all the way into Denton due to an inflight death. The news report had simply said that an elderly woman had passed away on a plane. Addie had been glued to the television, strangely touched by the incident, but not sure why. Now she knew. That lonely old woman was Stella! And she was coming to see her.

Addie could feel her vision narrowing, and her breathing was quick and shallow. "What? How?" Her heart was racing while she struggled to make sense of what she had just learned. The room was just beginning to fade into darkness, and Addie quickly put her head between her knees in an attempt to stay conscious.

"Oh, good heavens!" A startled and frightened Woody flew around the desk and put his hand on her back. "Addie, are you all right? Do you need something to drink?"

After a minute, Addie's breathing slowed and she sat up slowly. Her face was flush and her hair was tossed about her head.

"That was interesting," she tried to joke, but she could see the concern on Woody's face. "I'm so sorry. That has never happened to me." She put her hand over her heart as though to calm her nerves.

"Are you OK?" Woody asked, his hand still on her back as though he were afraid she might fall over.

"I think so," Addie said with a small smile. "But if you have something cold to drink, I wouldn't refuse it."

"Of course, of course," said Woody hurrying from the room.

While he was gone, Addie tried to smooth her hair and shirt. What had just happened, she wondered. She waited for the steady voice of her mother to respond and was disappointed when it didn't.

"Here you go," said Woody handing her an ice-cold Coke. She popped the top with a fizz and took a sip, then held the cold can against her temple.

"I had no idea the news would affect you like that. You gave me a scare."

"Me too." She looked at him apologetically. "You see, Stella's death made the news where I live, and I remember watching it on TV. They didn't mention her name, but it really struck me as so sad. I remember almost crying at the story and having no idea why it was hitting me like that. I didn't even know who it was." She took a deep breath to steady herself. "Now I do."

Woody just looked at her and shook his head slightly. "That's unbelievable."

They both sat in silence for a minute.

"So, where is Stella now?" asked Addie.

"She was returned to San Antonio after a viewing here for local people so we could pay our respects. She was buried in her family plot on the south side of town. I don't think anyone from Destiny made the trip, except Travis. He helped with the transport and some of the arrangements."

"How nice. Were he and Stella close?"

"I think so. I know she always spoke very fondly of him, as though he were special to her, but I don't know much about their relationship. He did chores for her, and I know they were neighbors. Maybe there was more to it. That's probably why she named him in her will."

"Do you know Travis very well?" She was curious about the arrogant fireman. It seemed like there might be more to him than her initial impression allowed.

"I suppose. He's a great guy. Played football in high school. I think he played with Cole. He was a hell of a tackle. We all thought he might play ball in college, but he really wasn't interested in it. He went to college at Texas A&M to study agricultural engineering and then joined a firm in Houston. I heard he was doing really well, working in their research division. But he came back home about six months ago to take care of his daddy. Red has Alzheimer's, and Travis came back once it started getting dangerous for Red to live by himself. Their house is not too far from the Destiny Ranch. You should get to know him now that you're neighbors."

She looked at him and shook her head. "That's so weird to think about. I have neighbors here."

"We take that seriously around here. We sometimes have to rely on each other a bit more than city folk do."

"I can see that," she said nodding her head.

"One more thing. Stella used to be our town librarian, and she was all set to volunteer at Destiny

Days. She reads stories to the kids. They all love it, and she's been doing it for years. Anyway, the librarian wanted me to ask if you'd like to do it this year."

"Oh," she paused to think. "Well, I am an English teacher, and I love kids. And, since I'm going to the festival anyway, sure. Why not?" She was still amazed that this little town seemed to be embracing her so completely.

"Great! I'll let Ms. Hunter know to expect you," he jotted something on a notepad before continuing. "So, you're going to the festival. Are you going with Marsha? I hear you two are becoming fast friends."

Small town gossip spreads fast, thought Addie. "No, actually. I'm going with Cole. He and his father showed up at The Hushpuppy just after you left last time and invited me."

"They did, did they? I'm not surprised." Woody hesitated as if he was going to say more and then thought better of it. "Well, I think I've covered enough for today. Maybe a little too much," he said patting her hand. "But you're welcome to sit and stay as long as you need."

"Thanks, but I'm feeling much better. And I have a lot to think about," she said and stood up to leave. Suddenly she stopped and turned back to Woody. "I'm sorry, but did you say Travis was named in the will?"

"Yes, I did. He's the other party I spoke about. He doesn't know it yet, but I'll meet with him later today, and then you two can sort that out between you. But if you need any help, all you have to do is holler. And let me know if you decide you want to sell. I can help put you in touch with the right people."

"Thanks, but I think it's too early for me to think about selling. Somehow I feel I owe it to Stella to go slowly and make the right decisions with her things." She paused for a second and then added. "My things, I guess." She was still having trouble believing she had just inherited a ranch. "Please tell Judge Wescott that I'm not ready to sell just yet. And thanks for everything, Woody. Really. You're making this much easier than it might be." She put her hand out, and he grasped it with both of his and squeezed warmly.

"Any time, my dear. Any time."

It was just about lunchtime when Addie finished, so she decided to check on Marsha. She was relieved to see that life had returned to normal at The Hushpuppy with Junior back in the kitchen and a slender girl with a huge ponytail bounding from table to table. Marsha certainly was good at her job.

Addie slipped into an empty booth near the front and waited for her friend to notice.

"Hey, girl," she said handing Addie a Dr. Pepper in a tall icy glass. "I guess you're finished with the legal eagle."

"I am, and I have a bunch to tell you. But first, are you OK? What happened?"

"Oh, the usual with me. I'll tell you about it later, but right now I've got a bunch of orders to take around, and I better get to it before Junior starts squawkin'. You hungry?"

"Actually, I could eat."

"Let me grab you a menu."

"Don't bother. Just surprise me."

"Boy, you are brave," Marsha called out over her shoulder with a wave.

With a few minutes to herself, Addie began replaying the facts in her head. Was Stella really coming to see me? Why didn't she let me know? And what was she coming for? People don't really just drop dead like that without any notice, do they? She felt like a crime scene investigator on one of those horrible TV police dramas. Rubbing her temples, she was hoping for some words of wisdom from her mother, who was still conspicuously absent. I guess I'll just have to call and talk to the real thing, she thought.

Addie took a sip of her drink when Marsha appeared with a plate of meatloaf, mashed potatoes, and green beans.

"It's the blue plate special today. Pretty good, and really fast," Marsha said sliding into the booth across from Addie. "So, what's the hot news?"

"Where do I start? Turns out I'm not just the executor of Stella's estate, I'm the sole heir."

"No!" squeaked Marsha. "This is huge! Bigger'n a polar bear in a mousetrap! How do you feel about getting' all that stuff?"

"I don't know, really. I've never owned a ranch before. I've never even owned a house. I don't even own my own car outright. It's just so overwhelming." Addie put her hands on her temples again and shook her head.

"Are you kidding? It's one of the best places in town! And all that land? Shoot, girl. You were pretty hot stuff when you came to town. But now you just shot up to most eligible bachelorette in four counties!"

"But I don't even live here," Addie said in hushed tones as though she was worried someone would overhear her. "I love the ranch, but I live in Denton."

"Forever?" Marsha shot back. "You so sure you're gonna live there forever? Just think about it. You just inherited a mansion full of art. That's what I was doing this morning. After seeing all of those amazing pieces at Stella's, I got inspired. I was out rock hunting so I could finish a project I was working on. You can't tell me that place doesn't inspire you too."

"Yes, it does," admitted Addie. "But moving my whole life for it? I don't know."

"You've done it before. That's how you ended up in Texas in the first place."

Before Addie could respond, she saw Cole walk in. Following her gaze, Marsha turned to see what she was looking at.

"You moved to Denton for a man, why not Destiny," she said nodding her head toward Cole.

Cole walked into the restaurant and scanned the tables until he spotted Addie. When he saw her watching him, he waved in greeting.

"I saw your car as I drove by and thought I'd stop and say howdy." He placed a hand gently on her shoulder to reach down and give her a sweet kiss before sliding into the booth next to Addie.

"Hey Marsha," Cole nodded a greeting toward her.

"Would you mind getting me a cold RC Cola and a fresh moon pie?"

Realizing she was still on the clock, Marsha scrambled up to fill his order.

"Lots of ice," Cole said as she scurried to the back. He moved around the table and took Addie's hands in his.

Cole was again dressed in an ironed button-down shirt, but this time he wore pleated black slacks. His Wayfarer sunglasses crowned his head, and Addie noticed the bronze tanning on his face showed a slight patch where the glasses protected his eyes. He was gorgeous, as usual.

Addie felt a little more comfortable next to his dazzling looks today. Since bumping into him was becoming a more frequent occurrence, she had taken to applying make-up and dressing a bit more carefully when she went out. She wore figure-flattering faded blue jeans and white canvas wedge sandals that showed manicured toes with pastel pink polish. A tight red tank top under a white short-sleeved shirt complimented her blonde hair, which she had left down to fall around her shoulders.

"Aren't you a sight for sore eyes," Cole said smiling at her.

"Back at ya," she said smoothly flashing a smile of her own.

"I was just running back to the office from the courthouse, so this is a welcome break. What are you up to today?"

"Not too much. More organizing and cataloging out

at the ranch."

"Sounds fun," he said and then shook his head. "Actually, sounds ghastly."

"Yes, I'm so looking forward to it. But I'll feel better once I know exactly what's there. I just hope it doesn't take months!"

"Oh, I think it will definitely take months," he said with a grin. "Maybe years. You really can't rush these things." Cole's smile was charming as he leaned back in his chair. Marsha delivered his pie and drink, and he motioned toward Addie.

"Actually, the pie's for her," he told Marsha and handed her a $20 bill. "And lunch is on me." He smiled and downed about half of his drink before sliding from the booth. "Ladies," he said with a nod as he turned to leave.

"At least he's a good tipper," said Marsha still upset after being pushed from the booth.

"I wonder what else he's good at?" said Addie suggestively.

"Oh girl, you got that lost puppy in a kindergarten at lunch time look on your face."

"No I don't, but that is a damn good looking man."

"Looks ain't everything," Marsha reminded her.

"OK... looks, money, a white horse, and looks."

"Oh sister come back to earth and eat your lunch. Remember you're a ranch owner now and quite good looking yourself."

"Just think of the beautiful babies we could have," said Addie looking into the distance with glossy blue eyes and the hint of a smile curving her mouth.

"Eat," Marsha commanded one more time with a roll of her eyes before heading back to the kitchen.

CHAPTER 14

The next morning found Addie once again sleeping a little later than she wanted. But she woke well rested and ready for another day of organizational madness. Actually, she had a pretty good system going, but it did require a lot of running up and down stairs and moving objects. Since the upstairs bedrooms were essentially empty, she used them to sort and categorize pieces. She had even written signs on the doors so she didn't get confused. One room was for paintings, photography, and drawings of any kind including frames. The next room was for sculptures, pottery, textiles, metal works and any other type of three-dimensional art. She had a room for ordinary household items and another for small furniture.

Working this way kept her on track, and she was

beginning to make a dent in one corner of the attic. Marsha said she would stop by after her shift late this afternoon, so Addie wanted to make sure she had a system that would allow them to work productively.

But, first things first. She headed to the kitchen to make coffee. When she opened the back door for Mel, she saw that more of the land surrounding the house had been cut down. Travis, no doubt. But when did he come, and why did she not hear him? Was he some kind of stealth landscaper? She really needed to thank him, and since they also needed to discuss the will, she decided a little neighborly visit was in order.

Addie turned to her newly cleaned and organized pantry and pulled out supplies for making chocolate chip cookies. She had made a trip to the grocery store yesterday, deciding that she needed to stock up for at least a couple of weeks. Throwing chocolate chips in her basket had been an impulse buy, but now she was glad she had them. She would take a plate of cookies to Travis and his father as a thank you for helping out.

Addie was dressed casually in faded denim shorts and a pale pink and white baseball t-shirt. She had her hair neatly tucked into a ponytail and had applied mascara and a little lip gloss. Even though her first meeting with Travis hadn't been that smooth, she couldn't deny that he was a good-looking man and it never hurt to look presentable.

"*Yes, indeed,*" agreed her mother's voice. "*Present yourself as though you're proud to be you. You never know who you're going to run into.*"

"There you are," said Addie to the voice in her head. "I hate to say it, but I actually missed you!"

Addie looked again at the directions she had gotten from Woody and slowed the car. Everything here was so spread out, and she wasn't sure where she was supposed to turn. She saw a mailbox up ahead on the left, and as she neared it she saw it matched the address she was given. Spying a house at the end of a long dirt drive, she turned assuming that was the place.

As she drove closer, she saw a one-story ranch-style home painted a pale yellow accented with white stones. An older green pick-up truck was parked in front of the garage. The house looked like it was built in the 50's, and though it was old, it looked well maintained, and the yard surrounding it was clean and tidy.

Holding her plate of cookies, Addie rang the doorbell and waited. When no one appeared, she knocked several times. This time, she heard some scuffling behind the door, which was finally opened by an elderly man with a short grey beard. He was taller than Addie by a few inches, and his denim overalls hung loosely on his thin frame. The blue plaid shirt underneath looked faded and worn, but his overall appearance was of a man who had once been robust, maybe even good looking, in his younger years.

Addie smiled at him in greeting, but he looked at her with confusion. "I'm sorry, do I know you?" he asked a bit hesitantly.

"Not yet," she said. "I'm Addie Butterfield, and I live just around the corner at the Destiny Ranch. I was looking for Travis Granger." She smiled again hoping a friendly face would put him at ease.

"The Destiny Ranch, you say? I thought Stella was gone. Are you staying with her?"

Addie remembered Woody telling her that Travis' father had Alzheimer's disease, and she hoped she was not upsetting him.

"Yes, I'm staying there. You must be Mr. Granger," she said and held out her hand.

"Yes, yes I am," he said reaching to shake her hand. "Would you like to come in?" He relaxed enough to smile back at her.

"Thank you, that would be great."

"And please call me Red. No one calls me Mr. Granger anymore."

Addie followed him into a large entryway that held a round glass-topped table with a star etched elegantly into it atop a stunning driftwood base. The entryway opened into an expansive living room that held a large leather sofa facing a wall of windows that showcased a view of the patio and the undulating hills behind it. The room had a western decor that might look kitschy in another place, but in this setting was both comfortable and appropriate.

"What a lovely home you have," Addie exclaimed taking it all in.

"This is all my wife's doing," he said fondly. "She loved to decorate, and I haven't changed a thing since she's been gone." He looked off into the distance, and Addie wasn't sure what to say.

"I brought this for you," she said holding the plate

out for him. "I wanted to thank Travis for helping out at the ranch." He took the plate from her and looked at the cookies under the plastic wrap. "I hope you like chocolate chip cookies," she said feeling a bit foolish for explaining what they were.

"I do, yes, I do," he said and put the plate down on the entry table. Then he turned back to her. "Did you say you were here to see Travis?"

"Yes, is he home?"

"He is, yes he is. He's out back in the barn," he said pointing out the window. "You can go out there if you want."

"I don't want to disturb him if he's busy," she told him.

"You can go out to see him there. He would like that, I think. Yes, go out and see him."

"OK, thanks," she said and followed him to the back door. She felt him watch her as she walked out, so she turned and waved.

A well-worn pathway led to the barn, which was a good fifty yards from the house. The large barn doors were closed, and she wasn't sure if she should knock. Addie pulled the rope on one of the huge doors and it creaked open. She stepped inside and was surprised by what she saw. Instead of the farm equipment, bales of hay, and pitchforks she expected, she saw several rows of long tables that held aquariums. Some of them were under lights of various colors, and all had something growing in them. A large fan at the back of the barn circulated cool air, which she could just begin to feel from across the room. A computer and printer along with stacks of papers and books sat on a table near the fan, and she saw Travis hunched over the keyboard staring at the glowing screen.

"Hello," she called out to him from the door. Startled, he looked up and was clearly surprised to see her.

"Addie," he rose as he said her name. He bent to pick up a pencil that fell from the table when he stood. "What a surprise. What are you doing here?" He smiled at her as he walked across the room to welcome her in.

"I came to..." she couldn't finish her thought and looked around in confusion. "The better question is what are you doing here?"

"Welcome to my secret lair," he said with amusement standing about a foot in front of her. She had to look up to see his face. Addie hadn't noticed how tall he was when they first met. As on that day, he was again wearing jeans and a white t-shirt.

"I..., I...," she started and then looked around again at the equipment she saw lining the sides of the barn. Trying again, she said, "I thought you were a fireman."

"I am," he said and tried to sound serious. "One of Destiny's finest. Oh wait, that's the police department."

She looked up at him and saw the corners of his eyes crease when he grinned. She couldn't help but smile back at him. "Seriously," she continued. "What is all of this stuff?"

"You first," he said. "Not that I'm not happy to see you, but I am surprised. What brings you out this way?"

"I brought cookies," she said pointing back toward the house. "As a 'thank you' for all of the work you've been doing at the ranch. I left them with your dad."

"That's terrible," he said and turned to walk back to his work. "You should have brought them in here." He looked over his shoulder and grinned, motioning for her to follow him. "I guess you could call this my lab. I've been experimenting with creating a new approach to biofuels using different types of organic materials, you know, like algae and micro algae and other stuff. It's really very top secret. If I tell you any more, I'll have to kill you."

"That's amazing," she said taking a closer look at the tanks. She could swear she saw something move in one of them and stepped back apprehensively. "Don't look now, but I think your biofuel is about to climb out of its tank."

"Well, if it bites me, maybe I'll get to have super powers. I'll be able to fuel small cities and charge car batteries for damsels in distress."

She laughed at this and walked over to the fan while he sat behind the make-shift desk. "How do you get it to blow cool air? It feels great in here."

He seemed pleased that she had asked. "I built a geothermal heating and cooling system right behind the barn. It works pretty well, but this room is not well insulated, so the effects are not as good as they might be."

"You built a geo-what?"

"It's a way to use the earth's natural temperature to heat or cool the air inside a structure."

"And how does one build such a thing?" she asked curiously.

"Basically, you did a big hole and put tubing in it. See here," he said pointing to a pipe coming out of the ground. "The air underground stays at a constant temperature so when you circulate it down there and exchange it with the air in here it either heats or cools depending on if your air is warmer or cooler than the underground temperature."

"Ingenious," she said genuinely impressed. "And what got you started with the biofuel?"

"I worked in the renewable energy division of a firm right out of college doing research and development. We were doing some breakthrough work, really advanced stuff, and I just wanted to keep it going." He walked over to the computer and typed in a couple of numbers.

"Yes, Mr. Dudley said you moved back home to take care of your dad. I'm so sorry about that, but it's wonderful of you to want to care for him yourself."

Travis shrugged. "He's my dad. Of course I'm going to take care of him."

"You don't have any other brothers or sisters?"

"Nope, just me and dad. Mom passed away about four years ago, and he was diagnosed with Alzheimer's about a year later. It was pretty mild at first, but then it became clear he couldn't live by himself, so I moved back."

"Still, you had to put your life on hold for it, and I think it's quite selfless of you," she said, bending over to peer into a nearby tank. "So, how do you like being back in Destiny?"

"I like it a lot better now." He grinned and leaned back in his chair taking a long look at her.

Feeling her cheeks begin to warm under the scrutiny of his gaze, she turned and walked around the barn, pretending to take an interest in the instrumentation.

"My, my, Travis, you are quite the package. You're a fireman, an engineering whiz kid, a caring son, and a helpful neighbor. How do you manage it all?" It was her turn to flirt a bit and make him squirm. But she had the feeling she was playing with fire.

When she turned back, she found herself standing right in front of him. "There are a lot of hours in the day. The trick is to make each one count." He looked down at her with an intensity she found unnerving. She stepped back to get some breathing room, and her smile was a bit forced. Sensing her discomfort, he continued. "What about you. How do you like Destiny?"

"It's interesting," she said honestly. "I've never experienced a place quite like it. It's been an adventure." She laughed a little at this, and he grinned.

"A non-committal answer," he observed.

"I like it," she hurried to assure him, "but honestly, I've only been here a few days, and it feels like I've been here for weeks. Everyone has been so open and welcoming and, well, unguarded. It's just not what I'm used to," she said and looked up at him. "And I don't really know what I was expecting, but everyone I've met has so much personality, so many dimensions, you know?"

"I think you can find people like that in any place," he offered.

"Right, I'm sure people like Marsha Brady are a dime a dozen! And Stella who started an art community and built a town around it." She flung her arms wide and looked around the barn. "And firemen who turn out to be scientific geniuses. Yes, it's quite the ordinary run of the mill town."

Travis looked like he was trying to swallow a smile. "I'm sure a gorgeous school teacher turned ranching heiress will fit in just fine." Addie peered up at him, and he continued. "I know you spoke with Woody yesterday. He told me about the will. How do you feel about your new inheritance?"

"Well, to tell you the truth, I feel a bit awkward about it. Stella, I'm finding out, was quite an amazing woman and a bit of an eccentric. But I didn't really know her. It's odd that she picked me to leave all of her treasures to. I feel honored, but strange at the same time." She had been wandering around the room while she spoke, but now she stopped and faced him. "Were you two close?"

"Close enough, I suppose. I grew up around her and spent some time out at her place. When I was younger, my friends and I would play down at her pond. Sometimes she would let us spend the night in one of the guest houses. I have a lot of great memories from those times. My dad helped her when everyone left the ranch, and I pitched in when I was home in the summers. And I've been doing chores for her since I came back home. She spoke of you often. I know she thought of you as the daughter she never had."

"It's an odd bond, to be sure. I was born in her bedroom, and she helped deliver me. I guess it gave us a special connection." She paused before continuing. "I know you helped with her funeral. You must miss her."

"I think the whole town will miss Stella. She was a big presence here."

Addie looked at him closely. "A non-committal answer," she said, but then continued before he had a chance to reply. "So, she named you in the will also. How would you like to handle it?"

"We've got plenty of time for that. Right now, I'm feeling the need for a cookie. Come back to the house with me?" He smiled charmingly, and she couldn't refuse.

"Of course," she said, and he followed her out of the barn closing the door tightly. "Your house is wonderful," she said waiting for him to join her. "At least, what I saw of it."

"It's getting back into shape. When I came home, I arranged to have a woman from town come out to clean it every week. It was kind of shocking to see how much Dad had let things go. But it's better now."

"Your dad is delightful. How's he doing?"

"Like most people in his condition, he has his good days and bad days."

"I've heard its hardest on the relatives." When he didn't respond, she changed the subject. "What a great view you have back here. Some people like the beach or the mountains, but this type of western scenery with rolling hills and plateaus in the background has always been my favorite."

"Mine too." He put his hand on the back door when they heard a dog barking in the distance. They turned, and Addie saw a huge white dog lumbering toward them with its tongue hanging out the side of its mouth.

"There you are," Travis said as the dog ran toward him at full speed. He put his hand out as a signal telling the dog he was not to jump on the company.

"Who's this?" Addie said completely smitten by the smiling dog. She held out her hand for him to sniff then stroked his back.

"This is Shiner," said Travis. "He's only a few years old, so he's got a considerable amount of energy."

"He's beautiful. What kind of dog is he?"

"He's a Labrador-Great Pyrenees mix. He's more than 90 pounds, but he thinks he's a lap dog."

Addie laughed and put her arms out. Shiner happily trotted over and leaned against her while she scratched him behind the ears, giving her the best canine hug she'd ever had. "You're quite the charmer, aren't you Shiner," she said.

"Come on, mutt," Travis said reaching down to grab the dog's ear playfully. "Let's go inside." Addie and Shiner followed him into the house.

"Hey dad," he said to his father who was sitting in a chair near the window. "I see you already met Addie, our new neighbor."

"Yes, Addie. Yes, I met her. She came to see you."

"And," he added crossing the room to the front entry, "she came bearing gifts." He picked up the plate of cookies where Red had laid them. He pulled back the wrapping and helped himself to a cookie. "Wow, now that's good," he said holding the plate out for Addie. She took a cookie, and he turned to hand one to Red, who just held it in his hand.

"Well, they're not exactly difficult," said Addie, pleased that he liked them.

"On the contrary. I'm quite a cookie aficionado. I grew up eating the most delicious homemade desserts, and I have to confess that a well-made chocolate chip cookie has always been my favorite." He set the plate on the coffee table and sat on the sofa while Shiner lay down at his feet.

Addie took a seat in the chair next to Red's. "Hey," she said, "you earned them. I don't even think I'd be able to see out the back window if not for you."

"What are neighbors for?"

"It's been a big help, I can tell you that. Was he always so helpful at home?" She directed the question to Red, feeling odd not including him in the conversation.

Red looked over at her his eyes clouded with uncertainty. "Who?"

Addie had never spent time with an Alzheimer's patient and wasn't sure what the correct protocol was. She decided just to ignore it and see what happened. "Travis," she said nodding her head toward him. "Did he help out at home when he was younger?"

"Oh, yes. Yes, he did. He did a lot of chores around here. When he wasn't busy getting into trouble." Red chuckled and took a bite of his cookie.

"Trouble?" Addie asked peering suspiciously at Travis who just sat back and looked at her with a self-assured grin.

"Nothing serious, I assure you. Just boy stuff. You wouldn't understand." He said reaching for another cookie.

"Why are you so certain I wouldn't understand? Maybe I have brothers." She raised her eyebrows pointedly the way she did with an argumentative student.

"Do you?" he asked casually.

"Well, that's really not the point, is it?" He burst into laughter at this, and she smiled. "And as much as I'd love to sit here and listen to every detail about your sordid past, I really do have to go. Marsha is coming by to help me sort through the maze of odds and ends that are the Destiny Ranch."

Addie stood to leave and turned to Red. "Thanks so much for letting me stay and chat. And for your son's help at Stella's. I really appreciate it."

Red stood and shook the hand she extended toward him. "Any time dear."

"I'll walk you out," said Travis following Addie to the front door. Shiner trotted out after them.

She opened her car door and turned to face him before getting in. "This was fun," she said and seemed surprised to find it was true. "And I am grateful for your help."

"It's no bother. I find riding a tractor gives me time to think."

"We'll have to add 'thinker' to your growing list of

qualities." She climbed into her car, and Travis closed the door.

"Thanks for the cookies. And drop by any time."

She smiled and waved as she turned the car around and headed back to the ranch.

CHAPTER 15

"Woody that's simply unacceptable. I need that property. Isn't there anything you can do to convince her to sell?" Anderson hoped he didn't sound desperate, but he was almost beyond caring. He shifted the phone to the other ear. "Have you told her that this offer is well above market?"

"I'm afraid you don't understand. She told me she is planning *not* to sell the property. Once probate is finished, she has decided to keep it. What she does with it after that I have no idea."

"Are you saying she plans to live there?" questioned Anderson. "I know she is the executor and beneficiary of the will, but certainly she doesn't plan on living there? For God's sake, why on Earth would she do that?"

"I don't know Anderson. Maybe she likes the place.

Maybe she is looking for a change. Maybe she is looking for a husband. I have no idea. All I know is that she told me she was not going to sell the property to anyone after I presented her with your last offer."

Anderson's nostrils flared, and he worked hard to keep from screaming. "OK, thanks Woody. I guess I'll just have to give up on it then. I'll see you at Destiny Days, right?"

"I wouldn't miss it for the world. You have yourself a good day Anderson."

Anderson took a deep breath, trying hard not to throw the phone across the room. Though he may be giving up on the idea of buying the property legitimately, he certainly wasn't giving up altogether. If the woman couldn't see reason, then it was time to approach this from a different angle.

He leaned back in his chair and stared up at the ceiling for a minute. Anderson's home office was his sanctuary. Both his wife and the housekeeper knew he was not to be disturbed when he was in his office with the door shut, as he was now. The room was overtly masculine and had been his father's study when he was young. Anderson had the room repainted and had replaced some of the furnishings, but the heavy antique desk that had belonged to his father was now his. It sat at one end of the office facing the doorway and was the focal point of the entire room.

Anderson leaned forward and picked up the phone again. "Cole, where are you?"

"I'm at the office, why?"

"I need you to come by the house. We need to talk,"

Anderson said curtly.

"Sure, Dad. What's the matter? Is everything OK? Is mom all right?"

"Your mother is fine, son, but I need your help with a business matter. When can you get here?" Anderson asked looking down at his Rolex.

"I'm just finishing up a couple of things. I can be there in about half an hour or so."

"That'll be fine. I'll see you then, son."

It took Cole nearly 45 minutes to make it back to the ranch. Anderson was sitting on the front porch waiting for him, smoking a cigar. He only smoked in two situations, either he was celebrating something great or worried about something really terrible. Lately, he'd been smoking more than usual, and it wasn't because of any unexpected windfall.

Anderson rose and shook Cole's hand. The two walked into the office, and Anderson closed the door. Cole took a seat across from the desk and waited for him to start.

"Thanks for coming, son. I know you're very busy at work, but this is important." Anderson ran his hand through his hair and wondered how to start. A lifetime of lies and deceit was about to swallow not only him but his family as well. He reached into the mini refrigerator behind the desk and handed Cole a Lone Star beer.

"It must be important if you're breaking out the good stuff," joked Cole reaching for the beer.

Anderson grinned and sat behind the desk. "You know I've been interested in Stella's place for some time now. I tried to buy it from her directly, and I've even tried to negotiate a deal with that Denton girl, Addie.

"I've never told you why I'm so interested in purchasing that ranch, and I'm not at liberty to tell you today. But it is very important that I make this deal happen."

"Dad, it's just 1,700 acres. Why the big concern?" Cole looked puzzled.

"I can't tell you that. But, I can say that the property is for a third party that I can't afford to disappoint." Anderson looked over at his son, not bothering to hide the worry in his face.

"What do you mean 'you can't disappoint them'? You're a wealthy semi-retired rancher. Who do you have to please at this point in your life?"

Anderson closed his eyes and tried to calm his frustration. "I can't talk about that. I just need you to try to convince that girl to sell her property to me. It's vitally important and not something I would ask if it weren't so serious."

Cole leaned back in his chair and peered at his father over the beer bottle. "How long have you had this idea? Did you want me to take Addie to Destiny Days so that you could get her property?"

"What if I did? She's pretty, smart, and available, all qualities you should be looking for. And she's about to be rich, too. Richer if she would just sell me the ranch."

Cole put his beer on the desk. "I don't feel

comfortable with this, Dad. It doesn't—"

"I don't care how you feel about it," thundered Anderson cutting him off. "I need you to do this. Do you hear me? I need your help. And if I don't get it, there will be trouble."

"Trouble for who?"

"For all of us," Anderson nearly spat the words. He stood up and turned his back to Cole. "For me," he said quietly. "And for my family."

Cole looked at his father. He had never seen him like this before. It wasn't just worry he heard in his father's voice. It was fear. Anderson finally turned back around and faced his son.

"Dad, what's wrong? You can talk to me," Cole pleaded.

"I can't. Son, please believe me, if I could say more, I would. But it's better—safer—if I don't. It's enough that I ask a favor of you. I don't have to explain."

"Dad!"

Anderson put both hands on the desk and leaned forward. "Son, you're old enough to know that in life you make a series of decisions. Some are good, some are bad, and some you really regret. This land deal is the result of something I deeply regret. But it's too late to try to undo what's been done. I need your help. That's all you need to know."

"You're in real trouble, aren't' you?" The creases between Cole's eyes were pronounced as he stared directly into his father's eyes. Anderson could feel a knot forming deep in his stomach.

"You have no idea," Anderson said dropping back

into his chair. "I need you to convince Addison Butterfield to sell her land to me. Because if we can't…" He shook his head and left the idea hanging. Anderson could feel tears beginning to well in his eyes and he blinked them away. "Cole," he said trying to regain his composure, "are you with me or not?"

"Of course I'm with you, Dad. I'm not sure what I can do, but I'll talk to her. I'll do my very best." Cole reached over and patted his father on the arm.

"I need it done quickly, son. The clock is ticking, and I have only a few days to make this happen."

Cole left the house and headed back into town, his lips taught and worry etched in his forehead. What in God's name had his father gotten involved with. Of course, over the years, he had heard some of the rumors about his father and his shady practices, but he had dismissed it as jealousy. Now, he didn't know what to think. The only thing he knew for certain was that his father needed his help.

Out in the deserts of West Texas, with the big sky and wide-open spaces, people often overlooked the fierceness of the place. It was a hard place to live, with hard weather and hard men living hard lives. Though he did not want to admit it, he knew his father had made a grave mistake and desperately hoped they all would not have to pay a high price for it.

But Cole knew what he had to do.

CHAPTER 16

Addie had spent most of the morning fretting over what to wear. She finally decided that a bright floral sundress that hit just above the knees was both figure flattering and appropriate for a festival. She added strappy platform sandals and a jangly bracelet to complete her summer look. She had spent more time than usual on her makeup, which complemented her features without appearing to be overdone. She had even curled her hair, and it fell in soft waves around her face. Taking a last glance at herself in the mirror, she was generally pleased.

The week had passed by in a blur. She was making good progress on her inventory list and had more than half the attic completely cleared out. It was slow, tedious work, but she had some great helpers. Marsha worked with her on a couple of days, and Travis stopped by one afternoon to help them move some of the bulkier pieces. Cole came by every afternoon to check on her. Usually, it was during the day when he was working, but he brought little gifts to help lift her spirits. One day, he brought icy soft drinks for both Addie and Marsha, and the next day he dropped off a big bouquet of fresh daisies, which were sitting on her front porch. Yesterday, he brought a plate of brownies beaming proudly as he handed them to her saying, "Made them myself." She tried not to squeal out loud at discovering that he could cook and now met four of the criteria on her husband list.

Addie was just finishing with her lip gloss when she heard a knock at the front door. She had a last-minute fear about being overdressed, but since there was nothing she could do about it now, she answered the door to a stunningly dressed cowboy in khaki slacks, plaid shirt, and slick boots.

"Wow," said Cole, obviously captivated with her appearance.

"Wow yourself," she said with a playful tone.

"Are you ready to go?"

"I'm not at all sure I'm ready to go, but I have nothing left to do, if that's what you mean." Addie was only half teasing as she grabbed her bright-orange straw purse and headed out the door.

"Addie," Cole said with a soothing grin, "you have nothing to worry about. It's just a bunch of locals getting together for some fun. And I'll be by your side during the entire presentation."

"Promise?" she asked grinning back at him.

"Pinky swear," Cole said, holding out his hand. Addie wrapped her pinky around his, and they chuckled.

The entire town square had been roped off for Destiny Days. Vendors of all kinds had set up booths in the streets, and there was a stage in front of the courthouse for music and other festivities. A wooden dance floor at the base of the stage was already crowded with dancers, young and old, enjoying the country and western sounds of Johnny Rocket and the Flattops. The other side of the courthouse lawn was packed with games, a bounce house for kids, and a mechanical bull.

Cole had to park several blocks away, and he and Addie strolled hand-in-hand toward the festival. As they got closer, the noise level grew considerably, and Addie was amazed at the number of people she saw.

Watching her, Cole laughed. "I told you. Destiny Days is a big deal around here. People probably started showing up around ten o'clock this morning, and it will go until midnight. And they'll be here all day tomorrow too."

"It's fantastic!" Addie exclaimed with a wide smile.

"We're supposed to meet the town founders at the main stage at noon. They'll have an official opening of the festival and make a few announcements. The mayor will introduce the city council and the town founders. Now, if you don't—"

Addie held up a hand to stop him. "It's OK. I've been practicing my curtsey ever since you told me I'd be introduced."

Cole squeezed her hand tightly. "That's the spirit. Oh, look. I think I see Dad over there."

They walked toward the side of the stage where a group of local dignitaries had gathered. Addie was relieved to see that the women were dressed much like herself in sundresses and sandals, although she was the youngest among them by about 30 years.

The band finished, and a group of young high school students wearing navy blue and gold shirts arranged the stage for the opening ceremony. A row of chairs was set up in front of the musical instruments, and a podium was brought out.

"Addie," said Anderson, motioning her to join him. "I'm so very glad to see you again. I'd like to introduce some folks to you."

He took her around to each of the council members and founders, presenting her as if she was a visiting princess from some far-away exotic land. She smiled and shook hands and hoped there wasn't a quiz later about who was who. Cole was true to his word and stayed by her side also shaking hands and exchanging greetings with people he obviously knew quite well.

A large crowd had gathered in front of the stage, and Addie put a hand over her stomach to calm herself. She suddenly felt as nervous as she did on her first day of teaching when she had looked out at a sea of students expecting her to know what she was doing. She took her place in line, and the VIPs climbed the steps onto the stage and sat in their designated seats. The president of the Destiny Benefit League thanked everyone for coming to the festival, which had the largest attendance of any festival in the town's history. The crowd cheered loudly at this news. She introduced the mayor, who said a few words about the bright future that awaited their growing hamlet. He then introduced the city council members, who each stood and waved as their names were read.

"Of course, our opening ceremony would not be complete without a word of thanks to the people who helped start our thriving community. Ladies and gentlemen, may I introduce our town founders."

Again, each person stood and waved while the audience clapped. Then it was her turn.

"Now, as you all know, Stella Pennington passed away recently. She was truly the heart and soul of our town, and she will be missed greatly by all of us. But we are so delighted to have her Goddaughter with us today. Let me introduce the newest member of our community, Ms. Addison Butterfield."

The mayor clapped as Addie stood. Much to her relief, the townspeople applauded loudly, and several cheered and waved at her in greeting. Addie smiled and gave a small wave before once again taking her seat in relief. The mayor officially declared the start of Destiny Days, and everyone cheered boisterously.

"That wasn't so bad, was it?" Cole leaned down to whisper in her ear.

"Not at all. And now that it's over let's have some fun!" Addie was almost giddy with excitement. She had been welcomed as part of the community, and she was being escorted by the most eligible bachelor in town.

Before they could step away, she heard a familiar voice behind her.

"Well done, Addie!" Woody squeezed her arm with affection.

"Woody, how great to see you. Have you been here long?"

"Actually, we just got here. I would like you to meet my wife, Dodie," he said putting his hand on his wife's back affectionately. She was probably a few years younger than Woody and had her graying hair pulled into a tight bun at the back of her head. She was a little rounder than her husband and no less friendly.

"I've heard so much about you. It's great to finally meet you in person." Dodie smiled sincerely and gave Addie a welcoming hug.

"Your husband has been a life saver! Really, I don't know what I'd have done without his help."

"That's my Woody, always ready to help as long as it doesn't involve doing the dishes!" They all chuckled.

The group around her seemed to be growing. Cole introduced her to the high school principal and the school board president. She also met some of the ranchers from the area and their wives, a couple of Cole's law associates, and several of Destiny's business owners.

"I'm starving," she said to Cole when he was able to pull her away from the group. She'd spent so much time worrying about the day that she hadn't eaten a thing. "How about we find some festival food and a place in the shade?"

"You read my mind."

Cole led her through the maze of people, some of whom stopped to say hello and welcome her to Destiny. They finally found the food booths and tried to decide what they wanted.

"Well, as you can probably tell, Elena's Taco Truck is one of the most popular. And, for good reason. But the line is about a football field long. How about a hamburger?"

"A hamburger! I can eat that any time. I'm torn between the cowboy sushi and the deep-fried ice cream."

"You are brave," Cole said with a laugh.

"Of course, there's one thing I always crave when I go to a festival of any kind."

"A corn dog?" asked Cole.

"How did you know?" Addie was surprised and hoped he wasn't teasing.

"It's my favorite, too. I never eat them anyplace else, but when I'm at a fair, I have to have a corn dog."

"With lemonade," added Addie.

"Two corn dogs with lemonade coming up."

They found a table under one of the tents and sat side-by-side munching their exceptionally tasty corn dogs.

"Are you having fun?" asked Cole.

"I am. I'm amazed at the number of people who came out for this. Destiny seems like such a friendly little town."

"It is," said Cole. "But just like anyplace, it has its

dark side as well."

"Dark side!" said Addie with a laugh. "Please don't go all Darth Vader on me."

Cole had to chuckle at that. "No, it's just that we're not all festivals and fun. Making a living in West Texas can be tough. There have been several years that were especially difficult for ranchers. Dad lost almost a quarter of his herd to disease one year. It put several local ranches out of business. And look what happened to Stella. She had a thriving community at one time, but now it's gone."

"And you're telling me this because…"

"No reason, really. I guess that's why we love our festivals and celebrations. We work hard, so we feel like we've earned them."

Addie and Cole sat in silence for a minute before he continued.

"Speaking of working hard, how are things going at the ranch?"

"I had an extremely productive week, and thanks to your thoughtfulness, I haven't yet torn out all of my hair, thank you very much," she said smiling at him. "There's just so much stuff there, you know? I really want to sort through every last piece before I can decide what to do with it. I owe that to Stella."

Cole took a sip of his lemonade and looked over at Addie. "Why?"

"Why, what?"

"Why do you feel you owe it to Stella? You didn't really even know her."

"I know, but it's weird. The longer I'm here, the

more I'm learning about her. She was interesting and eccentric and everything in between. And she wanted me to take care of her estate. And not just legally. She wanted me to care for it, you know, personally."

"Do you think that's why she named you as her sole heir?" Addie looked at him with wide eyes, and he grinned. "It's a small town. Word gets around."

"Does it?" asked Addie wondering how he could possibly know. She had only found out a couple of days ago herself. Was it possible he knew before she did?

"So, you own a ranch, Ms. Butterfield. Maybe we should go shopping and get you a pair of boots."

"And a hat," Addie added pointedly. "I definitely need a hat."

"But seriously, what are you going to do with all that land?" Cole bit into his corn dog but didn't take his eyes off Addie.

"You know, I have no idea. I actually thought about trying to get the art colony started again. But that's really not me. I can't see myself running a hippy art retreat. Besides, I wouldn't know where to start."

"What about your life in Denton. Do you miss it?"

Addie had to reflect for a minute before answering. "My life in Denton is comfortable. But the more I think about it, I'm not sure that's what life is really about. Comfort."

"I know what you mean. I love my family, and I have a lot of friends in Destiny. But I feel like it's on my trips to Houston where I really shine. There's so much to do there. The work is interesting, and I really love the energy."

"Have you ever thought of moving there?"

"All the time. But my Dad needs me here, so here I am."

"I guess I'm kind of the opposite right now. The quiet of this place—Destiny Days aside, of course," she added with a grin, "is really appealing to me. And I've always been fascinated with small towns."

"Visiting one and living in one are two different things," he reminded her. "If I were you, I'd sell the place and never look back."

He stared off into the distance and seemed to be miles away. Addie studied him closely. When they first met, he seemed pleased that it would take time for her to settle the estate. Now, it sounded like he wanted her to go. But when he turned to look back at her, he had his familiar, charming smile. "Not that I want you to leave, but there are lots of places you could call home."

"Like Houston?" she asked, and he laughed.

"Hey, it's a great place. You can find anything you want there: quiet, loud, slow, fast. Not to mention you'd have your own personal tour guide to show you around." His smile was mesmerizing as he leaned over to nudge her arm impishly.

"There you are!" Addie didn't have a chance to respond as they were interrupted by an out-of-breath Marsha who walked up in a short denim dress that was cinched at her tiny waist. The scooped neckline was just low enough to reveal cleavage that had many heads turning in her direction. Blue and brown western boots replaced her usual heels, and she had left her hair down, which fell in thick brown waves below her shoulders. Addie was surprised by the transformation from bouncy waitress to cute cowgirl.

"Look at you!" she said with genuine enthusiasm. "What have you been up to?"

"I just got here, but I'm fixin' to have some fun," Marsha said eyeing the crowd.

"Hey, Marsha," said Cole in greeting, and Marsha smiled at him.

"Well, just look at the two of you. If you don't just look like the blonde country and western Ken and Barbie!"

Embarrassed, Addie smiled awkwardly, but Cole laughed heartily. "Marsha, you always know exactly what to say!"

Addie touched his arm. "What time is it getting to be? I have to do that reading at the library."

"It's not quite 1 o'clock. I think you told me you had to be there at 2:30."

"See, you've got lots of time. Come stroll around with me for a bit. You can spare her for a few hours, can't you Cole?" Marsha said in a pleading tone.

"It's up to Addie," he said easily.

"Sounds fun," she said squeezing Cole's hand. "I'll be at the library until about 4. Maybe we can meet for dinner?"

"Oh," said Marsha biting her lower lip.

"What?" asked Addie.

"Well, I was sorta hopin' you could eat with me," she paused and looked pleadingly at Addie and Cole and then continued, "and my mama."

"Your mother's here?"

"Not yet, but she said she would stop by at about 5:30 to eat with me."

Addie looked at Cole, who was smiling. "Is that OK with you?"

He laughed and shook his head. "You don't have to tell me about family obligations! You girls have fun, and I'll meet up with you at the stage around 7 for some dancing," he said as Marsha linked her arm through Addie's and pulled her back toward the square.

"My goodness," Marsha said. "You two are certainly getting close."

"I like him," said Addie with a shrug, and then added, "a lot. Is that so terrible?"

"Nothing wrong with that," Marsha assured her. "But there's more'n one crawdad in the crik if you know what I mean. You sure you want to settle down with the first one you see?"

"Who said I'm settling down? Now hush," said Addie with a grin. "Let's wander around and find one for you."

The two strolled through the festival leisurely, looking at the variety of goods for sale. They poked through a booth that had beautiful handcrafted jewelry, and Addie bought a sterling silver ring. Another stall displayed the most unique tie-dyed scarves. They admired stunning Mexican pottery and sampled homemade jams and jellies.

As they turned the corner, Addie saw a firetruck parked along the side of the road. Firemen were hoisting young children onto the truck so they could explore it.

"There you go," said Addie mischievously. "Let's go over and have that fireman show you how to climb his ladder."

"Don't tempt me," said Marsha eyeing the firemen closely.

"Oh, look. There's Travis," Addie said watching him throw a toddler up in the air. The child squealed with delight. When he set him on the ground, Travis put his fireman's helmet on the child's head, and he and the boy's mother chuckled at the spectacle the youngster made spinning in circles with his head completely covered. Addie laughed silently, and the two of them walked over to say hello.

Travis spotted Addie and Marsha walking over and waved in greeting.

"Well don't the two of you just look delicious," Travis teased.

"Down boy," Marsha scolded but grinned nevertheless. "Aren't you going to introduce us?"

Travis looked around him and said, "I think you already know everyone."

"Not everyone," said Marsha eyeing an unfamiliar face.

Travis followed the direction of her gaze, and said playfully, "Down, girl."

When Marsha sneered at him, he just laughed. "That's Victor Delgado. He joined our little group a few days ago. He still hasn't moved here completely, but he came in for Destiny Days. He works for Texas Mart at the distribution center and is transferring from Graham. He was a firefighter there, so we're lucky to have him."

"I don't need his resume, Travis. Just introduce us."

"Yes, ma'am," he said. "Hey, Victor. Come over here for a sec. I'd like to introduce a couple of friends of mine. This is Marsha and Addie. Marsha's lived here forever, so anything you want to know about the town, she's your man." He smiled when Marsha looked at him sideways. He left Marsha to chat with Victor, while he introduced Addie to the other members of his team.

"So," Addie said to Travis when they were alone, "is this a normal part of your firefighting duties?"

"One of the best," he said scooping up a little girl who was probably in kindergarten and setting her inside the cab of the truck. He showed her where the lights and sirens were and had her honk the horn. She giggled and put her hands over her ears both thrilled and embarrassed at the loud sound it made. Addie giggled as well.

"You like kids?" she asked.

"Sure. Do you?"

"Of course, I'm a teacher."

"If that were a prerequisite for being a teacher, I would have liked school a lot better."

"True enough, I guess. I'd like to say that all teachers only have their students' best interests at heart, but I've known some who were just mean bullies," she said shaking her head. "But, speaking of kids, I need to get going. I have to do a storytelling thing over at the library."

"I always loved those. Stella had quite a way of making a book come to life."

"I won't pretend I can even do half as good a job as Stella, yet off I go, once more unto the breach. Wish me luck." She waved and stopped to tell Marsha she was headed to the library and would find her later.

Addie sat in a large wooden rocking chair surrounded by a circle of young children. Their parents sat in chairs off to the side.

"If you give a mouse a cookie," she began reading the beloved book from her childhood. Each time the mouse needed something more, she sighed loudly and hit her forehead in frustration. The children giggled and shook their heads at the silly mouse and the exhausted little boy. They clapped and cheered in appreciation when she was done. There were cookies and milk at the back of the room followed by an arts and craft project Ms. Hunter, the town librarian, had set up for them.

Addie met several of the children's parents after the reading and told them how glad she was to be in Destiny and how much she loved helping at the library. Several of them said they knew Stella and would miss her a great deal. After a minute or two, she looked around the room and saw Travis leaning against the door frame watching her.

She walked over to him. "How long have you been here?"

"Long enough," he said. "You're great with kids. I bet you're an awesome teacher."

"Aw shucks," she said with a grin.

"No, really. You did Stella proud."

"Well, it's not exactly hard, reading a children's book."

"Reading a book is not difficult. Making squirming little rascals sit still for it is."

"So, did you come by for the cool air in here, or for the cookies?" They walked over to the refreshment table, and he took a couple of sugar cookies.

"All of the above and more," he said popping a cookie into his mouth. "But I better get back or the guys will think I ditched on them." As he walked out, he stopped to chat with a couple of the parents. There was another storytelling in an hour, so Addie decided to stay in the coolness of the library and help with the art projects.

"Relax, he'll find you," said Marsha waiting with Addie by the stage, where the headline band was about ready to play. Addie was busily scanning the crowd, but when she looked over at Marsha, she saw she was doing the same thing.

"Are we looking for anyone in particular, Ms. Brady?" she asked with a grin. "A certain fireman who is new in town and needs the assistance of a local expert, perhaps?"

"He's probably already gone. He said he didn't know how late he was going to stay," she said without taking her eyes off the surrounding throng of people.

"How long did the two of you talk?"

"Long enough for me to find out he's 26 years old

and single. Need I say more?"

"Now, now. No need to settle for the first crawdad you see."

"Very funny," said Marsha. "Don't look now, but I think your crawdad is headed this way."

Addie turned to see Cole walking toward her. He had changed and was now wearing dark jeans and a long-sleeve grey paisley shirt.

"Howdy," he said with a smile. "You been having fun?"

"I have. I see you went home to change."

"Well, my place is not far from here, so I figured I'd run home and get a little work done before coming back to meet you."

"I thought you lived at your dad's ranch," Addie said looking up at him.

"I stay there occasionally. But since I moved back to Destiny, I thought it would be good to have my own place. I have a house just a couple of miles from here."

"How convenient," said Addie with a provocative smile.

The band started up, playing an upbeat version of Boot Scottin' Boogie that made the crowd holler in appreciation. Couples headed for the dancefloor, and Cole bent down close to Addie's ear.

"How about it?"

"Well, I'm not a great dancer, but I'll give it a go."

Cole took her hand and led her to the dance floor. Marsha watched the two of them move together. There was no denying they made a handsome couple. She turned when she felt a tapping on her shoulder.

"Would you like to dance?" Victor asked a bit nervously.

"Do roosters crow at sunrise?" He looked at her in confusion, and she linked her arm through his. "Of course, I want to dance," she said pulling him toward the floor.

Addie spotted Marsha and Victor across the floor and smiled. Watching her, Cole bent his head lower.

"So, you and Marsha seem to be pretty good friends."

"We are," Addie said. "I've never met anyone quite like her. She's very comfortable with herself. It's infectious."

"How was dinner with her mother?"

"It was fun. Marsha really loves her mother, even when she pretends to be frustrated by her. It reminded me of my mom and me."

He smiled down at her, then twirled her twice before pulling her close again. When the song ended, she was slightly winded. Cole led her to a table and went off in search of something to drink. Addie watched the dancers, unaware that Travis was watching her from a table across the dancefloor. He sat with some of the other firemen drinking from a long neck bottle. When a few of them left to find partners for the next dance, Travis went to buy another round of beers for the guys.

Cole returned carrying four bottles. "I figured Marsha would join us at some point."

"You're a great dancer," she said as she sipped her beer. "Do you go dancing often?"

"Well, you might have noticed that there's not a lot else to do around here."

"I guess," Addie said with a small chuckle.

The sun was melting behind the horizon, and twinkle lights that were strung through the trees and around the dancefloor were now the main source of light. Cole pulled Addie close and put his arm around her as they watched the crowd of dancers. He smelled like a forest after a cleansing storm, and she leaned against him and relaxed her head against his chest.

Marsha came up breathing heavily and smiling broadly.

"Is one of these for me? I sure could use one about now."

Cole passed her a bottle, and Marsha drank thirstily. She and Addie exchanged a knowing look.

"Marsha, the table is yours. I'm going to spin Addie around the dancefloor for a bit."

"Have fun," she called as they walked away.

They danced for three songs before they returned to the table for a rest. Marsha had been chatting with Victor, and they headed back to the dancefloor as soon as Cole and Addie were back.

Cole brought them fresh drinks, and they chatted easily about nothing in particular when Travis appeared at their table.

"I wonder if I might have this dance," he asked Addie. She looked hesitantly at Cole, who stared back at Travis. "You don't mind, do you Cole?"

"Of course not. It's up to Addie."

"Well," she said. She hadn't spent as much time

with Cole during the day as she had hoped. Addie was about to decline so she could spend more time with him, but Travis took her hand.

"It's just one dance. I'll have her back safe and sound in no time."

Travis led her to the dancefloor where the song was now a waltz. He took her confidently in his arms and led her through the steps.

"You know, I've never been big on dancing, but the waltz was always my favorite."

"Why is that? Because you only need to count to three?" She was slightly miffed at the way he had taken her away from Cole.

"Relax, it's just one dance. Surely you can give me one dance. Think of it as payment for the mowing."

She had to tilt her head back to look up at him. "I've already paid in cookies," she reminded him, still not ready to forgive him.

"Well then, payment for the mowing I will do in the future," he was grinning, and she had the feeling he was playing with her. She wasn't sure she liked it.

"I'm beginning to think your landscaping services are too expensive," Addie said turning her head to the side trying to ignore how close she was to him.

"Well, maybe Mr. Pressed Jeans and Shiny Boots there will do it for you. I'm pretty sure his services are much cheaper."

Addie looked up at him, taken aback by his annoyed tone and narrowing eyes that were looking in Cole's direction. "Travis, what's wrong with you? Are you drunk?"

He looked down at her. "Why is it when you tell a woman the truth she always thinks you're drunk?"

"What are you talking about? You are the one who asked me to dance, and now you seem bent on insulting me."

Travis stopped at the edge of the dancefloor and pulled Addie off to a darkened corner.

"I'm not trying to insult you, Addie. It's just that I know Cole. I've grown up with him, and he has a lot of great qualities. But he's not the guy for you."

"And you know this how, exactly? Travis, we just met. Do you really know me that well?"

"Maybe not, but I know him." Travis once again looked in Cole's direction.

"So, what are you trying to tell me. He's dangerous?"

"Of course not. But—"

"Look, Travis, I appreciate that you think you're trying to look out for me if that's what you're doing. But I can take care of myself."

"I know you can. I never meant to imply that you couldn't," he hurried to assure her.

"OK, then. Let's just leave it at that." She crossed her arms and looked up at him with her head tilted. It was the same look she used to silently tell a student that it was time to stop talking and do as she said.

He looked down at her, and then looked away into the darkness. Addie could see his chest rise as he took a deep breath. "OK," he said softly, but when he looked back at her, she had the distinct feeling that she was most definitely not in charge. He was not one of her students, and the fact that he was backing down had little to do with what she wanted.

Travis continued to stare at her, and while she couldn't see him clearly in the night shadows, she could feel the intensity of emotion radiating from someplace deep within him. They were standing close, watching each other through the darkness. Finally, it was Travis who broke the silence.

"I'm sorry, Addie. I have no right to comment on your personal life," he said without moving, and then added, "Forgive me?" The simple question completely disarmed her.

"Yes, Travis, I forgive you," she replied gently wishing she could see his face.

"Thanks," he said sincerely and pulled her close. The hug was friendly, but she couldn't ignore the power she felt as he enfolded her in his arms. There seemed to be much more complexity to this man than she had originally thought. "I'll let you get back now."

Addie watched Travis walk back to his friends, then she turned and stared into the darkness. She stood there for a few minutes to calm herself. There was something between Cole and Travis, she could feel it, but she didn't know what it was. They were friendly on the surface, but there was tension between them. Was Travis trying to warn her about something, or was he simply hoping to cause trouble for Cole?

Addie rolled her head from side to side to relieve the stiffness in her neck. She looked back in the direction Travis had gone, but she couldn't see him any longer. Feeling the faint tickle of some sort of flying insect brushing against her face, Addie waved her arms instinctively and took a step back. She saw the faint glow of the firefly and watched it fly off into the distance until she could no longer see the flickering light.

CHAPTER 17

Addie woke early on Sunday morning. The glowing clock told her it was only 6:22. She lay with her head on the soft pillow staring up at the ceiling in the dark room. It was just a little over a week ago that she had first arrived in Destiny. Since that time, she had made a close friend, learned she had inherited a ranch and a houseful of art, and met a handsome cowboy on a white horse, and she was hopelessly infatuated with him. The trouble was, she wasn't at all sure he felt the same.

Cole and Addie had danced and laughed at Destiny Days until almost midnight. He had stayed with her exclusively and was attentive to her every need. And then he had taken her home, kissed her sweetly on her porch, and left.

She was so hoping to spend the night at his home

in town. Addie knew it might be moving fast, but what was he waiting for? She was ready and willing and had even said outright that she would love to see his place. The only thing she could come up with is that he didn't feel the same about her as she did about him. He said all the right things and his smile could melt her heart, but she was afraid she might be misreading his level of interest.

It just can't be true, she groaned to herself. She had come all the way out here, and had finally found a man who looked like he really might be the one—white horse and everything! She had been so busy searching for him, it had never even crossed her mind that she might finally find him and he wouldn't want her.

Still tired, she turned over in bed and pulled the pillow on top of her head.

Addie woke much later to the sound of Mel's bark echoing through the bedroom. She sat up and rubbed her eyes and saw that it was now past ten o'clock. The sunlight was beaming brightly through the window, and she knew Mel had to go out. She sat on the side of the bed willing her body to stand up and move when she heard a banging on the front door.

Who could be knocking on the door at this outrageously considerate time? she thought, grabbing her robe. She ran a brush quickly through her hair and tied it up behind her head in a high ponytail. Maybe Cole had stopped by to bring her breakfast in bed. That idea had her moving faster.

As she opened the door, she caught a glimpse of her reflection in the mirror and shrugged. "Not my best, but I did just climb out of bed."

She stepped forward and nearly tripped over Mel, who had stopped as if frozen. His ears were pasted to his head, and Addie could hear a low growl rumbling from the little dog.

"Mel?" she asked softly. "What is it, boy?" Addie was motionless as well trying to determine what he was reacting to. Then she heard it. A faint rattling sound coming from the hallway outside the room. The pounding on the front door startled her so much her entire body tensed. Carefully, she peered around the doorway and into the hall seeing the cause for Mel's apprehension. Just outside the door to her room was a bulky snake with a diamond shape adorning its long, coiled body. Both the head and tail were raised, and the snake rattled and hissed ominously.

Addie's breath caught in her throat, but when she peered down the hall and realized this rattlesnake was not alone, she exploded in an involuntary scream. The entire hallway floor was filled with slithering movement. She snatched Mel into her arms and jumped back reflexively.

"Addie! Addie, what's wrong?" She heard Travis' muffled voice from outside the front door.

Still too frightened to move, she clutched Mel tightly and yelled, "Snakes! There are snakes everywhere!"

"Don't move!" he commanded. "Addie, don't move, I'll be right there."

She wasn't sure how he was planning to get into the house or what he was going to do, but just the assurance that he was there calmed her a bit. Addie did as she was told and did not move a muscle, even when the slithering demon crossed the threshold to her room. She whimpered softly and held onto Mel so tightly she thought he might pop.

It seemed to take an eternity before she heard Travis again, though she knew it was less than a minute.

"Addie, where are you?" His voice was much closer now, and she knew he was in the house.

"I'm down here in Stella's bedroom. There are snakes all over the hallway! And there's one coming into the bedroom." She knew her voice was frantic, but she was too frightened to care.

"Don't move. Sudden movements will cause them to strike. Just stay still. I'm coming."

She didn't know how he managed it, but she could have cried with relief when she saw him tiptoe softly into the bedroom holding a garden rake. He looked at her trembling in the middle of the room holding onto Mel with desperation. Her legs and feet were bare. Travis looked around the room and could see no other immediate threat aside from the snake now coiled near the door. But he pulled the covers back from the bed gently and used the rake to shake the ivy canopy just to make sure.

"Addie, I want you to stand on the bed and stay there. And keep your dog with you." His voice was calm and authoritative, which helped sooth her nerves.

She watched with wide eyes as Travis used the rake to guide the snake out of the room. He worked on clearing the hallway. She could hear rattling and hissing and the muffled sounds of his boots against the wood floors as he herded the snakes out the opened front door.

After about five minutes, she heard the front door close and more deliberate footfalls in the hall. Travis set the rake by the bedroom door and crossed quickly to check on Addie. She was still standing in the middle of the bed, and her breathing was uneven.

"Addie?" he asked softly. "Addie, are you OK?" He held out his hand to help her down. "They're gone."

She took his hand, and he lifted her off the bed and onto the ground. She looked up at him, and tears were already welling in her eyes and spilling down her cheeks. He pulled her close and put both arms around her. He rubbed her back tenderly, and finally, she lifted her head.

He looked down at her and gently wiped strands of hair back from her face.

"Take a couple of deep breaths," he coached as he breathed with her. Finally, she could feel herself steadying. "Better?" he asked with a small smile.

"Yes," she said softly. Mel squirmed in her arms, and Travis took him from her and held him at eye level.

"Don't take it personally little guy. I know you would have stepped up if I hadn't come along."

"What just happened?" she asked, still feeling as if she were having an out-of-body experience. She sat on the edge of the bed. "How did all those snakes get in?"

"Snakes are a pretty common sight in West Texas. I've even seen them in the house a time or two, but I've never seen anything like this before. Usually, the air conditioning keeps them away. They don't like it as cold as we do." Travis put Mel on the floor and straightened up looking down at Addie. She was staring straight ahead and missed the concerned look on his face.

"Do you think they'll be back?" she asked with a shudder.

"Doubt it. Snakes don't really like living in houses, especially ones with dogs in them."

"Then why were they here?" she looked up at him with wide eyes.

"I'm not sure. But I'll make a point to keep the field around the house cut low. That should keep them away."

"Do you think there are others in the house somewhere?" she asked lifting her feet onto the bed.

"I don't think so. Some of the snakes looked like they were already headed out the door when I came in. But I'll call some of the guys to come over and check everything out."

"I don't want to cause trouble," she said but was silently thankful for the offer.

"It's no problem. Just one of the many services provided by your friendly neighborhood firemen."

Her eyes locked with his and she fought against tears. "Thank you, Travis. Thank you, thank you, thank you!!" She stood, and this time she was the one who pulled him into a hug. Then she tilted her head back to look up at him.

"Why are you here, by the way? Not that I'm not absolutely thrilled to see you."

"I came bearing gifts," he said with a smile as if he just remembered why he was there himself. "I seemed to have left them on the porch. Hang on a sec." He dashed from the room and returned less than half a minute later holding the plate she had taken to him and his father. It was full of cookies.

"I hope you like oatmeal raisin. It's my mom's award-winning recipe," he said proudly handing the plate to her.

"How nice. You didn't have to do that," she said smiling sweetly at him.

"Mom taught me to never return an empty container to someone who brings you food."

"Thank goodness for mothers who raised their sons right!" she said. "And as much as I want to dig into a cookie right now, there's one thing I think I need more. Care for a cup of coffee?"

"I would love one," he said.

She turned to go out to the kitchen but hesitated at the door. She turned to Travis with a creased brow and wide glistening blue eyes that made her look like a little girl who was certain ghosts were hiding in her closet. He smiled and took the lead. She followed him to the kitchen looking back down the hallway and into every corner of the kitchen. Mel trotted along with them and stopped at the back door.

"He hasn't been outside yet." She stated it as fact but didn't move to the door.

"Then, maybe we should let him out?" Travis asked.

"But the snakes. They're still out there!"

Travis glanced out the back window and shook his head. "They won't be back here. Too much sun." When she still didn't move to open the door, he asked, "Would you like me to stand outside with him?"

"Would you?" she asked biting her lower lip. "I know it's silly, but—"

"No need to explain. Come on, Mel."

The two went out the back, and Addie watched from the safety of the kitchen. At least, she thought it was safe. Once again, she scanned the floor for any slithering movement. Seeing none, she walked over to the coffee maker then took the plastic off the plate he'd returned to her. When Travis and Mel walked back in, the kitchen smelled comfortingly of fresh coffee and delicious oatmeal cookies.

Addie was sitting at the kitchen table, and Travis joined her. She reached for a cookie off the top of the huge pile.

"Yummm, these are wonderful. And you said you made them?"

"Don't look so surprised. I'm not a total moron in the kitchen."

"I never said you were," she said looking at him thoughtfully. Another cowboy who could cook? After spending years searching for her dream list man, she had already met two in the wilds of West Texas who were surprisingly close. Maybe everyone in West Texas is a match, she thought. Then how would I choose? Wondering if she might actually be close to madness,

Addie took a bite of her cookie and tried to calm her nerves.

Travis reached for a couple of cookies, and she looked at him closely. "Travis, I'm so grateful you stopped by when you did. Really," she put her hand on his arm, "you may have saved my life."

He put his hand over hers and squeezed it. "I'm not sure about that, but you're welcome. We take snake bites very seriously out here. The medical facilities stock plenty of snake antivenom since they are a part of life in West Texas. Even if you had been bitten, you'd probably have been fine."

"Maybe so, but thank you. I thank you, Mel thanks you," she was finally feeling a bit more relaxed and reached down to scratch Mel behind the ears. She looked up at Travis and grinned. "By the way, have I said thank you."

"Maybe once or twice." He grinned at her.

She sat up as a thought hit her. "By the way, how did you get in here? I didn't hear any glass breaking or boards cracking."

He fished in his front jeans pocket and pulled out a silver house key. "It was actually my other reason for coming over. Stella gave Dad a key when he was helping her out. I wanted to return it."

Addie stared at it for a couple of seconds and then shook her head. "No, I think you should keep it. Having a neighbor with a spare key might be a good idea."

Travis nodded his head and stuffed the key back into his pocket. "I think that coffee may be ready. You sit; I'll get it." Before she could stop him, he was up and pouring coffee into the mugs she had left on the counter.

"How do you take your coffee?" he asked.

Addie could feel her face reddening at his question. She had started drinking coffee when she was young, and the only way she liked it was with tons of milk and sugar. It was really more of a coffee flavored sweet milk, and she was always embarrassed when she fixed it that way in front of a stranger.

"Black," she blurted out not sure of what to say. "I'll take it black."

"Black it is. I hope you don't think less of me as a fireman, but I take it sweet—really sweet—with cream."

"You know, that sounds good. I'll try it that way," said a relieved Addie.

Travis prepared two cups of coffee and sat down next to her.

"How are you feeling?"

"Better," she said reaching for another cookie. "Wow. Snake attack and oatmeal cookies for breakfast. This is starting out to be an interesting day."

Travis smiled, and they were both interrupted by a knocking on the front door.

"That'll be the guys," he said to her as Addie pulled her robe belt tighter. "You can stay here."

She heard Travis open the front door, and about two or three firemen came in. Travis was talking to them, but Addie couldn't hear their conversation clearly. After a couple of minutes, he came back to the kitchen carrying a large long-handled flashlight.

"Alan and Pete are going to start checking the upstairs levels, and I'll go through everything down here."

"You should tell them there's a litter of kittens on the third floor."

He looked at her with an amused expression. "Why, do you think they won't know the difference between a cat and a snake?"

She chuckled, feeling a bit silly. "Do you think you could check the bedroom first? I'd like to get changed."

"Sure."

Addie followed him to the bedroom and watched him thoroughly search every corner, crack, and crevice. He checked the vents and the plumbing and finally declared it serpent free.

He left to poke through the rest of the house, while Addie quickly changed into snug faded blue jeans and a green UNT t-shirt. She pulled running shoes onto her feet, wanting to stay covered as much as possible. She brushed her teeth and hair and was just about to go back to the kitchen when she overheard Travis speaking to the other firemen through the vent.

"I know, but there had to have been more than 20 of them. And they were all in the hallway, and there appears to be no way for them to have gotten in."

"And you say they were diamond backs?"

"Every one of them. And they weren't small."

"I don't know, Travis. But they don't seem to be here now."

The men walked off, and Addie could no longer

hear their conversation. Although she didn't hear much, she could hear the concern in Travis' voice. Could it be that this was not some freakish act of nature? Perhaps not everyone in Destiny was so glad she was here.

Addie walked back to the kitchen and poured another cup of coffee. She could hear the firemen coming down the hallway, and she smiled gratefully when she saw them.

"I can't thank you enough for coming all the way out here," she walked over and shook their hands. "There's hot coffee and wonderful cookies, made by the man himself here," she said gesturing to Travis.

"And you're eating them?" joked Alan. "Pete, maybe you better go get some antivenom after all."

They laughed and took several cookies off the plate. "Thanks," said Pete, "but we have to get back."

Addie and Travis followed them to the door and watched them climb into the truck. When they were back in the kitchen, Addie took a sip of her coffee, staring at Travis over her cup.

"So, you don't think these snakes just wandered in here, do you?" He looked at her in surprise, and she pointed toward an air vent. "It's an old house."

He nodded his head and realized she had overheard them. "No, Addie, I don't. Is it possible for a snake that size to end up in a house? Maybe. But not that many of them."

"Then what do you think happened?"

He sat without speaking. Finally, he said, "Addie, I think you should talk to the sheriff." He hurried on as he saw her eyes widen. "I'm not saying there was any foul play or anything. It might have been some sort of prank. I don't know. But it's unusual, and we like to report things that are unusual to the sheriff."

"If you think I should."

"I do," he told her. "And I'll go with you. We can go tomorrow morning."

She nodded her head but kept her gaze fixed on Travis.

"What?" he asked. "You look like you want to say something."

"I do, but you've already done so much."

"Try me," he said with a confident grin that had her smiling back.

"Well, I know it's an imposition, but do you think you could stay for a bit? Marsha is coming over for lunch, but just until then?" She looked at the floor feeling weak for asking.

He put a finger under her chin and lifted her head so she could see into his glittering green eyes. "It would be my pleasure."

She smiled at him with relief and his expression changed slightly, but she couldn't read it. Addie knew he was smitten with her, and she hoped she wasn't taking advantage of him. He broke into her thoughts by standing.

"You know, I had another reason for coming over. I was going to do some mowing. Would you like to learn to drive a tractor?" Travis asked.

"That's one I've never been asked before," she stood, smiling up at him. "I'd love to. Just give me a minute to freshen up a bit."

"You really don't know anything about riding a tractor if you think you need to freshen up to drive one," he called out to her as she ducked into the bedroom.

She came back out a couple of minutes later wearing a grey t-shirt that had seen better days and had her ponytail stuck through a baseball cap that had the Texas Rangers logo on it.

"How do I look," she asked striking a pose.

"You get my vote for Ms. Tractor USA," he proclaimed pulling the brim of her hat down playfully.

Addie took to tractor driving surprisingly well, and the two of them were covered in sweat and dirt as Marsha pulled up the drive. Addie sat behind the wheel with Travis standing behind her. They both waved as Addie steered toward the house.

"Girl, you look messier than a plate of spaghetti in a blender," Marsha quipped as the two approached.

"Why, thank you, Marsha. You're so kind," Addie shot back at her, feigning insult. "What about Travis?"

"Oh, he looks about normal."

Travis smirked at her. "Love you, too."

He hopped off the tractor and helped Addie climb down.

"I think that's enough mowing for one day. I'll put the tractor back in the barn and head on home."

"Travis, please stay for lunch. After all the mowing and saving my life and everything, it's the least I can do," pleaded Addie. "Look, Marsha even brought food," she added pointing to the plastic bags Marsha was carrying.

"Please don't tell me it's gopher dogs. That's all she ever makes!"

"That's not true. I can make plenty of things," protested Marsha.

"So, what did you bring today?" asked Travis.

"Well, I'm not sure that's any of your business, Mr. Nosey Pants!"

Travis laughed loudly when he peered into one of the bags spying hot dogs and hot dog buns. Addie grinned while Marsha seemed to be working hard to look indignant.

"As much as I'd love some of that down home Southern cookin', I really should get back. But thanks for the offer."

"Say hello to your father for me, and thanks again. For everything!" Addie said.

Travis climbed onto the tractor, and the girls waved as he drove back toward the barn.

"What do you mean, 'saved your life'?" asked Marsha turning to look at Addie.

"You are not going to believe what happened to me this morning," said Addie grabbing Marsha's hand and leading her into the house.

CHAPTER 18

Addie and Mel were sitting on her front porch when Cole drove up. She was wearing a form-fitting black dress that hit her mid-thigh. It really wasn't an evening dress, because she hadn't packed anything very dressy. But with black heels borrowed from Marsha, a stunning white-gold diamond pendant that she always took with her on trips, and hair that was swept back from her face with small white floral hair pins, she was ready for dinner at the country club.

Cole climbed out of the truck looking stylish in dark grey chinos, a black blazer, and black and grey pinstriped shirt. A dark teal silk tie punctuated his outfit. He smiled when he saw her and pulled a large gift-wrapped box out of the truck.

"Hey, there," he said climbing the steps. "I'm looking for a date for dinner. Know anyone who might take pity on a poor cowpoke?"

"I know lots of people who would take pity on a poor cowpoke. I just don't see how that's going to help you." She smiled and stood up, and he leaned over to kiss her, pulling her close. Addie closed her eyes and could feel her breasts pressing against his chest. He lifted his head slowly, and Addie opened her eyes sighing contentedly. It had been a rough day, and seeing Cole was exactly what she needed.

"Hi," he said smiling down at her.

"Hi," she said with a slightly husky voice.

"I have something for you," he said holding out the box.

"I can see that," she said taking it from his hands. "But what have I done to deserve this?"

He just shrugged his shoulders and looked at her with a confident smile.

"Should I open it here?" she asked sitting on the swing with the giant box in her lap.

"Sure," he said sitting beside her.

She ripped the wrapping from the box and read 'Lucchese Bootmaker' on the cover.

"You didn't!" she squealed with delight. Addie opened the box and saw the most beautiful pair of western boots she had ever seen.

"They're goat leather, and all of the details are handmade and hand sewn," he seemed very pleased that she liked them.

"They look like they cost a million dollars," she said glancing at him sideways. "Cole, I really can't accept them."

"Of course you can! Every ranch owner needs a good pair of boots. Think of it as a welcome to Destiny gift."

"Well, they are beautiful," she said caressing the leather and looking closely at the floral details. "I hope they fit."

"I'm pretty sure they will. I had help with the sizing."

Puzzled, she looked up at him, then nodded as realization hit her. "Marsha?"

"Who else?"

Addie kicked off her shoes and slid her feet into the boots pulling them up. She stood and walked several steps. "They fit perfectly," she beamed, "and they're so comfortable. I think I'll wear them to bed tonight."

Cole laughed softly. "I'm glad you like them." He stood up and grabbed her arm to twirl her several times, then pulled her into a sweet kiss. "Now, let's get going. I'm starving."

When Cole had called her that afternoon and invited her to dinner at the country club, she had eagerly agreed. A night out at a nice restaurant away from the ranch was just what she needed after the day she'd had. Her earlier anxiety about Cole's level of interest faded the moment she saw him.

The country club was not exactly what she was used to from her days in Connecticut. As part of their work with the arts, her parents had use of the local country club, and she had grown up eating dinners and attending weddings and other functions at the exclusive establishment.

"Our little club is smaller than most, but the golf course is pretty challenging for such an out-of-the-way spot," Cole informed her on the drive over. "And the restaurant is the best in town. Daddy actually started the club with a couple of other business associates, and as a charter member, he gets the best seat in the house."

Walking in with her arm linked through Cole's, she felt relaxed and happy. It was a typical West Texas evening with a soft breeze that fluttered her hair and gently tickled her face. Long strands of feathery orange clouds brushed against the horizon creating a soft contrast to the darkening blue sky. It was hard to believe she'd had such a horrifying start to the day.

The country club was a modest but elegant stucco and stone two-story building with a stunning Mexican tile roof. It was situated on a hill that sloped back toward the golf course. The entrance was on the second floor, and the back of the clubhouse offered a grand two-story view of the grounds. Cole escorted her to the restaurant, where the maître d welcomed them.

"Cole, how nice to see you again. We have your table ready if you'd like to follow me."

They stopped to greet a few of the members, most of whom Addie had met at Destiny Days. They shook her hand warmly and asked how she had enjoyed the festival. With the pleasantries behind them, they sat at a table near the second-floor windows that offered a stunning view of the sunset.

"Well, you weren't kidding. This is definitely the best seat in the house." Addie laid her napkin in her lap and let the soft piano music and soothing beauty of the setting sun melt the stiffness from her entire body.

"*A beautiful man and beautiful scenery. Relax and enjoy yourself, Addie.*" Her mother's voice was approving and encouraging. "*And, whatever you do, don't think so much!*"

Amen to that, thought Addie and looked wistfully at her handsome date.

"What are you thinking about," Cole asked softly watching her.

"I'm thinking how right this feels. I think I needed a night away from counting and stacking," she smiled lazily at him. "Thanks for inviting me."

"My pleasure," he said easily reaching across the table to hold her hands.

They both straightened when the waiter appeared at their table. They ordered drinks, and Cole suggested an appetizer of prosciutto wrapped asparagus.

"Sounds wonderful," agreed Addie.

He ordered the pan-seared pepper crusted tenderloin with port wine sauce and she selected the grilled mahi mahi topped with lobster Florentine.

"I wasn't expecting such fine dining right here in Destiny," she said after their drinks had arrived.

"The country club has been here for over 20 years, but with the growth our town has seen recently, they were able to steal a chef from Austin who totally revamped the menu and the whole restaurant for that matter."

"Cheers to progress," Addie said with a grin as she

lifted her glass.

Cole lifted his as well and took a sip. "Addie, I wanted to let you know that I've got to go to Houston for about four or five days. I leave tomorrow morning and hope to be back by the end of the week, depending on how everything goes." She was disappointed that he would be gone but also pleased that he had wanted to tell her.

"Big case?"

"You could say that," he frowned and looked out the window, but Addie got the feeling that he wasn't admiring the view.

"Sorry, didn't mean to bring up business," she said, trying to pull him back into the room.

"No worries. It's an occupational hazard," he sat back in his chair and ran a finger slowly around the rim of his glass.

"Tell me about the most interesting case you've ever handled."

"Well," he said thoughtfully, "that's a tough one. There was one case I had when I was fresh out of law school. I was assigned as the public defender of a man—a kid really, he was only 18—who was suing his high school because his SAT scores were too low to get him into the college he wanted to attend."

Addie looked at him skeptically. "Really?" she asked.

"No joke. His grades were good; he mainly made A's and B's in everything, but his scores sucked. He felt he had received an inferior education, so he sued the school. And, he named every school board member, every superintendent, and every teacher and principal he could find."

"Surely that was thrown out. Tell me it was thrown out."

"It never even made it that far. Rather than have a public relations scandal, I convinced the school district to settle. They agreed to reimburse him for the cost of the test and paid for a test prep course."

She shook her head. "I guess it takes all kinds."

"The guys at the firm were laughing over that one, and I knew I got it as kind of a rite of passage. But, in the end, they were impressed that I was able to settle it, so I counted it as my first win," he said with a grin.

"Wonder whatever happened to him. Maybe, because of your help and inspiration, he went on to graduate and dedicated his life to helping the downtrodden."

"Actually, I heard he got his girlfriend pregnant and never even went to college." They both shook their heads and chuckled.

They enjoyed their dinner, and Cole ordered another round of drinks. They chatted and laughed and had a wonderfully relaxing evening. Addie decided not to tell Cole about the snakes. She really didn't know what to make of it herself, and she didn't want him worrying about it. Honestly, she wanted it completely out of her head tonight. She'd deal with it tomorrow. Dinner at the classiest restaurant in town on the arm of a handsome attorney did wonders for her mood.

They listened to music on their way back to her ranch, and Addie sat close to him enjoying the way her perfume mixed with the masculine scent of his cologne. When he pulled the truck to a stop in front of her door, she placed her hand against his chest, enjoying the firmness she could feel beneath her fingers.

"Want to come in for a nightcap?" she asked trying to sound sultry.

"I'd love to, but I'm afraid I can't. Ten hours from bottle to throttle."

She looked over at him curiously. "Say again?"

"I'm flying tomorrow morning. I need at least ten hours separating my last drink and my take off."

"You have a plane?" she asked wondering how that had never come up before.

"It's Daddy's, but I'm a licensed pilot." He smiled when her eyes widened in wonder. "Don't look so impressed. It's actually not that uncommon when you live out this way."

"Is that so. You cowboys certainly have a lot of hidden talents."

He chuckled and leaned down to give her a quick kiss. Then he slid out of the truck and reached for her hand to help her slide out.

"Allow me to escort you to your door, Ms. Butterfield." He was overly gallant, but she was beginning to sense that another night with him was about to end at her front door.

"Certainly," she said grabbing his arm seductively. "I know you can't drink, but how about a cup of coffee, or maybe some iced tea." She didn't have iced tea, but she was prepared to throw some together if he would agree to come inside with her.

"Another time," he said and could feel her shoulders drop. "I promise. I really need a good night's sleep, and I'm pretty sure that's not what I would get if I stayed." He looked at her teasingly. "But I'll come by as soon as I get back to town."

Cole put his hand on her back and pulled her against him. She leaned into the kiss wrapping one arm around his neck and the other around his waist and sighed with satisfaction. Finally, their lips parted, and they smiled into each other's eyes.

"Have a good trip," she said reluctantly.

"I'll hurry back," he assured her.

CHAPTER 19

T ravis picked her up early Monday morning, and the two of them filed a report with the sheriff. He too, like Travis, was surprised by the snake incident.

"I have to admit, that's pretty unusual," Sheriff Tom Healey said, looking over at Addie and Travis through dark-rimmed glasses with thick lenses. "Last year, Gabe Daley found that copperhead coiled up next to his front door. But I can't say I've ever heard of anything like this around here. And I've been sheriff for more than 20 years. But you see some strange things in this job. My guess is it was probably some kind of joke or prank. You're new in town. Maybe it was some of the local kids trying to have fun."

Travis suggested he have a deputy drive by once in a while to scare off any kids. Although he gave no outward sign of it, Addie had the feeling that Travis was not at all convinced the snakes had been a practical joke.

She tried to make small talk on the way back to the ranch, but he seemed pretty distracted.

"Thanks for going with me," she said when he pulled up in front of her house.

"Want me to come in for a bit?" he asked. "I don't mind."

She slid out of the truck and held the door open to peer back at him. He looked like a parent who was dropping off a child at day care for the first time, and her face softened with a sweet smile.

"Travis, of course you're always welcome here, but I'm fine. Really. Marsha is coming in a couple of hours, and we're spending the whole day together. I promise I'll call at the first sign of evil." She grinned, but he stared back at her without smiling. Finally, he nodded his head.

"OK. But let me know if you need anything," he said and waved when she closed the door. She waved back as he headed down the driveway.

The next day, Addie carried two statuettes of Greek goddesses down the attic steps and placed them in the sculptures room, which was now nearly full of pieces. She had gone through most of the attic storage, and only bulkier items remained. Hot, sweaty and exhausted, she decided she would quit for the day. She was pretty pleased with her progress. Marsha had been a big help on Monday, and Addie spent most of today stacking items in their appropriate rooms. Her inventory list was so huge, she had to start a second notebook.

Addie had been working diligently all afternoon and didn't notice that the sky was darkening earlier than usual until she headed for the stairs. She flipped a switch at the bottom of the steps and made her way to the kitchen. The clock on the stove told her it was still early evening. Looking out the large kitchen window, she could see that angry storm clouds had crowded out any traces of blue from the sky, and small trees and shrubs were straining against a wrathful wind.

"Mel," Addie looked down at the dog by her side. "I think you better go outside now. Looks like you might not get much of a chance later."

She opened the back door, and a gust of wind ripped it from her hand and slammed it against the wall, rattling the panes of glass in the door. Mel took a step back, but Addie called for him to follow her onto the patio. Her hair was whipping wildly around her head, and she held onto the sturdy table to keep from blowing over. The wind was thick with dust and grass, and Addie lowered her head to keep it from stinging her eyes. Mel walked about five steps and quickly lifted his leg, seeming to decide that now was not the time to be picky about where he went.

The two rushed back inside, and Addie pushed the stubborn door closed just before the first huge drops of rain splattered on the pavement. Within half a minute, rain engulfed the landscape as though the clouds had burst open all at one time. Every window in the house seemed to tremble against the violent deluge, and Addie could hear the hiss of wind through the vents.

She opened the pantry door and retrieved the flashlight she had seen when she was cleaning. Rushing up to the third floor, Addie closed the window in the cat's room and saw drops of water gathering on the ceiling. A small puddle of water was collecting beneath them on the wood floor.

"Oh, great," Addie sighed. "Just great." She ran into the hall and checked on the other rooms, finding similar leaks in two of them. Dashing into the bathroom, she found a stack of plastic bowls. At least Stella had been prepared for the leaky roof, but Addie found herself wishing she had just repaired it.

After rearranging the piles in each room so they were clear of the growing puddles, Addie placed bowls to catch the falling water. The storm gave no indication of slowing in intensity, and a bright flash of lightening followed by an explosion of thunder had Addie covering her ears instinctively.

She checked the rooms on the second floor and found that two of them had leaks similar to the rooms above them. Again, she moved heavy piles of boxes to keep them dry and placed more plastic bowls beneath the steady stream of drops.

The first floor seemed relatively dry, but there were a few leaks around several windows, and Addie shoved towels around them. Another crack of thunder had her flinching impulsively, and she almost expected the entire house to fly apart board by board.

Addie hurried to the bedroom to check her cell phone for a weather report but instead found that it had no signal. She tried the radio she used as her main source of news and entertainment but could find only static up and down the dial.

"Perfect," she said still clutching the flashlight. She wasn't sure what to do. She ached for a bath and the comfort of her bed but instead settled for washing her face and brushing her hair and teeth. She pulled off her sweaty t-shirt and replaced it with a simple white knit blouse. Addie had never experienced such a vicious storm and wanted to stay alert in case action was needed.

She didn't have long to wait. The entire sky outside her window suddenly flashed with brilliance, and the lights inside the house flickered twice and then went dark. Addie jumped to her feet and heard what sounded like pebbles hitting the window. Using the flashlight, she made her way to the kitchen and pointed its faint beam outside. White balls of ice were hurtling from the sky and crashing onto the patio. They seemed to be about the size of ping pong balls and made a horrible cracking sound when they hit the windows. Hail was already piling up like snow against the outside wall.

Addie heard the shattering of glass somewhere upstairs and screamed. Another upstairs window splintered, and she couldn't tell if it was on the second or third floor. She was torn between running upstairs to investigate and taking shelter in the bathroom. This could be a tornado; she had no way of knowing. Addie didn't hear any weather sirens, but perhaps Destiny didn't have any. Deciding there was very little she could do upstairs, she grabbed a blanket from the bed and sat huddled on the floor of the bathroom with Mel. Addie grabbed her knees and softly rocked back and forth listening to the fury Mother Nature spat down upon her.

The hail finally slowed, but the wind and the rain kept a steady tempo. There seemed to be a bit more time between lightning and thunder, and Addie could feel her breathing begin to slow. Was that the worst of it? Oh, please God, she silently prayed, let that be the end of it.

Heavy pounding on the front door made her breath catch in her throat. She listened silently, and after a few seconds, it sounded again.

"Addie!" she heard Travis' voice behind her front door for the second time in three days. She scrambled to her feet and followed the bouncing beam of her flashlight down the hall. She unlocked the door, and Travis pushed his way in, water sliding from his slicker to stand in a pool at his feet.

"Addie, are you OK?" he asked, shining his larger, brighter flashlight up at the ceiling. It cast the entryway with a pale glow, and he could see the concern on her face. "I wanted to come by and make sure you were all right," he said carefully removing the slicker and laying it at his feet.

"I am," she said with a tremor in her voice. "Yes, I am. How did you get here?" As soon as she said it, she felt silly. "I mean, you didn't drive over here in that, did you?"

"I missed the worst of it," he said, wiping water from his face.

"Let me get you a towel."

He followed her down the hall and into the bedroom. She handed him a towel and sat on the edge of the bed watching him dry his face and hair. He tossed it on the edge of the tub and turned to face her.

"Do you have any matches?"

"There should be some near the sink."

Travis lit the candles sitting around the tub and picked up the blanket from the floor.

"I thought it might be a tornado, so Mel and I were riding it out in there," she said to his unasked question. "Is it a tornado?"

"No, but it's a hell of a storm. We don't often get hail like that out here." He sat on the bed next to her. "And I'm not sure we're through the worst of it."

"What about your dad? And your house? I don't want to pull you away if you're needed there." Addie placed a hand on his leg and looked up with eyes that were wide with concern. She was beyond comforted to have him there but knew he had other obligations.

"I dropped Dad off at a neighbor's house. And our place is pretty solid. I'm a bit worried about the barn, but it's been through worse and came out unscathed," he said patting her hand.

"I heard glass breaking upstairs. I know at least two windows are broken. And there are leaks all over the place."

"I'll go up and check on things," he said standing.

"I'm coming with you."

They climbed the stairs and checked out each room on the second floor. One of the rooms had a smashed window and rain was streaming in, drenching the nearby boxes. Travis looked around the room for something he could use to block the rain. Finding nothing suitable, he went into the hallway and returned with a cabinet door from the bathroom. Placing it over the cracked window, he secured it with a stack of boxes. They found another broken window on the third floor, and Travis was able to construct a make-shift repair in that room as well.

When they were back downstairs, Addie stopped in the kitchen. She remembered she hadn't eaten all day and could feel the emptiness inside her rumbling.

"Are you hungry?" she asked and didn't wait for his reply. "I haven't eaten all day, and I'm going to make a peanut butter and jelly sandwich. Want one?" she said turning toward him.

"Sure," he said easily. While she worked on the sandwiches using her little flashlight to navigate the kitchen, Travis poked around the house and returned with a handful of candles.

He took them into the bedroom, and when she walked in, the room was glowing with flickering light.

"Bed picnic?" she asked playfully.

"Sounds romantic," he said.

She missed the huskiness in his voice as she kicked off her shoes and put plates on the bed. "Dr. Pepper OK with you?" she asked over her shoulder as she headed back to the kitchen.

"Works for me."

Addie returned carrying two cans and a chew bone for Mel.

They sat on the bed with the storm raging outside.

"How long do you think this will last?" she asked between bites.

"I was looking at the satellite before we lost power, and it looked like it would probably last for a few hours."

"Do you think we'll get more hail?"

"Not sure."

"I desperately hope not. I'm not sure my house can take it." She was about to take a bite of her sandwich and hesitated, holding it in midair. "That's funny. My house. This is my house. I still can't believe it."

"Have you decided if you're going to keep it?"

"I want to. I think it's what Stella wanted," she paused.

"But," Travis prompted.

"I've been going over Stella's finances, and I honestly don't know how she managed to keep it herself. And I can't see how I'm going to either."

"You could always sell some of the assets. This place has a ton of those."

"I could," she said taking a bite of her sandwich. "I know that's not what Stella wanted, but I really don't see any way around it. I don't suppose you know anything about her money situation, do you?"

"Afraid not. We talked a lot over the years, but I don't remember her ever talking about money," he said and lifted his can. "Now that I think about it, it does seem a bit improbable—her, living in this big house with a whole community of artists to support on a teacher's salary. I know they grew food and had a couple of animals, but still. Creating art takes resources," he looked at her quizzically.

"And now it's all mine to figure out," Addie threw her head back and could feel the tightness in her neck and shoulders. "I want to do the right thing. I just don't know what the right thing is. Did I ever tell you Stella left me a journal?" Addie asked him.

"No, you never mentioned it," Travis said waiting for her to continue.

"She'd kept it for me since I was born out here. She wanted me to understand the ranch and the philosophy by which they all lived. It sounded so incredible, and I'm sure it was. She wrote a letter to me asking me to take care of her things," Addie let her voice trail off.

The two sat in silence for a minute listening to the storm.

"I just don't know what to do," Addie repeated. "How did all of this happen? Two weeks ago, I was a middle school teacher living in Denton. Now, I'm out here in West Texas, and I own a ranch house that may not survive the night!" It sounded comical, even to her, yet tears were welling in her eyes.

Addie stood to put their plates on the dresser, but a sudden deafening crack of thunder made her entire body jerk. The plates rattled in her hands, and Travis sprang from the bed reaching out to keep them from falling. Thunder boomed again, and Addie lurched forward. She looked up at Travis in the soft light. Every emotion she had ever felt in her entire life churned inside her body, and she breathed heavily matching the ferocity outside. Without thinking, she put both of her hands behind his head and pulled him to her. His lips met hers as she pressed her body into him. The kiss deepened as man and woman came together with violent passion while the storm raged in fury.

Travis bent his knees and reached down to lift her up, holding her with one arm while the other grabbed her hair and crushed her lips hard against his. She wrapped her legs around his torso, and he carried her to the bed, laying her gently on her back while their embrace tightened. Travis lifted his head and pulled his t-shirt off in one hurried motion, letting it drop to the floor. Addie reached over to unhook his belt while he unbuttoned her shirt spreading it open to caress her bare shoulders. Her hands moved behind him digging into his back, feeling his muscles move beneath her touch. His lips found hers again while he reached under her pulling her close against him. She could feel her breath catch in her throat, feel his heart beating with hers.

Addie threw her head back drunk with sensation. His warm breath brushed her neck as his lips and tongue teased a path slowly along the column of her throat. He reached behind her with one hand to unhook her bra while burying his head between her breasts. Strong hands closed around her ribs reaching nearly all the way around her as a low moan rose from deep within her. She felt delicate, feminine, passionate, hungry. Twisting her fingers through his hair, she pulled him up to cover his mouth with hers.

The radio interruption was worse than if they had been thrown into a pool of ice water, and Travis froze as he listened to the page.

"Fire 236, there is a report of a vehicle accident near Highway 62 and Campbell Road. EMS is en route."

Travis lifted his head and stared down at her, taking a ragged breath. Without taking his eyes off her, he fumbled in his front pocked for the radio.

"Fire 236 acknowledges page," he responded in a monotone voice.

"10-4 fire 236."

"Fire 236 is en route." Travis shoved the radio back into his pocket and looked down at her with a pained expression.

"Addie—" he started.

"No need to explain," she said hastening to sit up and pull her shirt closed. "You need to get going."

He yanked his t-shirt back over his head and reached over for a last kiss.

"Thanks for coming out to check on me," she said softly as he turned to leave. He hesitated for a moment at the door and finally turned back to look at her.

"I'll see you tomorrow," he said and left. She couldn't see his expression in the dim light, but his voice was lower than usual.

Addie took a long, calming breath and lay back against the pillows. What would have happened if he hadn't been called away? She had been frustrated and confused and emotional, and she had thrown herself at him. And he had reciprocated quite fully. She could feel the hunger in his touch. She would be lying to herself if she said she had not been aroused or that she didn't find his rough masculinity wildly exciting. But where did this leave them now? And what about Cole?

Mel jumped up on the bed and lay his head in her lap as though he knew she needed a friend. She rubbed his head absently and listened to the rain outside her window. The storm was beginning to calm somewhat, and concern over the state of her house was replaced with fatigue. Addie fell asleep soundly with the candles flickering softly.

CHAPTER 20

Addie was still on her back when she woke early to light flooding in through the windows and from every fixture she had left on the previous night. She moved stiffly still dressed in shorts and a t-shirt and decided she would start the day with the bath she so dearly needed last night. While the tub was filling, she made coffee and let Mel out the back door. The sky was a friendly light blue without a single trace of the storm that had nearly demolished her house, though she could see standing water in several low spots across the ranch.

Addie turned on her radio to the local station and stepped into the steamy bath. Talk of the storm monopolized the newscast.

"Destiny was hit hard by a severe storm last night. Residents experienced power outages, large hail, and major flooding in most parts of the town. Public

Works Director Diego Rios said he was watching storm reports closely all evening. 'Storm trackers were saying that the storm was moving mainly to the east, but suddenly it changed course. When they said it turned south, I knew we'd get hit with hail.'

"A flood watch was issued from 9 o'clock last night until 5 o'clock this morning. Rios said the sheriff's department worked with firefighters to block off unsafe streets. There was one storm-related car accident, but only minor injuries were sustained. Although the storm didn't cause significant damage, officials say there were some broken windshields and house windows as well as roof damage across the town.

"City Manager Daniel Vickers says Destiny will now deal with the aftermath of the storm. 'We're left with some debris like dirt, tree limbs, things like that. The major work now is clean up. Our crews will be out on the streets starting today getting things back to normal.' If you have debris in your area, please call Destiny City Hall."

Travis probably had a pretty late night, thought Addie as she rinsed shampoo out of her hair. Thinking about Travis had her stomach quivering. She wasn't sure what reaction she should have when she saw him again. She could tell him it had been a mistake, but Addie dismissed that idea almost as soon as it occurred to her. She always hated that response when she saw it in the movies, thinking it made the woman look kind of manipulative. But, what if he said it to her? She really didn't see Travis as that kind of guy. Probably the best thing to do is just to be friendly. She enjoyed Travis' company, and if it went further than that, she would deal with it at the time.

Addie climbed out of the tub and wrapped herself in a towel, glad she had made a decision, but the nervousness in her stomach was still there.

"*Just keep yourself busy,*" advised her mother. "*Things will sort themselves out in time.*"

"Good thinking, Mom," Addie said aloud. "And I know just what I need to do."

Addie had decluttered the first floor of the house having moved a lot of the art and collectibles to the other rooms upstairs. Giving the downstairs a thorough cleaning would brighten her spirits and make more of the house livable. She was getting tired of spending all of her time in the kitchen and bedroom.

After devoting a couple of hours in the front living room dusting, wiping walls, sweeping, and polishing, she declared the room fit for habitation. She had dragged a huge area rug to the back patio and pulled old dusty drapes off the windows and now didn't feel the urge to sneeze every time she walked into the room. The furniture was old but functional. She sat on a lime-green wing backed chair with spindly legs that was now vacuumed and cleaned and admired her work.

Addie heard a car engine rattling outside and opened the door to see Travis climbing out of his truck. He walked around to the back and pulled out several boards that he lugged up the steps and lay on the porch.

"Morning," he said with a smile and headed back to the truck.

"Almost noon," she corrected following him. "What's all this?"

"I thought I'd board up those windows until you can get them fixed," he said pulling out a circular saw and small toolbox.

"I was listening to the news on the radio. Sounded like you had quite a night."

He raised his eyebrows and followed her into the house. "It wasn't too bad. The accident turned out to be a car that had skidded off the road. No real injuries. And then we just went around blocking off roads that had high water. We've pretty much got that down as we know exactly which roads tend to flood in hard rains." Travis looked around her at the living room.

"Somebody's been busy," he said with a smile. "I don't remember that room ever looking this good."

"Well, I don't think it's ready for the cover of *Better Homes and Gardens*, but at least you can breathe in here now."

"Hey, I have something for you," Travis said and went back to his truck. He came back in carrying a large box that had Justin Boots stamped on the top of it. He handed it to her. "I hope you like them. Marsha helped me pick them out. If you're going to live on a ranch, you need a good pair of boots. They'll protect you from snakes and other critters that might be hiding in the grass."

Addie opened the box and saw a cute pair of practical western boots. She could feel her face flush as she imagined Marsha helping both Cole and Travis buy boots for her.

"They're wonderful!" she said and smiled up at him. He was grinning with pride.

"Try them on. Marsha said she was pretty sure they would fit."

Addie sat on the newly cleaned sofa and pulled them up. Her second pair of boots fit as nicely as the first. "Like a glove," she said taking a few steps in them.

Travis looked at her from her boots up her tanned legs to her tight pink t-shirt and finally to her eyes, which were staring back at him. They looked at each other without speaking. Finally, she smiled softly.

"Thanks so much, Travis. It was really thoughtful of you."

"You look great," he said, and then cleared his throat as if he were trying to restrain himself. "OK if I get started?" he asked heading for the stairs.

"Of course. Do you need some help?"

"Naw, I got it. I don't mean to interrupt your day."

"It's hardly an interruption when you're coming over to fix stuff," she called after him.

After a few seconds, he came back down the stairs empty handed and headed for the porch to get the lumber. "At least let me buy you lunch when you're done. The Hushpuppy?" she asked.

"I'll be sure to work up an appetite," he said with a twinkle in his eyes and disappeared up the stairs.

So, nothing physical, Addie thought. I guess we're both pretending nothing happened last night. She knew she should be relieved.

Standing alone in her new boots in the middle of her newly cleaned living room, she sighed. Addie stood for a moment listening to Travis move around upstairs, then she turned and walked back to start cleaning the den.

A couple of hours later, Addie and Travis walked into The Hushpuppy. "Miss Addie," exclaimed a young girl sitting at one of the front tables. She hopped out of her chair and ran over to give Addie a big hug. Addie remembered her from the storybook readings she did at the library and squatted down, so she was eye level with the girl.

"Mia, how are you?" Addie smiled at her then waved a greeting to her parents.

"I'm doing great, but that storm woke me up last night. Wasn't it scary?"

"Yes, it was. I'm so glad it's gone now."

"Me too. We have to go get some stuff to fix our fence after lunch. Part of it fell down," Mia said matter-of-factly. Her parents waved at her to come back to the table, and she said, "I have to go back and finish now. Bye!" Addie and Travis watched as she skipped back to her table.

"You're quite the celebrity," Travis teased as he led her to a window booth where they waited for their favorite waitress. It seemed the storm was all anyone was talking about. There were still a couple of roads closed due to high water, and on the drive over they saw a lot of tree limbs scattered on the sides of the roads and several broken and downed fences.

"It's pretty crowded in here for a late lunch on a

weekday," Addie commented.

Travis looked around. "A lot of them have been out helping clean up and clear the roads. Big storms like that don't happen every day, but we usually get a couple of them a year. The next morning, folks pitch in to help, whoever can take time off work. And some of them are ranchers who have probably been fixing fences since early this morning."

A group of middle-aged men sitting at a table in the back stood up to leave, stopping to speak with Travis on their way out.

"Thanks again for helping us out last night, Trav," one of them said shaking his hand. "Yeah," said another. "We'd probably still be stuck if it hadn't been for you."

"I really doubt that, Charlie," said Travis smiling. "You guys take care."

After they walked out, Addie looked at Travis. "What was that all about?"

"After we cleared away the accident, I drove over to Barren's Bridge Road to block it off and saw them stuck in mud that was almost completely covering their back wheels. I was able to radio a couple of the guys, and we used the winch on the truck to pull them out."

Addie sat back and looked at him with her head tilted to one side. "Always taking care of everyone," she said softly and then leaned forward. "Tell me, who takes care of you?"

He never got a chance to answer as a flustered Marsha all but flew up to their table and set two glasses of ice water in front of them.

"Whatever you do, don't tell me a sad story about the storm last night. My goodness, it's as if no one had ever seen rain before," Marsha looked over at Travis and grimaced. "Sorry, Travis. I know you've probably been workin' all night. I'll put on my best happy waitress face now."

"Great," he said looking back at her. "I'd love to see what that looks like."

"Very funny. Now, what'll you have?"

"Burger and a DP for me," said Addie.

"Are you sure? Junior's in the kitchen today."

"No, I really just want a burger."

"Make it two," said Travis putting the menus back behind the ketchup bottle. "But make mine an iced tea."

"Comin' right up." Marsha took a step back and looked at the two of them together. Saying nothing, she headed back to the kitchen.

"So, did you get any sleep last night?" Addie asked taking a sip of her water.

"About four hours or so."

"So, you'll be ready for a long nap after lunch." Addie could feel her cheeks warming as she realized it sounded like an invitation, but Travis either didn't notice or pretended not to.

"No, once I'm up, I'm up. If I sleep during the day it really messes me up."

"How did you become a fireman anyway?" Addie asked.

"I actually got involved with it when I was in college. By the time I got my undergrad, I had already logged some hours with the local department, and I just kept it going after that. I really love it."

"You have a master's degree?" Addie asked. After so many years with her husband checklist, it was second nature for her to explore any of those qualities she saw in a man.

"After I got my bachelor's at Texas A&M in agricultural engineering, I was asked by the dean to work on my masters. Then I joined a company in Houston and ended up in their biofuels research department."

"The dean asked you to do graduate work? You must have been a very good student."

He shrugged. "I guess. Were you?"

"I guess," she echoed him. "But I didn't do graduate study."

"Did you always know you wanted to be a teacher?"

"Not always," she started. Addie didn't feel like revealing her failed dreams of becoming an artist. "But it's what I went to school for. I have a degree in English and am certified to teach all secondary grades."

Marsha interrupted their conversation with plates of food and two cold drinks.

"Sorry it took a bit. This place has been a madhouse today!" Again, she turned her head to look at each of them, and when they said nothing, she just raised her eyebrows. "You two enjoy your lunch."

Travis chuckled and squirted ketchup onto his plate.

"How long have you known Marsha."

"Forever," he said with a laugh. "She was always

such a hoot. She was too young to be in high school with me, but I knew her brother Greg pretty well. I would hang out at their house, and she would flirt with me," he said simply without bragging.

"Did you two ever date?" Addie asked biting into her burger.

"No. I think we ended up thinking of each other as brother and sister. But she's great. And a lot smarter than she lets on."

Addie was pleased with this assessment of her friend and nodded her head in agreement.

"You two seem to be pretty close," Travis observed.

"For someone I really just met a few weeks ago, I sometimes feel like I've known her forever. She's quite easy to be with."

"She says the same about you," Travis said with a lopsided grin.

"Does she?" Addie said straightening, her teacher voice in full force. "And do you often gossip behind people's backs?"

"Only when the backside is so lovely," he said leaning forward.

She looked at him sideways, not sure what to make of him. He liked to flirt, that much was obvious, but there was so much more beneath the surface.

"It must be tough," she said changing the subject, "being a fireman. Have you ever had to save anyone?"

"You'd be surprised how rarely that happens. Mainly we just run around saving people's stuff." He took a bite of his burger and dunked a fry in ketchup.

Addie leaned toward him. "I know you don't like to

talk about yourself."

"And you do?" he questioned just as evenly.

She sat back eyeing him slyly. "OK, tell me one of your most exciting rescues, and I'll tell you something you want to know."

Travis looked at her through squinted eyes, then said, "Deal. But you have to answer anything I ask you, right?"

Addie just nodded her head with a grin.

"Well," he said. "Probably the most impactful rescue I ever made was before I was a firefighter. I had just graduated from high school and was helping Stella with stuff around the ranch that summer before I went off to college. I went over one afternoon, and she was sitting on her front porch. I could tell right away that something was wrong. She just didn't look right. She had been sitting on a chair, and then I saw her slump over onto her knees. I jumped out of the truck and ran up to her. I thought she might be having a heart attack, but then she moved her hand to her throat, and I knew she was choking. I was able to do the Heimlich maneuver on her, and it worked. She told me later that she had been close to passing out. That really scared me. She could have died if someone hadn't come along.

"That's when I decided to become a fireman. You know, to be able to help someone when they really need it, like Stella did." He had been looking off to the side while he told the story, but then he focused back on Addie. He shook his head slightly. "It still bothers me when I think about it. The moments that separate life and death and how important they are. Sometimes I wonder about the times that people aren't able to call us or didn't have someone show up on their porch at just the right instant." He took a sip of his iced tea and looked at her.

Addie looked back at him as if seeing him for the first time, glimpsing the caring, thoughtful man beneath the witty and charming exterior. Finally, he grinned at her and said, "My turn."

She laughed and picked up a french fry. "OK, a deal's a deal."

"So, why is such a good-looking girl like you not married?"

"That's what you want to know about?" she asked teasingly. "My love life?"

"Yes," he said without hesitation. "Spill it."

"Maybe I'm just a career-obsessed mad woman who's impossible to get along with."

"Perhaps, but I don't want to deal in maybe's and could of's. I want the truth according to Addie Butterfield."

She sat back and looked up. "The truth," she said reflectively and put her elbows on the table resting her chin on her crossed hands. "The truth is, I'm not married because I haven't met him yet. And I know what you're thinking—that I'm waiting around for some imaginary guy that only exists in the confines of my vivid imagination." As she said the words, she couldn't help but wish it was just an imaginary list. Maybe then she would be able to crumple it up and forget about it. How nice it would be to meet a nice man, date, fall in love and have a life together instead of waiting for her dream guy to ride up on a white horse and say *I love you* in another language as they ride off into the sunset.

Her cheeks warmed slightly as she realized Travis was watching her closely. "I've dated and had relationships," she continued. "Just none of them were meant for forever." She shrugged her shoulders and reached for her drink. "You're the one who asked."

But Travis wasn't willing to give up so easily. "So, you've met plenty of the wrong guys. What kind of guy would be right?"

"Well, let's see," she said playfully. "He'd have to be a man of letters, that's a given. Education is very important to me. He'd be tall. And handsome would be nice, but that's not a deal breaker," she sipped her drink while Travis grinned between bites of fries. "Texan," she said definitively. "I find I like the men in Texas. All that horseback riding is very primal. He'd need to be handy in the kitchen. I need someone who can bring me breakfast in bed once in a while. And he'd speak another language." She nodded her head, pleased that she was able to sum up her list so succinctly.

"Well, I guess that leaves me out. I only speak English." Travis shook his head, and Addie laughed.

"You wanted the truth."

They ate slowly and chatted easily, and when she had a break, Marsha joined them placing fresh drinks in front of them and sliding into the booth next to Addie. She picked up a fry from Addie's plate and leaned back with a sigh.

"My feet are killing me," she complained.

"That's because you wear spikey pointed shoes," Travis shot back without hesitation.

"Excuse me, they're fashionable," she replied giving him a look that said he must be the biggest dope on the planet. "I work on tips," she reminded him.

"Well, here's a tip. Don't wear spikey pointed shoes when you have to be on your feet all day." He swallowed his last bite of burger and then stood up. "If you ladies will excuse me for a minute."

"There is absolutely no excuse for you Travis Granger," Marsha shot back as he walked away.

Then she turned back to face Addie. "So, I guess your footwear collection is growing."

Addie sighed and rolled her eyes. "I have no idea what I'm doing. I hope I'm not leading them on."

"So, what if you are? Relax and enjoy it." Marsha said with a lazy smile.

"You really don't know me at all if you think I could do that." Addie frowned.

Marsha punched her arm lightheartedly. "Come on. It's not the end of the world. A couple of cute guys gave the new girl in town some boots. Someone call the cops."

"But what do I do if they find out about each other's gifts. They'll think I'm some kind of tease."

Marsha looked at Addie with surprise. "Haven't you ever had two guys fighting for you before?"

"Of course not," Addie replied indignantly as

though someone had just suggested she kick a puppy.

"Girl, you have not lived," Marsha replied shaking her head.

"Quiet," Addie said elbowing her friend. "He's coming back."

"OK, OK. I won't say another word about 'bootgate'." Marsha stood up and glared impishly at Travis as she passed him.

Addie pushed her half-eaten burger and fries to the middle of the table. "I'm stuffed."

Travis pulled the plate over and helped himself to her leftovers. "You'll never get fat eating like that," he said with a smile. Addie self-consciously crossed her arms in front of her wondering if that was a crack aimed at her small chest. She knew it was silly, and usually she enjoyed her slender frame, but how she wished she could fill out a low-cut top. Shaking it off, she looked over at Travis.

"What are you doing with the rest of your day," she asked as he finished off her burger.

"I've got stuff to do in the lab at home. What about you?"

Addie didn't answer him, and sat staring straight ahead. She saw it, she knew she did. An image so fast she almost couldn't tell what it was. Something on her bed. It was the bedroom at the ranch. It flashed again, and she saw it was Mel's collar sitting on her bed.

Travis had stopped eating and was looking at her closely as she continued to stare as if in a trance.

"Addie?" When she didn't respond, he put his hand on her arm. "Addie?"

When she moved her focus to him, he could see the concern on her face.

"It's Mel," she said. "We have to go. Now. Something's wrong with Mel."

CHAPTER 21

Addie burst through the front door followed closely by Travis. Two of the paintings that were hanging in the living room were on the floor, the canvases slashed and the frames broken. Several of the figurines she had carefully cleaned and displayed just this morning were smashed on the floor.

"Mel!" Addie screamed, and Travis yanked on her arm to keep her back.

"Wait, Addie," he said sternly. "Someone may be in the house. Let me check." He stood still and listened for any noises. Hearing nothing, he held up a finger signaling her to keep still.

"Stay right here until I can check things out."

"I have to go to the bedroom," her voice was shaking.

"Let me look first," he tried again.

"No, I'm coming with you," she said stubbornly.

He decided to give in so he could keep her in sight. She followed him down the hall as he looked inside the rooms and closets. There were more damaged items in the den, and when they crossed into the bedroom, Addie's hands flew up to cover her mouth. The statues of Stella and Ven had been spray painted in red. Stella's bookcase lay on the floor in splinters, her cherished collectibles shattered as though someone had unleashed a lifetime of hatred and evil upon each of the treasured pieces. And, in the middle of the bed was Mel's collar, just has she had seen it in the restaurant.

She reached down to pick it up and saw that it had been unhooked. In the entire time she'd had him, Mel had never gotten out of his collar. Travis seemed to understand what she was thinking, and his nostrils flared when he looked at her.

"Stay right here. I'll check the rest of the house."

Addie stood stiffly holding the collar and listened as Travis moved through the rooms. She heard doors open, his boots on the floor boards, the crunch of glass as he stepped on broken trinkets. But what she didn't hear was Mel.

After a few minutes, she heard him running back down the stairs.

"There doesn't seem to be anybody here. And I didn't see Mel anywhere."

"Are you sure?" Addie's voice shook, and her eyes were glassy. "Maybe he's hurt and lying in a closet or under something." As she said it, she dropped to her knees and looked under the bed.

"That's possible. I only did a very quick search."

When she stood again, he wrapped her in his arms and stroked her hair. "We'll find him, Addie." He looked down into her soggy eyes, and she could see the resolve on his face.

"I'll radio Sheriff Healey so we can get an investigation underway. I'm going to round up some of the guys and see about searching the entire ranch. I need you to stay here and wait for the sheriff. You can look for Mel in the house, but don't leave," he pulled his radio out of his pocket as he spoke. "You and I will stay in contact with our cell phones. If you find Mel, let me know." Before he left the room, he turned back to look at her. "Do you understand, Addie?"

She nodded quickly. "Yes, and thanks."

"We'll find him." His confident leadership was reassuring.

She could hear Travis talking on his radio as he moved down the hall and out the door. Addie went through every inch of the bedroom that could hold a small dog and then moved into the kitchen. She searched the first floor thoroughly, opening closets, moving furniture, and calling Mel's name. Nothing.

Travis opened the front door and strode in purposefully. "The sheriff's on his way, and I have a couple of buddies that will be here in a few minutes. Do you know if those guest houses are locked?"

"They should be. I checked them all myself. Let me get you the keys," said Addie running to get her purse.

Travis walked the grounds near the house while Addie started searching the upper floors. After a few minutes, she could hear Travis coming in the front door speaking with someone.

"Addie," he called up to her. She came to the steps and saw one of the firemen he had introduced her to at Destiny Days. "Luis is going to check the outbuildings, and then he and Pete are going to start combing the grounds. I'm going home to get Major. I can cover more ground on horseback."

She nodded her head and tried her best to hide her distress. "Thanks so much for coming over to help," she said to Luis.

"Of course," he said with a comforting smile.

Addie meticulously searched every room on the two upper floors but could find no traces of Mel. She looked out one of the large windows in a third-floor room and saw Travis on a chestnut horse riding across the ranch. He was wearing a dark cowboy hat, and it occurred to Addie that she had never seen him like this—in a hat, on a horse, looking like a cowboy. He had never even mentioned that he had a horse. She watched him trot over to the pond and walk the horse slowly around the perimeter. He looked very comfortable in the saddle, but that was probably typical for a man who had grown up in West Texas.

The sheriff pulled up just as Addie was walking out the front door for some fresh, if not hot, air. She showed him in and walked through the house with him pointing out damage. A deputy scribbled in a small notebook and then went upstairs while the sheriff sat in the living room with Addie.

"Would you like some coffee or water?" she asked.
"I also have Dr. Pepper."

"You know, a Dr. Pepper sounds wonderful," he
said. "Thanks."

"The cans are cold, but would you like a glass with
ice?" Addie asked heading down the hallway.

"A can is fine," he told her and pulled a small pad
out of his shirt pocket.

When she returned with the drinks, he was busy
jotting notes on a blank page.

"Thank you kindly," he said with a friendly smile.
Pushing his glasses up his nose, he continued. "How
are you doing?"

"I'm OK. A little shaken up and worried about my
dog."

"I understand Travis and a couple of others are out
looking for him?"

"Yes, that's right." She said sitting in the chair next
to his.

"Are you up to a few questions?" he asked popping
the top on his can.

"I suppose so."

"What time did you and Travis get here today?"

"Umm, I think it was just a little after 2:30. We
walked in and saw that some of the art in the front
room had been damaged. Travis went through the
house to make sure no one was here. And then I found
Mel's collar on the bed. He has never once gotten out
of his collar on his own."

"Was the front door locked?"

"I locked it when we left, and it was still locked

when we returned."

"Do you know if anything is missing?"

"I'm really not sure. It's such a mess. But Stella had some jewelry in the bedroom, and it's still there."

"Once you get to cleaning things up, if you notice that anything is missing, please give me a call." He reached into his shirt pocket and handed Addie his card.

"Addie," he said looking at her carefully, "do you know of anyone who would do this? Maybe someone who has a grudge against you or had one against Stella?"

She looked back at him with wide eyes. "I don't think so. I don't even know that many people, and everyone's been very welcoming. As for Stella, the people I've met seemed to like her very much."

Sheriff Healey patted her hand. "I just have to ask. It's all part of the routine. But I would like to get to the bottom of it. We'll take some fingerprints and see if that leads us anywhere."

Addie nodded. The deputy came downstairs and spoke with the sheriff.

"There is more vandalism on the two upper floors, but only to the things closest to the doors. You have a lot of stuff up there," he said looking at Addie.

She explained her situation and why she was in Destiny and at the ranch, while they both wrote in their notebooks.

"Maybe someone was looking for something in particular," offered the deputy.

"Could be, but that doesn't explain the dog," the

sheriff replied. "I'll take a look around the outside of the house, while you get started with the fingerprinting."

"Is there anything you'd like me to do?" Addie said standing up.

"Not in particular, but please try not to touch anything until we give you the all clear."

She sat outside on the porch and called Travis on her cell phone.

"Hey," he said on the other end.

"Hey. The sheriff is here, and they're going to get some fingerprints."

"That's good."

"Have you seen anything on your end?" she asked hesitantly.

"Not yet, but we still have some ground to cover."

"What should I do? I feel so useless just sitting here."

"I know, but we need you to stay there in case the sheriff has questions. And Mel might still just show up at the house. If you want something to do, you could have cold drinks ready when we get back. It's blazing hot out here!"

"That," she said, "I can do."

After getting the OK from the sheriff, Addie busied herself in the kitchen making a pitcher of iced tea, since it seemed to be the national drink of Texas. As she heated water in the microwave, she wondered if she was the only one in the entire state who didn't drink it.

Bradley had liked sweet iced tea, so she always kept a pitcher of it at her apartment.

Thinking of her apartment back in Denton had her frowning. When she left for West Texas, she had assumed she would be gone for about a week, two at the most. Now, she was in Destiny and was actually considering moving here to live on her inherited ranch. When she told her mother about the inheritance, she had been thrilled for Addie and had immediately assumed that she would sell it all off. She even offered to come out to assess some of the art. Addie had been able to stall her easily saying that she was still taking inventory and would let her know when it was done.

The microwave beeped at her, and she poured the hot tea into a tall pitcher, filling the rest with water. Since she still had nothing to do, she decided to make another one, sweet this time. She also pulled chocolate chip cookie dough out of the refrigerator and heated the oven. Addie had made a batch of dough the other day when she and Marsha were cleaning, but only baked a few cookies. At least she could offer the guys fresh cookies and cold drinks when they returned empty handed.

"No," she told herself. "Stay positive. Travis said he would find Mel. Believe in that." But even as she gave herself the pep talk, she frowned and all but shoved the trays of cookies into the oven.

Addie finished in the kitchen and decided to wait on the front porch. After a couple of minutes, she could hear Luis and Pete talking as they neared the house. Their faces were wet with sweat, but they seemed relaxed.

"He's behind us," said Pete pointing into the distance. Addie shielded her eyes with her hand and squinted to see Travis on horseback trotting toward them. He held the reins with one hand and cradled Mel in the other. The dog squirmed occasionally and didn't appear to be hurt. Addie nearly cried out with relief as man, horse, and dog came to a stop at the bottom of the steps.

Travis held his horse completely still as he handed Mel to Addie. "Yours?" he asked with an easy smile.

"You bet," she said laughing, reaching up to take the dog into her arms. She held him close and spun around with him while he alternately barked and licked her face.

"Where have you been?" she asked looking at bits of hay and grass stuck in his coat. "You're a mess!"

Travis climbed off his horse and patted the side of its neck. "I found him clear on the other side of the ranch. Luckily, he was barking like mad at Major or I might have missed him. He was all but invisible in the tall grass." Travis leaned over to scratch the top of Mel's head.

Addie looked at all three of the men, who were smiling back at her, and tears welled in her eyes. "Thank you," she said shakily and took a calming breath. "Thank you so much!" Regaining her composure, she said quickly, "Come inside where it's cooler. You guys look hot and tired. I have cold tea and warm cookies."

"Sounds perfect," said Travis wrapping the reins

around the porch railing and following her inside. Pete and Luis walked along behind them.

"Mind if I grab a towel?" asked Travis stopping by the bedroom door.

"Help yourself," she said and put Mel on the floor. "I've got sweet iced tea, regular iced tea, Dr. Pepper, water," she smiled at the other men.

"Sweet tea for me," said Pete taking a seat at the table.

"Same," said Luis.

Travis walked back in and tossed towels at the other sweaty men. Addie placed a plate of cookies in front of them and delivered their drinks. She handed a regular tea to Travis.

"The sheriff's around here somewhere. They're taking fingerprints."

Travis nodded and grabbed a couple of cookies off the plate.

"Good," said Pete holding his cookie up and nodding at Addie.

"I'm glad you like them."

"So," said Luis looking slyly at Travis. "The least you could do is let one of us find the dog. It's just like him," he said to Addie. "We do all the hard work, and he rides in like the hero at the end." Travis threw his towel hitting Luis in the face.

"You're all heroes to me," she said, then grinned self-consciously when she realized how corny it sounded. "Really, you have no idea what this little guy means to me."

The three men turned when they heard voices down

the hall. Sheriff Healey and his deputy joined them in the kitchen.

"Please help yourself," Addie said motioning to the cookies. "Would you care for anything to drink?"

"I think we're good," said Sheriff Healey, "but I'll take you up on your offer of a cookie," he said reaching across the table.

Pete and Luis looked at each other and stood at the same time.

"If you're all set here, we'll be getting back," said Pete leaning down to give Addie a quick hug.

"Thanks again, guys," Addie said giving Luis a hug. "And please take some cookies with you."

Travis walked with them to the front door, and Addie could hear them laughing at something he said. But when he returned to the kitchen, his expression was more serious.

"What do you think?" Travis asked the sheriff.

"Well, my first thought is that it was kids again. But Addie said she had to unlock the door when you two got here. There's no sign of forced entry anywhere. My guess is, whoever did this had a key."

"What about the room with the cats? Could someone have gotten in that way?" Addie asked anxiously.

"We checked it, and it doesn't look like it. But we dusted for prints just to be sure. Travis, I know your prints are on file. Addie, what about you?"

"I'm a teacher, so mine are on file as well."

"Very good. We'll be able to rule out your prints and see if anything else matches. But, to be honest,"

Sheriff Healey looked at them both and pushed his glasses up before continuing, "I'm really not hopeful. If this was done by a career criminal, then we might get a lead. Other than that, we probably won't find a match. But, in any case, we're done here, and you can move about the house freely now." He looked at Addie. "Are you planning to stay here tonight?"

"I'm planning to stay with Marsha at her apartment in town," she said and then looked over at Travis. "I've already called her."

"Probably best," agreed the sheriff. "I'd advise you to change all of the locks as soon as you can. We'll have a car patrol this area over the next few days. And please let us know if anything else happens or if you find that something is missing. Doesn't matter how small or insignificant it seems. It will help our investigation."

"OK," she promised. "Sheriff, thanks for your help. Are you sure you don't want a drink for the road?"

"Naw, we'll be fine," he said shaking her hand. "You two enjoy the rest of your day."

"I'll walk you out," said Travis following them down the hall. She could hear him talking with the sheriff out on the porch but couldn't make out what they were saying. She picked up the towels the guys had used and threw them in the basket in the pantry then sat at the kitchen table and waited for Travis to return. When he sat next to her, he put his hand over hers.

"Are you OK?" he asked without taking his eyes off her.

"I am." She looked up at him and tried to smile, but the concern etched on her brow gave her away. "But,

who would do this? I'm beginning to feel very
unwelcome in Destiny," she said and then threw her
hands up. "But everyone I've met seems so nice. I have
no clue as to why anyone would do this? Do you
remember anyone bothering Stella this way?"

"No, not as far as I know. And we were pretty close,
so I'm sure she would have said something."

"And she didn't have any crazy relatives living
nearby who might be upset that she left everything to
me?"

Travis smiled softly. "I doubt it. I met some of her
family when I was in San Antonio for the funeral. They
were all very nice, and no one mentioned anyone living
out this way. But I guess we could put an APB out on
a deranged cousin Goober if that might help."

She looked over at him and saw he was grinning at
her. She chuckled and nudged his arm with her elbow
teasingly, but continued to stare at him. Even though
his hair was tousled and he had sweat stains on his
shirt, sitting there in dusty blue jeans and rugged work
boots, she was acutely aware that he was all man.

"Addie," he said and his smile faded. "How did you
know? About Mel, I mean, at The Hushpuppy." His
green eyes were clear and watching her closely.

She stared back at him evenly concealing all
emotion. Addie had never told anyone about her
flashlight, and she wasn't going to start now. It was a
part of her that she had never been comfortable with,
and she was pretty sure it would be the last time she
saw him if he knew.

Shrugging evasively, she said, "I don't really know.

I just had a feeling."

Travis continued to hold her gaze steadily, and Addie had the sense that he didn't believe her, but he left it alone. "When are you heading over to Marsha's?" he asked changing the subject.

"In a little bit. I need to pack some stuff," she said and stood.

"OK," he said and sat back in his chair.

"Travis, you don't need to wait for me. I don't want to keep you."

He shrugged and reached for another cookie. "Then pack fast, because I'm not leaving here until you do."

CHAPTER 22

Addie and Marsha sat together on the sofa in her apartment while Addie told her the events of the afternoon. Marsha's expression was serious, and her usual lighthearted humor was absent.

"So, the sheriff has no leads?" Marsha questioned.

"Not so far as I know. He told me to call him if I remembered something or found that anything was missing."

"How in the world are you supposed to know if stuff is missing in that stockpile of a house?"

"I could use my inventory list, but it's so huge it would take forever to go through everything." Addie took a sip of her ice water before continuing. "I asked Travis if Stella had ever had anything like this happen, and he said he didn't think so."

Marsha nodded her head. "I'd be surprised if she ever even locked her doors. A lot of people who live in the country don't bother."

"The sheriff said he thought whoever did this might have a key."

"Maybe," said Marsha and reached over to pat Mel who was happily curled into a ball on Addie's lap. "I'm just glad you got him back."

Addie narrowed her eyes slightly and looked at Marsha. "I'm pretty sure whoever did this knows how important Mel is to me. They didn't hurt him, thank goodness, but they wanted me to know they could have. I think it was a message."

Marsha frowned. "What message do you think they are trying to send you?"

"I think they want me to leave," she said and raised her glass to her lips. "And I think I'm going to do just that."

"What?" asked Marsha with wide eyes. "You're just going to leave it all behind?"

"It's not what I want to do, and it's not what Stella wanted me to do, but I think it's what I have to do."

"Addie, the sheriff will figure out who's behind this. You just have to be a little patient. In the meantime, you'll stay here with me," Marsha said comfortingly patting the blankets and pillow she had pulled out for Addie. "We'll be roomies. It'll be great! And you can take a break from all of that work you been doing."

Addie smiled sadly. "I hope the sheriff figures everything out, but it won't change the fact that I can't stay," she said holding up a hand to silence Marsha's impending protests. "It's not just the vandalism. I've been going through Stella's finances. Frankly, I can't figure out how she managed to keep the place. From what I can tell, she seemed to be losing money every month."

"So, you'll get a job here. We have teachers in Destiny too, you know."

"Even if I got a teaching job, I wouldn't be able to keep it."

"Then sell some of the stuff. The place is loaded with it, and some of it is pretty valuable."

"Even if I did that, it's just a short-term solution. It wouldn't change the fact that I just can't keep up with the place."

Refusing to give in, Marsha shook her head. "You're looking at this all wrong. The Destiny Ranch is a treasure! It means something to people around here. Maybe you could open a museum. That would bring in some extra money. It's got all those buildings. Surely we could think of something to do with them."

"The problem is," said Addie reluctantly, "I'm on a bit of a deadline. It's almost July, and if I'm going back to Denton, then I have to be done here by the beginning of August. That really doesn't leave much time to take care of things."

Marsha continued to frown, but couldn't seem to come up with anything that might change Addie's mind. "I just don't want you to go," she finally said in a small voice looking away.

Addie was touched. The Marsha she knew was quick-witted and head-strong. This softer side of her friend was new to her.

"It doesn't have to be forever," Addie said, rubbing

Marsha's arm gently. But even as she said it, she knew it was probably not true. How often would she be able to come all the way out to Destiny? And by then, the magic she was now feeling about the people and the place would be a memory.

"So, whoever it is that wants you to go, you're just going to give in to them?" Spirited Marsha was back. "I can't just sit by and watch you turn tail and run."

Marsha's words hit their mark. "I'm not running," Addie said defensively. "I was already thinking that I would have to sell everything before all of this happened."

"But don't you want to know who's behind this? If you put up a for sale sign, we may never know."

"Again, not what I want to do—"

"Then don't!" Marsha interrupted her. "At least, not quite yet. Just give it a little minute."

"I'll think about it," she responded but could tell Marsha was not convinced. "Tell you what," she added, "I have a meeting with Mr. Dudley tomorrow morning. I'll run everything by him and see what he has to say. And I'll wait to make my final decision until then."

Marsha stared at her without blinking. "Fine, but don't think for one second I'm not going to keep pestering you with all the delightful advantages your hometown of Destiny, Texas, has to offer." Marsha accentuated the word hometown and then curled her lips in a crafty smile. "Starting with the obvious testosterone-based pleasures you've already been tasting."

Addie grinned back at her. "Play fair," she admonished.

"Not for a second!" Marsha retorted. "Now come help me find something we can eat for dinner."

Addie put Mel on the floor and followed her into the kitchen.

"I was going to make spaghetti, but I could probably find something else in here."

"Spaghetti sounds wonderful," said Addie. "Let me take Mel out for a little walk, and then I'll come back in and help." She turned at the door and added, "And, you can catch me up on all things Victor."

Morning came early at the apartment. Marsha had a breakfast shift at The Hushpuppy, so Addie waited until she left to start pulling herself together. Even though Marsha's couch offered a reasonable night's rest, Addie found that sleep had eluded her nonetheless. She had lain awake for hours mulling over the events of the past several days trying to develop a plan that would allow her to keep the ranch and live happily ever after in Destiny. In the end, sleep had claimed her before any type of coherent strategy materialized. Now that she was awake, she knew why: the only plan that made any sense at all was to sell everything and move back to her life. Her real life in the real world.

She had a couple of hours before her meeting with Woody. Thinking about it made Addie's stomach turn. She was about to put an end to the beautiful dream of

Destiny and disappoint a woman who felt a deep connection to her and was certain she would do the right thing. Addie felt sick at the idea of failing to fulfill Stella's wishes. Even the thought that Cole had called last night to wish her sweet dreams did nothing to brighten her mood.

She had stacked the blankets and pillows carefully on the sofa only to turn and pound her fists on them in fury. Addie snatched the pillow with both hands and hurled it to the floor, letting out a small howl of anger. Why had Stella put her in this impossible position? Too enraged to even cry, she sat on the couch with her heart pounding in her chest, eyes staring blankly at the floor.

It shouldn't be this hard. She was doing the only thing she could do. After all, Stella had never actually said, keep the ranch and all of my stuff, did she? She said to take care of it. But what did that mean? Addie's breathing had returned to a normal rate. She needed another look at Stella's journal, and if she hurried, she would have time before her meeting with Woody.

Ignoring Travis' warning that she was not to return to the ranch without him or a deputy present, Addie opened the door cautiously wondering what today's malady would be. To her relief, everything appeared as it had yesterday, and there were no signs of an intruder. Her boot-clad feet moved hastily down the hall and into the bedroom. The journal was not at the side of the bed as she had left it. Addie searched the room and under the bed, but there was no sign of it. She rummaged through her purse, thinking she might have shoved it in at the last minute, but it wasn't there. After rifling drawers and hunting in various rooms in which she might have accidently left it, Addie stopped and stared straight ahead. It seemed something had been taken from the ranch after all.

"Woody," Addie said with a smile shaking the lawyer's hand. "Great to see you again."

"You too," he replied. The smile beneath his mustache was genuine and comforting. "How have things been going?"

Addie took a seat and looked at the floor for a few seconds before continuing. "Actually, not that great."

"I heard about some of the problems at the ranch. But you're OK?"

"I'm fine, but I'm afraid I've made a difficult decision." Addie's sad eyes revealed her distress.

"Oh?" Woody asked and sat back in his seat.

"This is not easy to say, but I'm afraid I've decided to sell the ranch after all. And before you ask, it's actually not because of the recent troubles I've had, although that didn't help anything." Addie took a steadying breath and then went on. "I just don't see how in the world I could possibly keep it. Financially, I mean. Even if I got a job, the math just doesn't work out. I don't even know how Stella did it all of those years."

"So, your decision is strictly financial?" asked Woody examining her closely.

"Basically," admitted Addie. "I have to confess that I've begun to feel like I may have worn out my welcome here lately. But I'm sure the sheriff could get to the bottom of that mystery," Addie said shaking her head. "To be honest, I was beginning to contemplate selling before anything had happened. It's not what I want to do," she hurried to assure him. "I believe Stella wanted me to keep the ranch and preserve her things, but I just don't see how that's possible."

"I may be able to help with that dilemma," Woody said picking up a brown envelop from his desk. "I've had a call from Conrad Schuster. He's an attorney in San Antonio that handled things for Stella every so often. He works for their family. Anyway, I just received the paperwork," Woody paused and looked directly at Addie. "What do you know about Stella's family?"

"Nothing, really. She wrote in her journal that her father had purchased land out here, and that's why she picked this place to start the Destiny Ranch. I don't even know what he did. She didn't write much about her family."

"Well, what I'm going to tell you may come as a bit of a shock. I mean, I didn't even know myself until just recently. Anyway, Stella's grandfather, Otis Zemlicka, started Rio Oil back in the twenties. Stella was one of only three grandchildren, and when he died about 20 years ago his fortune was split among the three of them." He paused, watching her closely. "Have you ever heard of Otis Zemlicka?"

"No," Addie replied, "but I've heard of Rio Oil."

"Yes, I imagine you have. We've all heard of it and for good reason. That company made Otis one of the top oil and gas men in Texas. And when he died, Stella inherited a third of his fortune." He paused to let the news sink in. "Addie, Stella had considerably more resources than we knew. You'll be able to keep the ranch if you want it."

Addie's brow crinkled when she looked at Woody. "I still don't see how that helps me. Even with tens of thousands of extra dollars it won't help in the long run."

Woody pursed his lips. "It's more than that, Addie."

Addie stared at him. "So, it's more like hundreds of thousands of dollars?"

Woody reached across the desk and handed her the envelope. "It's more like hundreds of millions of dollars."

Addie's eyes widened, and both of her hands flew to her face. She sat very still for at least a full minute while Woody watched her. Finally, he broke the silence.

"Stella, as it turns out, had quite a portfolio. She owned or had part ownership in several companies. Her assets are held in a trust, which will now pass to you." Woody shook his head as if he were trying to understand it himself. "I honestly had no idea, but it actually explains a lot. She has been helping the town anonymously for years. She put up the money for the new library and school, the swimming pool, the fire house. It seemed like whenever we needed something, a large sum of money would just show up as a donation from an unnamed source. There was a lot of speculation about who was behind it. Many wondered if it was Judge Wescott. But I'll be damned if it wasn't Stella!" Woody smiled and shook his head again.

"That's unbelievable. She never wrote about any of this in her journal."

"She didn't want anyone to know. Conrad helped set it all up for her. As the artistic side of the ranch declined, Stella looked for other ways to help the community. In addition to her private donations, she started the West Texas Investment Corporation to help local businesses and creative enterprises. Junior got a grant to start The Hushpuppy from them. So did I," he said looking around the room nostalgically. "And so did several others in town. And she funded the West Texas Rising Star scholarship program. Travis got a full ride to college from it. Conrad told me she saw the citizens of Destiny as a creative collection, and she wanted to do what she could to help them."

"Remarkable," was all Addie could think to say.

"And now it's all yours," Woody said with a smile.

"I'm… I…" Addie stammered trying to clear her head. "I don't even know what to say."

"Now do you believe me when I say you don't have to sell the ranch if you don't want to?"

"Yes, I believe I do," Addie replied. She looked at Woody, and her eyes were still wide with disbelief. "I just can't take it all in."

"No doubt," said Woody truthfully. "There are some papers here you'll need to sign so I can take care of the trust. He slid a pen across the desk and showed her where to sign. After the paperwork was done, he looked over at her curiously. "So, do you still think you want to sell? Because, if so, Judge Wescott has been badgering me nearly hourly, and it would be great to give him a definitive answer."

"Here's a definitive answer for him. No. No, I will not be selling the ranch. Not now, not ever!" For the first time since Woody had told her of her new-found fortune, Addie smiled, and tears sparkled in her eyes.

"Sounds definite enough for me," Woody grinned broadly and walked around the desk. Addie stood, and Woody gave her a congratulatory hug. "This could not have happened to a more deserving person, Addie. Stella chose well."

Addie took a step back and wiped a tear from her cheek. "Woody, just one more thing. I don't want to tell anyone about this. At least, not until I've wrapped my mind around it. Stella didn't want anyone to know, and neither do I."

Woody placed a finger under Addie's chin with a fatherly gesture. "Your secret is safe with me."

CHAPTER 23

Addie left Woody's office and stood in the morning sunshine. She took a deep breath and sat on one of the nearby benches, not sure which way to turn. Since first arriving in Destiny, she had been off balance, but this latest news had her completely spinning. One moment she was worried about how to save Stella's ranch, and the next she was making more money in one month than she could possibly make in several lifetimes. How was she supposed to react to that?

And the funny thing was that money had never even been that important to Addie. Sure, she wanted to have a comfortable life and not have to count pennies for every little thing, but that was normal. What she had now was most definitely not normal. It was bizarre, strange, other worldly, perhaps, but not normal. She had always enjoyed her life, even with its uneven terrain. It was reasonable and familiar. She understood that life. Addie knew she was completely out of her depth now, and she wasn't sure what to do about it.

"Addie?" said a woman's voice, and Addie looked up to see the owner of the ice cream parlor coming toward her. They had met at Destiny Days. "Are you all right?"

Addie realized she had been deep inside her head and must have looked a little unsteady. She smiled a friendly greeting and stood up. "I'm fine, Grace. I think I was miles away. How are you?"

The two chatted for a minute before Grace went back to her store. Addie waved and turned toward The Hushpuppy. She may not have a clue as to what her life was going to be like now, but she did know one thing. She was going to keep the ranch, and that had her smiling.

She knew Marsha was working pretty much all day, but she couldn't wait until evening to tell her the news. Addie hopped off the bench and walked across the street to the café. It was a pretty slow morning, and she was able to catch Marsha's eye and motion for her to come outside.

Addie spoke quickly as soon as Marsha stepped out. "I know you're working, and I know you won't be home until late, but I couldn't wait to tell you the news."

"Girl you're about as jumpy as a toad on a hot plate. Spit it out."

"Woody was extremely helpful as it turns out, and I'm keeping the ranch. I'm not going to sell!"

"Halleluiah!" cried Marsha clapping her hands together as if in prayer. "What changed your mind?"

"We can talk about that later, but let's just say he helped me understand everything a lot better." Agreeing they would celebrate when Marsha got home later that night, the two hugged, and Marsha hurried back inside.

Addie nearly skipped back to her car. It wasn't even noon yet, and she didn't want to be alone. After a quick visit to the Sheriff's Department to report the missing journal, Addie stopped at the grocery store for a few supplies and then headed out to Travis' house. Even though she had decided not to tell anyone about her newest inheritance, she still felt like celebrating her decision to keep the ranch. And since Travis had done so much for her lately, she wanted to return the favor.

When she pulled up to his house, she saw the green truck parked next to a white mustang. Wondering if he had company, she wasn't sure if she should interrupt him. But she decided she could always just excuse herself if he was busy.

Like the last time she had visited, Red opened the door. He looked at her with confusion, so she took the lead.

"Hello, Mr. Granger, I'm Addie," she paused to see if he would jump in to the conversation. When he didn't, she continued. "I was wondering if Travis was home?" She said it with a big friendly smile and patted his hand.

"Yes," he said hesitantly. "Travis is home. Come in please."

Addie followed him into the living room, and she heard Travis coming from the back of the house.

"Dad, Emily will be here soon, so—" He cut off what he was about to say when he saw Addie. He had been drying his hair with a towel and was wearing blue jeans and nothing else. "Addie," he said with surprise.

"Hi," she said with a squeak in her voice, trying to slow her rapidly thumping heart. She hadn't taken her eyes off his bare shoulders and broad chest and hoped the longing desire she felt in every part of her body was not evident on her face. "I hope I'm not interrupting anything."

"Not a bit," he said with a smile. "I just jumped out of the shower. Let me grab a shirt." Addie stood in the living room uneasily not knowing what to say, or even if she could say anything.

"*Goodness*," said that all-too-familiar voice in her head. "*Do try to calm down Addie. You don't want to appear too eager.*"

Not wanting to have a conversation with her make-believe mother about her sex life, she tried to ignore it. Luckily, Travis came back into the room wearing a black Eagles Greatest Hits t-shirt, boots, and combed hair. But no matter how hard she tried, she still saw him bare chested. Red, who was standing next to her, seemed not to notice.

"Been busy?" she asked trying to sound casual.

"I did some mowing earlier this morning and then was working in the lab. How'd it go at Marsha's last night?"

"Fine, just fine," she said trying to think of

something else to say. "I brought some stuff. It's in the car. Anyway, I was wondering, if you have time that is, if you would want to eat some picnic. I mean, have a picnic. I have some stuff in the car." Stop talking, she commanded herself. Just stop! She could feel herself blushing, but she was too happy to be properly embarrassed. "Sorry," she said with a smile. "It's just that I'm in a pretty good mood and wondered if you had time for lunch."

"Of course," he said with a soft smile and seemed to be charmed by her awkwardness. "A man's got to eat, after all." Travis looked over at his father before continuing. "Emily, my dad's nurse, will be here any minute. I was just going to make sure he had everything. Dad, do you have that pillow? The small white one?"

Red turned to look around the room and found it on the sofa. "Here it is," he said and picked it up.

Travis turned to Addie. "Dad took a little spill the other day and hurt his knee. We have a nurse who helps us out several times a week, and she's been doing some basic physical therapy with him. They use this pillow." As he finished talking, there was a knock at the door. "That's probably her now," Travis said heading to the front door.

Emily Zapata was a short woman in her late fifties with shoulder-length dark hair and a kind face. She was what people would probably describe as pleasingly plump, and she seemed completely at ease with both Travis and Red. Travis introduced her to Addie, and Emily squeezed her hand warmly and winked at Travis.

When Red and Emily were all set, Travis turned back to Addie.

"There's a pretty shady spot behind the barn where we can sit," he offered.

"Sounds great."

Travis followed Addie to the car. "Whose car is that?" she asked when they walked out nodding toward the Mustang.

"Mine," he said. "I usually park it in the garage, but I haven't put it back in yet."

Addie looked from Travis to the car and back. A white mustang. A white horse? She stumbled, and Travis grabbed her arm to keep her from falling.

"What's the matter?" Travis asked seeing the confused look on her face. "You don't like Mustangs?"

She looked up at him with wide eyes. "What? No. I mean, I like them fine," she said still staring at his handsome face, her lips parted and brow creased as if she had just spotted a unicorn. He drives a white horse, she thought still dumbfounded at the idea that both Cole and Travis met nearly every psychic husband prerequisite. Still, he said he only spoke English. She hadn't had a chance to find out about Cole's linguistic capabilities.

Seeing that Travis was watching her closely, she smiled clumsily and tried to recover. "I hope you don't mind, but I brought Mel. He's been cooped up a lot at Marsha's, and I wanted him to get some fresh air."

"Of course," Travis said easily as Mel jumped out of the back seat. "He and Shiner can get to know each other."

Addie looked over at him and raised her eyebrows. "You mean if Shiner doesn't eat him first."

"Relax," said Travis taking the grocery bags from Addie. "Shiner's a big pushover."

"Do you have a blanket or something we can sit on? I didn't want to use anything from Marsha's."

"Let me run in and grab one. I'll meet you out back by the barn." He turned to walk into the house, but then paused and turned back to Addie. "Nice boots, by the way," he said with a pleased smile.

Addie had just made it to the barn when she saw Travis jogging toward her followed by an energetic white dog. He spread an old plaid bedspread on the ground while she pulled plastic plates, napkins, and tubs of deli food out of bags. Shiner and Mel lingered close by with wagging tails and drooling mouths, drawn by the tantalizing aroma of people food. They had quickly established that they could exist within close proximity of one another, even if they still weren't sure if they were friends. Travis threw a tennis ball far out in the field, and both dogs took off after it, giving Addie time to set up the food.

"Looks good," Travis said glancing over his shoulder.

"I just picked out food we could eat outside without too much trouble. Here," she said handing him a bottle of iced tea, "you can start with this."

Travis drank from the bottle and watched Addie scoop potato salad and coleslaw onto a plate. She added several deli meats and cheese slices along with a large dinner roll and handed it to Travis.

"Hope you like it," she said and turned to make a plate for herself.

"It's great," he said with enthusiasm. "I haven't eaten all day."

"Me either," Addie said popping the top on a Dr. Pepper can.

The dogs ran over exuberantly, but Travis set firm guidelines that they were not to sit on the blanket. When they obeyed, sitting on the grass at the edge of the blanket, Travis gave both of them a small piece of cheese as a reward.

"You're good with dogs," Addie observed.

"That's not all I'm good with," Travis said with a mischievous grin. He rolled up a piece of ham and popped the whole thing in his mouth.

"You're very sure of yourself, aren't you Travis Granger," Addie said eating a forkful of coleslaw. She was only half teasing.

"Aren't you?"

"You're kidding, right? Surely you know me well enough to know that I'm not sure about anything."

"No? I think you sell yourself short, Addie. I don't know many women who would move more than 1,500 miles from home to start a new life. And then you came out to Destiny on your own and didn't know anyone. That doesn't sound like someone who doesn't have at least a bit of self-confidence."

"Double negative aside, perhaps it's just stupidity," she said with a hint of a smile at the corners of her mouth.

"That's probably it," he said and ducked when

Addie wadded her napkin and threw it at him. "But seriously, aren't you going to tell me why you're in such a good mood?"

"I have finally made a decision," she said and paused for dramatic effect. "I'm keeping the ranch. I've decided that I'm not going to sell it."

Travis was about to bite into his roll and held it midair. "Really?" He seemed genuinely surprised. "That's fantastic! What changed your mind? Wait, I know. You just can't live without my extreme tractoring skills."

She laughed out loud at this. "Well, I have to admit that did tend to tip things in Destiny's favor." He waited for her to continue and she shrugged. "I had a meeting with Woody this morning, and he helped me figure out the finances," she said truthfully. "I feel so right about it. I know it's what Stella wanted, and I want it to." Then she sat and looked off at the rolling hills in the distance. "I just hope the sheriff can get to the bottom of everything."

"He will. Just give him a little time," Travis assured her.

The two sat in silence for a minute, and Addie lay on her back, enjoying the slight breeze. "How's it going in the lab? Have you solved the world's energy crisis yet?"

"I'm working on it," Travis said as he lay down beside her looking at the sky. "You know, a lot of people think the future is in solar energy."

"You don't?" she asked looking over at him.

"Not for everything. But I think biodiesel has some

real applications that can radically change the way we think about fuel."

"Why are you working with algae?"

"It's a great source of oil. About half of algae's composition, by weight, is oil. And they're easy to grow. But getting enough of it, and getting the oil out of it, are things we're still working on." Travis turned to look at her, and she could see the excitement in his eyes. "I'm pretty close to making a breakthrough, Addie. A real breakthrough."

Addie turned onto her side and propped herself up on an elbow. "Really? What kind of breakthrough?"

"I've been working on cross breeding some hybrid algae. And so far, the findings have been very interesting. I may have found a way to make algae that secrete oil into the water." Travis turned onto his side as well. "And that would be a game changer if it actually works."

"Travis, that's amazing. Have you thought about starting your own company?"

"Briefly, but just to do a proof of concept would probably cost about a million dollars. More likely, I'd have to sell the idea to another company or go off and work for them."

"Is that what you want to do?"

"Not really. I much prefer working on my own. Once you get inside a big company, it's really difficult to do what you want. But I'm getting to the point where I need more funding to really get this going." He looked over at her and shrugged. "Whatever, it will work out the way it works out."

"I'm sure it will." She smiled, then turned onto her back again. "This is awesome," she said lifting a knee and stretching her arms above her head. "Just laying here feeling relaxed for the first time in a very long time. I think I could fall asleep right here."

"Is that an invitation?" Travis said looking down at her.

"Not with the dogs looking," she said playfully, but Travis rolled over and put his knees on either side of her.

"Travis!" she said laughing and reached up to push him back.

"Hey, you started it," he teased and leaned forward putting his arms on either side of her. "Ms. Butterfield, I believe it's time for dessert."

Still laughing she squirmed out from under him. "I think you've had quite enough for one day, Mr. Granger."

"You can't blame a guy for trying," he replied, and his green eyes glinted in the light. He was staring intently at her and reached over to hold her hand tenderly. Addie stared back at him, and she knew she would not be able to refuse him if he pulled her close. They were both on their knees, and he continued to hold her hand. Why was he waiting? She wouldn't get an answer as Shiner took that moment to pounce with energetic enthusiasm on Mel, who was not pleased with his new friend's familiarity and snarled in reply.

Travis whistled and let go of her hand. "Shiner, knock it off," he admonished, and Shiner walked over to him with his ears back.

Addie chuckled. "He certainly pays attention to you."

Travis stared at Shiner with a scowl, and the dog lay down and looked up at him sheepishly. Finally, Travis smiled, and the dog stood up and wagged his tail. Travis stroked his back and pulled on his ears affectionately. "Play nice," he warned.

Travis threw the ball a few times for the eager dogs while Addie cleared the picnic. "You in the lab this afternoon?"

"Yup," he said and hurled the ball with the ease of a centerfielder making a play at home plate. "You got plans?"

"Yes," she said but went no further.

"Are they top secret?" he asked picking up the slobbery ball Shiner dropped at his feet.

"No, but you probably won't approve of them."

He looked over at her and then turned back to the dogs. "Is Cole back in town?"

A smile tugged at Addie's mouth. "No."

"Then please, do tell."

"I'm going back to the ranch this afternoon."

Travis threw the ball then turned to face her. "Addie—"

She stopped him before he could lodge his protest. "I'm just going by to get a few things and look over the damage. I'll keep my cell phone handy in case anything happens. But I think whoever is responsible for this doesn't like to do anything when people are home."

"You mean like when they snuck in and unleashed a bunch of deadly snakes while you were sleeping?" His tone was sharp.

"Travis, I'm not going to stay long. But it's my house, and I just want to spend some time there."

"I get it, but there'll be plenty of time for that after the perpetrators have been caught."

Addie tried to keep from giggling. "Perpetrators? Have you joined the police force in the last couple of days?"

"I'm serious. It's not a good idea. At least let me go with you."

"Travis, that's very sweet of you. And I'm not being reckless, but I just need a few minutes there by myself. I promise I won't stay past dark."

"I don't like it," he said staring down at her.

"I know," she said, "and I love that you're so protective, but I need to do this. I promise I'll be careful." She grabbed both of his hands and reached up to kiss him softly on the lips. She had meant it as a friendly gesture, but the touch of his lips against hers had her hungering for more. He put his hands on her lower back and pulled her against him and she leaned into the kiss. Her eyes were closed when he lifted his head, and when they opened, she couldn't read his expression.

"Addie," he said softly and hugged her close. He didn't say anything more, but held her tightly for a few minutes rubbing her back. His chest was hard against her face and she was completely wrapped within his embrace. In her entire life, she had never been held like this. He was tender, and strong, and masculine and loving. She moved her hands to his back and pulled him even closer. Finally, he reached down and kissed her sweetly on the top of her head and loosened his grip.

They stood holding hands, staring at each other, communicating without speaking. Addie looked down at his hands and squeezed them gently. When she looked back up to his eyes, she smiled sweetly. Finally, Travis bent down to pick up the blanket. He glanced over at her as he straightened up.

"I still don't like it, Addie."

"I know," was all she said.

"Well, we just had lunch. What about dinner?"

"I can't. I'm meeting up with Marsha at her apartment."

Travis rolled his eyes. "More gopher dogs!"

Addie chuckled as they walked back toward the house.

CHAPTER 24

Anderson arrived at The Hushpuppy about ten minutes before his scheduled lunch with Woody. The diner was crowded, but Woody's usual booth by the last window was empty. The lawyer ate lunch at The Hushpuppy nearly every day, so folks tended to leave it vacant for him. Anderson took a seat there to wait.

He had asked for this meeting in a final attempt to persuade Woody to help him secure the Destiny Ranch. He hoped his recent efforts to sour her on the area had finally born fruit. Anderson had one more play to make if she wouldn't sell. He didn't want to go there, but he would if he had to.

In the years since his first association with the Chavez family, Anderson had been very careful in his illicit activities, making sure nothing could be traced back to him. In his recent desperation, he worried that he was becoming sloppy. He didn't like to get his own hands dirty, but he was prepared to do so if needed. He was grateful for his long-time ranch hand, Manuel, who had been with him since the beginning and was willing to take care of the less pleasant affairs Anderson was sometimes called on to perform. Manuel was fiercely loyal to him, and Anderson repaid that allegiance with a house on his ranch and a generous salary that ensured his silence. It had been Manuel who had suggested kidnapping the dog to send a message to Addie. Anderson just hoped it had been enough.

He looked up and smiled when he saw Marsha approach his table. "My goodness, you look as fine as apple wine today, Ms. Brady," Anderson said trying to hide the fact that he was a twitching ball of nerves. He needed everything to seem perfectly normal, and flirting with women was something he was accustomed to doing.

Marsha returned the smile in appreciation. "The usual sweet tea today, Judge?" she asked.

"You read my mind," he said with a grin. "I'm meeting Woody, so I'll wait to order until he gets here. Is Junior in the kitchen today?"

"He is," replied Marsha, "so take your time and order anything you like."

Marsha moved to tend to another table, and Anderson turned to look out the window. He thought about his phone conversation with his son earlier that morning. Cole, of course, new nothing of his attempts to persuade Addie to leave. And apparently, Cole's attempts were yielding little success.

"Dad," Cole said, "the last time we talked about it, she seemed to be considering what to do. I've only talked with her a couple of times."

"That should have been more than enough time for you to persuade her to sell. Ask her to move to Houston with you! That's where you really want to be anyway. So go, and take her with you. She's more than a little infatuated with you."

"I can't do that," Cole said, and the frustration in his voice could be heard clearly over the phone.

"And we both know why, right?" Anderson spat the words into the phone, and there was silence on the other end.

"Look," Anderson said. "I'm not asking you to marry her. Just get her to move out with you, and you can break up later. It happens all the time. She's a good-looking girl. She'll bounce back."

"Dad, you can't be serious. Listen to yourself! You sound completely desperate."

"I am desperate," Anderson shouted. "I need you to do this, do you understand? I'm not asking, I'm telling you. Call her up and invite her to come down there today. Charm her the way you've charmed so many girls before, and then dump her. Then you can go off and live the life you've always wanted to live, and I won't stand in your way."

"Dad, I'm late for a meeting. I'm coming home early this evening, and we can talk more then. Just, please calm down and don't do anything until I get there."

"I'll do what I need to do. It might be better if you just stay in Houston."

Anderson closed his eyes as he replayed the conversation in his head. Yes, he was desperate. He needed to show that he was making progress, and he needed his son to shelve his own integrity for a few months and come through for him. And he couldn't care less if it was the right thing to do or not.

Woody arrived right on time breaking into Anderson's thoughts. The two men shook hands like the old friends they were just as Marsha arrived with their drinks. She placed a cold Coke in front of Woody and gave the judge his tea.

"What can I get you gentlemen today?"

"I'll have my usual," said Woody reaching for his drink.

"One chicken fried steak, mashed potatoes, and fried okra. And for you, Judge?"

"I'll have the cordon bleu, truffled potatoes gratin, and green beans amandine," Anderson said with a teasing smile.

"OK, that's one blue plate special and a hamburger with fries," replied Marsha stuffing her pen into her ponytail. "Ya'll let me know if you need anything else."

"That's one advantage to living in a small town. Everyone knows your name and your order," Woody said with a chuckle.

The two men exchanged pleasantries while they waited for their lunch, and it took everything Anderson could muster to appear relaxed and in control. Finally, the food arrived, and Anderson waited until after Woody had taken a bite before jumping in.

"I'm sure you know why I asked you here," he said with a grin, and Woody smiled back.

"I have a pretty good idea."

"Do you know if she's given any more consideration to accepting my offer?" Anderson posed the question calmly and took a bite of his burger.

"We were actually talking about it just this morning," replied Woody. Anderson cocked his head to wait for the news. "You know, I think she was considering selling to you, but today she told me she is going to keep it. She asked me to thank you for your generosity, but she's definitely not selling."

Anderson's jaw clenched slightly, but he nodded his head. "What changed her mind?"

"You know, I couldn't say really. She just told me to tell you she's planning to keep it." Woody watched the judge to gauge his reaction.

"Really," Anderson said fighting to remain calm. "I heard there was some trouble out at the ranch. Glad it was nothing to worry about." He smiled at Woody and took another bite of his burger.

"I know you're probably disappointed," started Woody, but Anderson shook his head.

"No worries. I just wanted to add to my holdings and thought that was a good way to do it," offered Anderson now anxious to the point of being ill.

"Well, I heard that Addie and Cole were getting kind of close. Maybe you could marry him off and get the ranch that way," Woody said with a wink.

Anderson looked at him and smiled awkwardly. His mind was racing. In spite of his efforts, she was not going to sell. It was time to shift to plan B.

A crash in the kitchen provided the distraction Anderson needed, and he palmed Woody's cell phone when the lawyer turned to look at the commotion. He knew Addie trusted Woody, and he could use that to his advantage. He slipped the phone into his pocket and waited for lunch to end.

Anderson sat in his truck, which was parked across the town square from Woody's office. He checked his watch and saw it was nearly 7:30. He'd had a very busy afternoon with Manuel getting everything set. Neither of them were very skilled arsonists, but Anderson decided it wouldn't matter if the cause of the fire was ruled criminal or accidental. All he needed was the result.

Finally, Anderson saw Woody walk out of his office and climb into his car. He waited about ten minutes to make sure the lawyer was gone before moving his truck to the alley behind the office. Anderson used a key to enter the building through the back door. Sitting at Woody's desk, he scanned the lawyer's cell phone until he found Addie's number. He carefully typed a text message:

"I've got important news. We need to talk immediately. Please meet me at my office at 8:30 tonight. I know who is responsible for your recent problems."

Anderson pushed the 'send' button and walked to the front lobby to unlock the door and turn on a light. The unstoppable wheels were now in motion. Fires, fatal shootings, and missing people were not uncommon in the outskirts of West Texas. And no one would miss a stranger from out of town.

Manuel would have everything set at the library by now. All he had to do was wait. Anderson sat behind Woody's massive desk and put the pistol Manuel had secured for him on it. As an avid hunter, Anderson had been around guns his whole life and had quite a nice collection of firearms. But he didn't want anything to trace back to him personally.

Cole had called him several times, and he had let it ring. Apparently, he had come home even though Anderson told him to stay in Houston. He didn't want Cole to know what he was doing, so he'd told his wife that he had business in Overton that would take him away until late that night. He had turned his cell off at about 5 o'clock and locked it in his safe at home.

The tension in his shoulders was so severe it was almost debilitating. He rubbed the muscles at the base of his neck and wondered how this had all happened. How had he become such a ruthless, desperate man? Because a foolish old woman and a silly little girl had refused to sell him some land. Anderson opened his eyes and glared into the dark hallway. Addison Butterfield would get what she deserved. His life would not be undone by a teacher from Denton. This act would surely show Chavez that he knew how to handle things.

CHAPTER 25

Addie sat on her porch drinking thirstily from a tall glass of ice water. She had spent several hours sweeping up broken glass and discarding the debris of artworks she deemed beyond repair. The late afternoon sun was just finishing its blistering punishment upon the landscape, giving way to its kinder evening façade. She savored the warmth that seemed to radiate through her body. Closing her eyes and inhaling deeply, a soothing smile softened her face. It was finally beginning to sink in that this was her house. It was her ranch. This mystical place that spoke to her as it had to Stella was hers. And she could keep it forever.

She was already contemplating different ideas for the ranch, and it excited her that none of them were now out of her grasp. And every one of them ensured that Stella's legacy and the artworks she had inspired would be preserved. Although Addie had not yet vocalized her desire to pick up and move to Destiny full time, she was beginning to think it was inevitable. Her life in Denton seemed far away, almost temporary. What was really keeping her there? Certainly less than what seemed to be drawing her here.

Addie downed the rest of her ice water and headed back inside. She had intended to do a little more work after her break, but now all she wanted was a nice bath before heading back to Marsha's. While the tub was filling, she checked her phone. Travis had sent a message: *Still breathing?* And she replied with: *Yes, and all by myself!* Marsha had sent a text saying she would be even later than expected. She had to finish a late shift for a sick waitress, but that she was still planning on celebrating tonight.

It was a little past 6 o'clock, and she was in no particular hurry other than to get Mel back to Marsha's where she had taken his food. When she had first arrived at the ranch and found that Stella's bathroom only had a tub and no shower, Addie worried that she would find it terribly inconvenient. But she discovered that she loved languishing in the bath, especially at the end of her day. It gave her time to reflect, which is something she almost never seemed to do in her previous life. At least, not as much as she did now.

Addie took time to dry her hair letting it fall straight and shiny around her shoulders. It was lighter than when she had arrived, and it contrasted nicely with the warm glow she had picked up from the sun. She changed into a new set of shorts and a navy-blue t-shirt and pulled up the boots Travis had given her. Addie looked across the room guiltily at Cole's boots. At some point, she was going to have to pick a favorite pair, so to speak. Having two handsome admirers was both thrilling and uncomfortable for her.

Checking her phone, she saw it was past 7 o'clock.

"You're probably starving," she said looking down at Mel who just looked up and wagged his tail. She scooped him up and buried her face in his fur. He was a reminder to her that whatever or whoever was behind her recent problems had not been discovered, and though she was feeling more and more at home on the ranch, it might not be safe to stay right now.

Addie stopped off for a couple of bottles of wine on the way to Marsha's apartment. She fed Mel, who scarfed it down as though he had not eaten in a week, and checked her phone, which had chimed the arrival of a new message when she was fumbling with the apartment key. She was surprised to get a text from Woody requesting such a late-night meeting, but she didn't really question it. She was about to send a text to Marsha but instead decided she could just pop over to the diner after meeting with Woody.

Addie crated Mel in the living room before heading to the law office. The town square was pretty empty at this time. Most of the shops closed at 7 o'clock, and only The Hushpuppy and a tavern on the corner had cars parked in front of them. The light was on in the front lobby of Woody's practice, so Addie walked in.

"Woody?" she called. She opened the door at the end of the lobby and saw that a light was on in his office. "Woody, it's Addie," she said as she walked down the hall. But when she turned to walk into his office, she froze.

"Close the door please, dear," Anderson said pleasantly, but neither the expression on his face nor the Smith and Wesson 9 mm pistol that was pointed squarely at her chest suggested he was in a cheerful mood.

Addie could feel every muscle tense, and she was careful not to move.

"Addie," he repeated. "Close the door." He continued to stare at her as she reached behind her for the door, too frightened to turn her back to him.

"That's better. Have a seat." He motioned with the gun to one of the chairs in front of Woody's desk. "I'm so glad you came alone. It makes things so much easier."

"Where's Woody?" Addie asked shakily.

Anderson raised his eyebrows as if to convey to her that he would ask the questions, not her. But then he answered. "I imagine he's at home with his wife. As it happens, I have a key to his office. And he conveniently left his phone out at the diner for me to take."

Too nervous to feel relief that Anderson had not harmed him, she sat and tried to keep her knees from knocking together while Anderson continued.

"You know," he said conversationally, "I was going to ask if you would change your mind about selling me the ranch. But I think we're a bit past that, don't you?"

Addie sat silently, waiting for him to continue. She had never looked down the barrel of a gun before and found it's menacing presence petrifying.

"I gave you and your aunt about a dozen chances to sell me that property, and you both stubbornly refused. I had my son try to put pressure on you. I had snakes put in your house and had the art vandalized. I even hid your dog to get your attention. But you were just too stupid to get the message." Anderson stood up but kept the gun pointed at Addie's head. "And now it's too late. Now I will simply deal with your executor instead of dealing with you. But, rest assured, I'm going to get what I want."

Addie sat without moving, her wide eyes never leaving Anderson or the gun. What kind of madman was he? Her little ranch couldn't be that valuable that he would go to such desperate lengths to get it.

"Judge Wescott," she finally found the courage to speak. "I'll sell you the ranch. I had no idea you wanted it this badly. We can—"

His insane laughter interrupted her. "We can what? Just forget this ever happened? As I said, dear, it's too late for that. Now, let's take a little walk over to the library."

Addie stood stiffly as though any wrong move would set the gun off. Anderson walked over and grabbed her by the arm dragging her toward the back of the office. His grip was surprisingly sturdy, and her arm throbbed under the pressure, but she barely noticed. All she could think about was what to do.

Nothing came to her. She knew if she screamed, she'd be dead before the sound left her mouth.

"It's only two blocks to the school library, but I'll shoot you in the liver if you try to fight me or call out."

The Judge pushed Addie through the back door and into the dumpster lined alley. The two walked side-by-side with Anderson still gripping her arm, the gun thrust into her rib cage. Addie's mind was racing as every step brought her closer to her impending doom. She hadn't told anyone she was going to meet Woody at his office. They might find her car parked out in front, but now she was going to the library. And no one knew to look for her there.

The street was empty, and not a single car drove by as they neared the building. Anderson let go of her arm and shoved her up against the door. He stabbed the gun into her back and fished a huge key ring out of his pocket to unlock the door.

"It's nice to be a trusted city official," he said opening the door and pushing Addie through it. "I've got access to all kinds of places. Woody's office, the library, even the Destiny Ranch."

Anderson pulled out a flashlight and guided her through the darkened room to the center of the reading area. The scent of petroleum permeated the room, and in the dim light, she could make out what appeared to be gas cans with cloth wicks hanging from them. Her breathing was fast and uneven.

"If you would be so kind as to take a seat," he said shoving her into a chair near a round table that held half a dozen candles, a box of matches, and several

large pull ties. "Hands behind your back, please."
When she didn't move, he grabbed an arm and
rammed it behind the chair. Reaching for the other
arm, he bound them with one of the ties. The straps
bit cruelly into her wrists, and Addie winced with pain.
Anderson reached for the matches and lit the candles
then stepped back. It was then she noticed something
else on the table: Stella's journal.

"You have no idea the pressure I'm under." He
hissed the words at her. "It never would have come to
this if you could have just sold the ranch and left. You
did this, Addie," he said holding his hands wide to
indicate the fire trapped room. "You! You don't know
the first damned thing about living out here, but you
waltz in and smoothly inherit some land and think you
know what you're doing. You don't!" Anderson
shouted the words and raised the gun as if he were
going to hit her across the face with it. Addie turned
her head away instinctively, but Anderson froze and
then lowered the weapon taking a calming breath.

"Do you like my set up? We came by earlier to get
things ready. Fires leave so little evidence behind. I
wanted to make sure it got good and hot in here. I even
made sure the fire alarm and sprinkler system were
tragically and unfortunately dismantled."

Anderson laughed and leaned over so his face was
only a couple of inches from hers. She smelled the
alcohol on his breath, saw the desperation on his face,
and heard the madness in his voice. Addie fought
against the nauseating panic that was building deep
within her. He walked to the table and picked up

Stella's journal.

"Nice of her to leave behind her sappy story of the Destiny Ranch. I have to admit it made for entertaining reading. I was particularly interested to find myself featured in her little fable. I found that her depiction of me was somewhat unflattering, and I don't want to leave behind anything that might point a finger at me. And now that I have it, I can make sure that every last memory of her is wiped away. Her journal, her precious library, maybe even the school if I get lucky." Anderson tossed the journal on the floor, and it landed near one of the gas cans. "It's kind of touching, though. I actually got the idea of a fire from her. All that talk of finding your way in the darkness. Tell me, how are your fireflies and flashlights going to save you now?"

Addie had been staring directly at him, but now she was seeing straight through him. She suddenly saw him engulfed in flames and writhing in pain. Confused, she focused her eyes on him and saw that he had not yet started the fire. Had she really seen it? She closed her eyes and again saw him in flames. She couldn't tell for sure, but she sensed someone else was with him. And then it was gone. Addie opened her eyes and knew. She knew he was going to die in the fire. But was she going to die right alongside him?

"Normally, I'm not a violent man," he continued, pulling Addie's focus back to the present, "but tonight I will finally erase Stella from Destiny once and for all. I've only had to deal with you for a couple of weeks, but I fought against that bitch and her ridiculous ideas for more than 30 years. I'm going to shoot you and burn this library to the ground. Then I'll get the ranch from whoever inherits it next. I'm willing to bet they're not nearly as foolish as you or your precious Aunt Stella."

Anderson raised the gun, and Addie screamed instinctively. At the same time, the front door of the library crashed open.

"Dad! Dad, are you in here?" Cole's voice echoed through the building, and Addie looked back to see him rush in.

Anderson lowered the weapon when he saw his son.

"Dad, what are you doing? Are you insane?"

"Get the hell of out here!" Anderson shouted at his son. "I told you to stay in Houston."

Addie's eyes met Cole's and his face contorted with rage.

"Put the gun down, Dad," Cole commanded.

"Or what? Son, you don't know what's going on here. I have no choice. She brought this on herself."

"Addie is innocent!" Cole barked. "We have to get out of here. Those gas cans are going to explode. If we all leave now, we can work everything out."

Anderson looked into his son's eyes and laughed. "You have no idea what you're saying. None!" his voice rose to a roar. "This is the only way I can protect you and your mother. And I've always protected you. I don't have any other options."

"So, your plan is to shoot Addie and burn down the library? Dad, you'll never get away with it. Do you know how I found you? I saw your car in the alley and knew this is where you would go. To Stella's library. Do you think I'm the only one who knows about your hidden feud with Stella? It'll never work."

Cole looked back at Addie and then continued. "Dad, I know about the cartel."

Anderson glared at his son. "If you really knew the people I'm involved with, you wouldn't question what I'm doing. Without my protection, you'd be dead already."

"Why," Cole was the one shouting now. "Because the Chavez cartel kills people like me?"

"The Chavez cartel kills everyone and everything in its path!" Anderson raged. "They'll kill you, me, and your mother if I don't do something. She's the only hope we have," Anderson snarled pointing the gun at Addie. "I've been controlled by the cartel for decades. They can't be bargained with. If I don't do this, we're all dead!"

Cole sprang forward and jerked Anderson's arm as he fired a shot. The bullet landed in the table leg sending splinters through the air. Another shot was fired as Cole and Anderson wrestled together. Addie was trying to free her arms from the chair when she felt a searing, throbbing pain in her thigh. She howled in agony and struggled to her feet with her hands behind her back as the two continued to battle for control of the gun.

"Cole," she screamed. "There's going to be a fire. You have to get out of here."

Cole trapped Anderson's arm between them, and Addie heard another shot followed by Cole's deep-throated moan. She knew he had been hit, but he continued to grapple with Anderson. Cole was working to pin Anderson's gun hand behind his back. They struggled for balance and tumbled into Addie, knocking her onto her back, as they fell onto the table. The splintered leg gave way, and the candles fell onto the gasoline-soaked carpet. In an instant, flames rose like dancing devils carving out chunks of oxygen and replacing it with thick dark smoke.

Before Addie could get to her feet, flames filled the room. She could hear both Cole and his father coughing, and she rolled over quickly away from the growing fire. She looked back when she heard a high-pitched wail that sounded like it was coming from some sort of animal. Anderson was bleeding and choking on the floor, his back and hair surrounded by flames as he shrieked in terror and agony.

Addie screamed in horror and tried to scramble to her feet. In the next instance, an arm had reached out and latched onto her shoulder jerking her up. The whole world seemed to turn upside down as Addie was carried out of the room.

"Hold your breath, Addie," shouted a voice. "Don't breathe the smoke."

Before she could comprehend what had happened, she was outside the library. She sat on the ground coughing and spitting, her lungs finally filling with beautiful, clean air.

Travis leaned down toward her. "Are you all right? Addie?" He pulled a small knife out of his pocket and cut her hands free.

"Cole," she choked out. "Cole is in there. And his dad."

"Stay right here," he commanded and ran back into the library.

Addie saw smoke billowing out the front door and heard the scream of a siren as a fire engine pulled up. Travis came out carrying Cole over his shoulder. He had just cleared the front steps when the library windows exploded, throwing the two men several feet forward. Cole's back was covered in flames, and Travis quickly rolled him over to smother the fire. He dragged Cole toward the curb and then collapsed in a coughing fit.

Pete ran up to Travis to check on him, and Travis waved him away. "I'm fine. Get an ambulance for Cole and Addie," he said between coughs. Then, looking up at Pete he said, "Anderson is still in there. I couldn't get to him."

Pete nodded in understanding and then sprang into action.

Travis removed Cole's boots and put them under his feet, slightly elevating his legs. Cole moaned incoherently and groped at his chest. Travis loosened his shirt and saw he was wearing a bullet proof vest. A bullet was lodged in it just above his rib cage. Several men came running over to check on Cole, while Travis turned back to look at Addie. The firemen had moved her to a safe distance, and she was wearing an oxygen mask.

"Where's Anderson?" asked one of the men.

Travis coughed and looked at them. "I'm sorry,

who are you?"

"We're with the Texas Rangers. Cole was helping us out with a matter."

"Anderson was in the library. I couldn't get him out before the roof collapsed."

"We believe excessive accelerant was used to start the fire," said one of the men.

"How do you know that?" questioned Travis. "You weren't inside."

"We sort of were inside," one of the men said and looked over at Cole. "He was wearing a wire." The man paused and shook Travis' hand. "Nice job, getting them out."

Travis nodded and went to check on Addie.

She pulled the oxygen mask down when he was near her.

"How did you find me?"

"Cole called me earlier looking for you," Travis said sitting on the ground next to her. "When you weren't with me or with Marsha, he said he was worried you might be in trouble. I headed to town to see if I could find you. I was driving by when I heard the gun shots. By the time I got inside, the place was on fire."

Addie grabbed Travis by the shirt and pulled him over to her. She kissed him hard and then put her head on his chest. "Thank you for rescuing me. Again."

Pete came over to check on them. "We have two ambulances here from Overton. They're loading Cole now and you and Addie will go in the other."

Addie looked over to see Cole on a gurney being wheeled into an ambulance. He seemed to be unconscious and was quite pale.

Travis stood and helped Addie up. She winced in pain. "My leg," she said pointing at her thigh. "Something's wrong with my leg."

Travis looked down and saw the blood on her thigh. He called out to the EMT to bring another gurney. Addie collapsed against him and he could feel her shivering.

"Addie, you're going to be all right. We're taking you to the hospital. Do you understand?"

"Yes," she said through chattering teeth.

The EMTs loaded her on a gurney and Travis helped them wheel her into the second ambulance.

"Travis?" she asked.

"I'm right here," he said squeezing her hand.

Addie looked out the back of the ambulance at the flames rising from the library. She watched sparks fly off into the black sky and then disappear. Like fireflies, she thought, and then fell into darkness.

CHAPTER 26

The ride to the hospital only took about 15 minutes, but it seemed much longer. The EMTs attended to and cleaned the gunshot wound on Addie's leg while Travis watched. Addie was still a bit groggy and had an oxygen mask over her face. She listened to their conversation, but her eyes never left Travis.

"Is it serious?" Travis asked.

"No," he said and placed a sterile wrapping on her leg. "You were lucky." He looked down at Addie with a comforting smile. "Just and inch to the right and it might have hit an artery and done serious damage. The bullet just grazed your thigh, but you did lose a little blood, so we'll need to move slowly."

Travis looked down at her and squeezed her hand. "Your leg will be fine. Your shorts, however, took a real hit. I don't think we can save them."

Addie smiled slightly under her mask. Travis was once again wearing a white t-shirt and faded blue jeans, and she couldn't help but think it never looked so good. Aside from a little soot in his hair and across his face, and a couple of scrapes on his arms, he looked perfect.

The ambulance pulled into the hospital, and the doors were opened quickly from the outside.

"She's got smoke inhalation and an abrasion on the upper thigh from a gunshot," the EMT said to the ER nurse. "She's stable and will need to see a doctor."

The EMT looked at Travis. "He also had smoke inhalation but is asymptomatic. He'll need to be cleared."

The medics wheeled Addie into the ER while Travis walked beside her. Once inside, they were shown into waiting rooms while nurses asked questions and typed information into their computers. Travis opened the curtains to both his room and Addie's so he could keep an eye on her.

After about a minute a doctor arrived to look at her, while Travis worked on paperwork with the nurse.

"You've had an exciting evening, I hear," the doctor said smiling down at Addie. He was probably in his mid-forties with a thick head of salt and pepper hair. Addie nodded under her oxygen mask.

"Well, it's all good news, Ms. Butterfield," he said after examining her leg. "We've cleaned your wound, and it's not too deep. I'll give you a prescription for the pain, and we'll put you on something to help prevent infection. The nurse will give you instructions. You'll need to make an appointment to see your local doctor in a couple of weeks."

Addie nodded again, and the doctor moved from her room to see Travis.

"I'm fine," Travis told the doctor.

"Well, let me check anyway," the doctor said with a small grin. He listed to Travis' lungs and had him breathe several times. "You know what?" the doctor asked and Travis looked at him, waiting. "You're fine." They both chuckled, and Travis shook his hand.

Travis walked over to Addie's bedside.

"We're going to leave her on the oxygen for a few more minutes, just to be safe. Neither of you shows any outward signs of inhalation toxicity, but it can develop over time, so I'm going to get you a list of warning signs," the doctor said poking through a drawer.

"It's OK, I'm a firefighter," Travis said, and the doctor turned to look at him.

"Oh, so you know all about it. Well, then you know to call if anything crops up."

"Will do," Travis promised.

The doctor left, and Addie could hear him giving instructions to the nurse.

"Addie, I'm going to get everything ready to go," Travis told her. "I've got a couple of buddies who are bringing my car over, and I'll go take care of everything with the nurse. I'll be back soon." He looked down into her eyes and held her hand as if reluctant to leave. He gently raised her hand to his lips and then set it back next to her as if he were afraid it might fall off. Finally, he turned and left.

Addie lay back on the pillow staring up at the industrial ceiling in the emergency room. She listened to machines that beeped and buzzed and heard the energetic footsteps of the medical staff. But all of that could not drown out Anderson's animalistic screeching that pierced her mind like broken shards of glass. Addie closed her eyes, and a tear broke from under her lashes and rolled down her face. She should be happy he's gone. He tried to kill her. But she knew it would be a very long time before the image of him twisting and screaming in burning agony would fade from her memory.

It took about 20 minutes before Travis came back in. The nurse was already unhooking Addie from the oxygen.

"All set on my end," he said as Addie sat up slowly.

"You OK?" Travis said when she winced.

"It's still a little sore."

"We gave her something for the pain," said the nurse handing Addie the discharge papers, "There are a couple of prescriptions for you as well as the instructions we went over for your leg. Remember, nothing too strenuous for the next few days," she warned looking at Travis.

After she left to get a wheel chair, Travis turned back to Addie. "Why'd she look at me?" he said putting a hand on his chest as though he were insulted.

Addie just shook her head and smiled. The nurse helped her into a wheel chair and was about to take her to the lobby when Addie stopped her.

"I'm sorry, but can I see Cole before I leave? He's the other patient that was brought in from the fire."

"Certainly," said the nurse. "He's just around the corner."

"Do you want me to wait here?" asked Travis.

"No, come with me," Addie said holding out her hand. Travis grabbed it but then let go when the nurse moved her down the hall.

When she pulled the curtain back, Addie saw him lying on a hospital bed. He was in a hospital gown, and his head was bandaged. Cole turned when they came in, but his usual stunning smile was missing.

The nurse left, and Travis pushed Addie closer.

"How are you doing?" she asked softly.

Cole looked at her and then up at Travis and shook his head. "Addie, I'm so sorry." He closed his eyes as if he couldn't trust himself to speak.

Addie picked up his hand, and he opened his eyes. "Cole, it wasn't your fault. Nothing that happened was your fault."

"It was my father who did it. Isn't that enough?" he said without making eye contact.

"No, it's not," Addie said putting both of her hands around his. "Cole, you kept him from shooting me."

Cole looked over at Travis. "Thanks for getting her out. Thanks for getting me out." He tried to smile but then just looked up again. "I still can't believe my father tried to do that. It was like he was a different person."

"Maybe he was," offered Travis. "Desperation can turn people into things they're not, make them do things they normally wouldn't do."

"This past week, I've been working with the Texas Rangers in Houston. I knew something was going on when Dad told me to persuade you to sell the ranch to him. He just wasn't himself."

"That's why you were in Houston?" Addie asked.

"I told you I had a big case. Well, this was it. It turns out the Rangers already suspected Dad might be working with a drug cartel. They had a file on him. Dario Chavez is the leader. He's wanted the Destiny Ranch for years, which was why my dad became so desperate to get it. A couple of weeks ago, Chavez said he needed to get the ranch, or he would kill his entire family." He stopped and looked at Addie.

"Why did he need the ranch so badly?"

"They wanted it for the water. Apparently, they were moving into farming and wanted the ranch so they could," Cole hesitated for a moment before continuing, "grow stuff."

"Why'd you go to the Rangers?" asked Travis.

"Because I knew Dad was in over his head, and I suspected it might be something like this. I needed the Rangers involved so the Cartel would leave all of us alone. I knew they wouldn't stop even if Dad were gone. They said they have enough now to work with the FBI and Mexican authorities on stopping them." Cole looked over at Addie. "I think you should be safe now, but they'll want to question you."

"That's why you were wearing a vest," said Addie.

"Yes. I'd probably be gone now if I hadn't had it on," Cole hesitated again. "Dad shot me in the chest."

Cole took a ragged breath, and Addie and Travis

looked at each other, not sure what to say.

"Anyway," Cole said trying to lighten the mood. "I guess I used up a couple of lives tonight. First with the bullet and then with the fire," he said but couldn't bring more than a weak grin to his face. "Seriously," he said looking at Travis. "Thanks." He held out his hand, and Travis shook it and nodded his head.

"Do you mind if I speak to Addie alone for a minute?" Cole asked Travis.

"Of course not," he said. "I'll wait for you in the front lobby," he told Addie, and she looked at him with gratitude.

When they were alone, Addie looked into his eyes. "Me first," she said with a soft smile. "Thank you, Cole. You saved my life." A tear rolled down Addie's cheek before she even knew she was crying. She stood up to reach over and hug him but stopped when she felt the bandages on his chest. "You're pretty banged up," she said, concern etched on her face.

"Just a couple of broken ribs and some minor burns. It might have been a lot worse." Cole took a deep, steadying breath before continuing. "Addie," he started. "I'm not sure how to say this. I guess you may be wondering what I meant when I told my father they kill people like me."

"People like you," she repeated. "You mean heroes that rush into danger to save people's lives?" She could see Cole shaking his head, but she continued. "Look, Cole, I know this may not be the time or place, but I don't think you and I were going to work out. I mean, I just can't see myself with a guy who has much better fashion sense than I do," she said with a teasing grin. Then she leaned over to put her face close to his. "I don't really care who you date, and I don't think it's anyone else's business either." She kissed him softly on the lips, then straightened up.

She looked at him lying on the bed, and her heart broke for him and all he'd been through. "Cole, I can stay with you. I really don't want to leave you here alone."

He shook his head. "You're a little banged up too. I think you need to go home and rest. Mom is on the way over," his voice caught in his throat, and he closed his eyes briefly.

"Your father loved you, you know," Addie told him. "I could tell when I met him. He was proud of you, and he loved you."

He opened his eyes and looked at her. "Thanks, Addie. You're a terrific friend."

"And neighbor," she added. "I'm keeping the ranch." Addie squeezed his hand then sat back into the wheel chair. "Oh," she added before she left, "and I'm keeping those boots too." She flashed a smile at him and finally got one in return.

"See ya' round, neighbor," he said with a small wave.

The nurse wheeled Addie to the lobby, and she was nearly turned over by an exuberant Marsha who rushed up to hug her.

"I thought we lost you," she whispered in Addie's ear. She straightened up and looked her over from head to toe. "You don't look too bad."

"I'm not," smiled Addie. "And I'd love to tell you all about it, but right now, all I want to do is go home."

"Of course, you do, honey," Marsha said. "We'll get together and gab all day tomorrow. I don't have to work."

Addie looked past Marsha and saw Travis speaking with a man. "Who's that talking with Travis?"

"That's my brother, Greg. He works here. Calls himself a phlebotomist, but we all just call him a vampire."

The two men saw the girls watching them, so they walked over.

"Addie, this is my brother, Greg," Marsha made the introduction.

"So nice to meet you. I've heard nothing but good things out of this one," Greg said pointing an elbow in Marsha's direction.

"Well, you can't believe everything she says," Addie added with a laugh.

"I don't, that's why I asked Mom about you. Believe it or not, I think Marsha might have been telling the truth."

"That might be a first," added Travis.

"Shut your trap, Granger. This young lady wants to get home," Marsha said and then turned back to Addie. "Do you want to come to my place?"

Addie looked at Travis, who answered for her. "No. I'll take her to her place. She'll be fine there."

"Oh, I see," Marsha said with a side smile. "Well, you just holler if you need something."

"I will. Thanks for coming all the way over here."

"Of course! What are friends for?"

Travis walked Greg back to the elevator, and Addie saw him make some sort of hand gesture. Travis responded with a different signal, and then they both laughed.

Addie looked at Marsha. "What are they doing?"

"Sign language," said Marsha. "My brother Bobby was born partially deaf, so we all learned it. And when Travis started hanging out with us so much, he learned it too. He and Greg would sign at school as a way to talk during class."

Addie's mouth dropped open as Travis neared her. "You know sign language?"

"Sure," he said easily as if everyone knew it.

"So, you speak another language?" she asked trying not to pee in the wheelchair at the idea that she had finally met a man who met all of her husband-to-be criteria. And it was Travis.

"I guess," he looked at her as if her medications might be causing her to hallucinate. "Is that a problem? I promise I don't go around randomly signing at people against their will."

Addie shook her head at him and smiled. "Travis," she said his name as though she were hearing it for the first time. "Take me home."

EPILOGUE

—★—

Travis sat at his kitchen table. It had already been two months since his father had died, and the place still felt lonely and empty. He hadn't changed anything in the house, hadn't seen the need. He inspected the ring he was holding one more time and shined it with the cloth the jeweler had given him.

About three weeks after the fire, he told Addie that he had finally decided what he wanted from Stella's estate.

"She always wore a ring on her right hand. I don't ever remember seeing her without it. If it's OK with you, that's what I'd like."

"Of course," Addie said. They'd been eating breakfast together at her place, and she ran to her bedroom to retrieve it. Is this the one?" she asked handing the ring to Travis.

"That's it," he said.

"It's beautiful," she said admiring it.

Stella had once told him that her grandfather had given the ring to her grandmother when he proposed. Travis knew exactly what he was going to do with that ring. Marsha helped him with the sizing, and he remembered being shocked when he took it to the jeweler.

"That's a beauty," he told Travis. "You don't see diamonds cut like that very often. It's a miner's cut, and it's done to help it sparkle. See?" He twisted the ring around so Travis could admire the shining diamond. "The solitaire is flawless and is probably about 4 carats. The setting is platinum, and it was from Tiffany's. This is quite a valuable piece. Can I ask where you got it?"

"It had belonged to Stella Pennington," Travis told him.

"Simply exquisite," the jeweler said holding the ring up. "My guess would be that this is worth around $100,000."

Travis looked at the ring now. He'd always liked it, but he had no idea it was so valuable. The band had a faint inscription that was still legible on the inside. It read, "My light in the darkness." He'd asked the jeweler to try to save it when he sized the ring, and he'd done an outstanding job.

Travis continued to rub the ring absently, thinking about that night. The night he almost lost her. The night he still had nightmares about and woke up in a sweat.

He'd been shocked to get a frantic call from Cole asking if he knew where Addie was.

"She's not with me. I think she's at Marsha's."

"I just checked Marsha's, and she's not there. She's not at her place, and she's not with you. Travis, I think something has happened to her. I can't really explain right now, but I think she's in danger. We have to find her."

Travis called Emily to sit with his dad and jumped into his mustang. He called Addie's cell phone several times but got no answer. He called Marsha's cell, and she answered right away.

"Hey you," she said.

"Marsha, have you seen Addie? Has she been to the diner tonight?"

"No, why?" she asked, hearing the concern in his abrupt tone.

"She's missing, and Cole thinks she might be in danger."

"What? What kind of danger?"

"I don't know. He wouldn't say anything. But, listen. When you're off, please go to your apartment. She may still turn up there."

He hung up wondering which way to go. He headed into town and hadn't gone but a mile or two when Marsha called him back.

"Travis, her car is here at the square. It's parked right in front of Woody's. Maybe she's just meeting with him. Do you want me to run over and check?"

"No, I'll do it."

Travis pressed the accelerator and called Cole to let him know about her car. He was nearby, so he said he would check it out. Even at this speed, it was going to take him more than 5 minutes to get there. He gripped the steering wheel tightly and flew along the highway. He slowed the car to turn down a side street that would take him to the square. As he neared the library, he thought he heard a gunshot. He rolled down the window to listen and heard another one. When he saw flames inside the building, Travis picked up his radio to call for help and jumped out of the car. The main room was in flames, and it was beginning to fill with thick black smoke. He spotted Addie on the ground, hands bound behind her back and all but threw her over his shoulder.

Travis put her on the ground outside and used a knife to cut her hands free. She was coughing and trying to say something.

"Cole is in there. And his dad."

Travis ran back into the building and found the two men. Anderson was surrounded by flames and screaming at the top of his voice. Cole, who had been attempting to pull his father from the fire, collapsed from the smoke, and Travis carried him out. When they reached the door, Travis heard the ceiling cave in and new it was too late to save Anderson when the screaming finally stopped.

Travis had a dream about the fire every night since it had happened. He'd been in dangerous situations before, but none of them had haunted him like this one. He knew he could have lost her. And that scared him more than any flames possibly could. Addie, too, had a difficult time leaving that day behind. On more than one occasion, he woke to her sitting up in bed screaming with her hands over her ears.

The library turned out to be a total loss, but thanks to the efforts of the fire department, the school had not sustained any damage. City officials were already working with the West Texas Investment Corporation on a grant to build a new library.

In the months since the fire, he and Addie had grown very close. She was so easy to be with, unlike any other relationship he'd had. Even when she was angry with him, which was almost never, he found her charming. Like when he decided she needed to learn to ride a horse.

"You'll love Major, Addie. He's very easy to ride."

"I don't know. He's very big. Are all horses so big?" she asked. "I mean, I always think they're beautiful when I see them running in a field, but when you get right next to them, they're huge."

It had taken some coaxing, but Travis finally got her into the saddle. As luck would have it, some of the guys took that moment to drive up in the fire engine and flip the siren, which spooked Major and he took off into the field at full gallop with Addie holding on for dear life. Travis had to jump onto his mount and take off after them. He finally caught up with her and was able to slow the horse, but the damage was done. Addie yelled at him in the field and sulked all the way back to the house vowing never to ride again.

Travis chuckled, thinking of it now. Addie had moved to Destiny full time about two weeks after the fire, which meant quitting her job. She was tremendously upset about that, but she met with the principals at both the middle school and high school in Destiny, and they told her she would be their first pick when a job opened up. Travis had gone with her to Denton to help her move, and she introduced him to her friends. They were all very excited for her and more than a little sad she would be moving.

When the last box had been unpacked at the ranch, Addie and Travis had celebrated the beginning of her new life well into the night. Travis adored making love with Addie. She enjoyed pleasing him and was extremely sensuous and responsive. Sometimes, he felt he had been waiting for her all his life.

But not everything in the past months had been good. His father passing away had been hard. Losing a parent is never easy, and losing the second parent is extremely upsetting. Red had developed a rare case of pneumonia about ten weeks ago, and he never recovered. He'd been hospitalized for about five days toward the end, and Travis had stayed by his side the entire time. Addie came up every morning and stayed until evening. Travis tried to tell her to stay home and that he would call if there were a change, but she refused. He'd actually been grateful for her company and her help with the funeral arrangements.

His father's death was a moment of passage for Travis, strengthening his determination. He knew what he wanted, and it was time to get it. He put the ring in his pocket and drove over to the ranch.

Addie and Travis walked hand-in-hand to the edge of the pond. He picked up a stone and skipped it all the way to the other side.

"Addie," he said turning to her. "Do you remember the day I taught you to skip stones?"

"That was you! Yes, I remember that. I had such a great time on that vacation."

"Well, that was one of the most important days in my life. I remember looking at you before you left and thinking about how much I liked you." Travis reached down and took both of her hands in his. "I was only ten years old and you were eight. You were such a cute little girl, but I decided on that day that I was going to marry you. And since that time, I've dated and had relationships, but none that compare to you.

"When you first came to Destiny and I saw you at The Hushpuppy, I couldn't believe you were finally here. I'm afraid I wasn't myself around you. I was so desperate to have you, but I didn't know quite what to do. You see, you had only just met me, but I'd been waiting for you for 20 years. And I'm not going to wait any longer."

Travis dropped to one knee and pulled the ring out of his pocket.

"Addie Butterfield, would you do me the great honor of becoming my wife?"

He slid Stella's ring on her finger. Addie looked at the ring on her hand and then down at Travis and closed her eyes while tears streamed down her face. She nodded her head and then opened her eyes and held out her arms.

"Yes, I will marry you," she said as he swept her off the ground holding her close while he covered her mouth with his. When he finally set her back down, she leaned against him, and they looked out at the water.

"I've always loved this pond," he said stroking her hair softly. "Addie, I know money may be tight, but we'll find a way to keep the ranch. I promise you that."

Addie turned to face him. "Actually, money is less tight than you might think."

"Oh?" he said puzzled. "You said you weren't sure how you were going to keep it."

"I did say that. But that was before Woody told me about Stella's secret. It turns out she had a bit more money than we originally believed. The ranch will be fine," Addie said and then continued, answering his unasked question. "It was family money. And she'd been using it anonymously to help the people of Destiny for a very long time."

"When did you find all of this out?"

"Woody told me on the day of the fire. Stella never wanted anyone to know, and neither did I, so I didn't tell anyone. You're the only one who knows. I mean, except for Woody."

"I'll be damned," Travis said scratching his head. "And all this time we thought she was a freedom-loving hippy."

"She was. She was just a freedom-loving hippy who was loaded," Addie chuckled. "She paid for the city park, the swimming pool, the library, the new school. And she set up a company called the West Texas Investment Corporation to help all kinds of people in

Destiny. Junior got a grant to start The Hushpuppy. I'm sure the corporation would be very happy to invest in a startup biofuel company that is going to change the world," she said with a smile. "And the West Texas Rising Star scholarship you got? Stella funded that as well."

"So, the West Texas Investment Corporation is funding the new library. That's really you?" Travis asked trying to understand what he had just learned.

"It is now. I inherited all of it," she said looking out over the pond. "It's still so unbelievable. I think, no matter how old I get, it will always be Stella's in my mind."

"Addie," Travis said, and she turned to face him. "How much money are you talking about?"

She shook her head. "I don't even know the exact figures, but if you're thinking about a number that has nine digits to the left of the decimal point, then you're in the ballpark."

Travis didn't speak and just continued to stare at her. That explains the ring, he thought.

"Travis," she said earnestly. "I need you. I can't possibly manage everything Stella had set up by myself."

He looked into her wide eyes. "It's just quite a lot to wrap my mind around," he said still a bit dazed by the news.

"The money doesn't change anything, does it?" she asked with a frown.

"Of course not," he hastened to reassure her, and smiled gently. "It'll just take me a minute or two to process it all."

"I know. That's one of the reasons I haven't told anyone. It doesn't seem real."

"So, you're telling me you never once considered chucking everything and living a jet set lifestyle?" Travis chuckled.

"Actually, I've thought a lot about what to do with it, but globetrotting is not one of them. The money never really changed who Stella was, and I don't want it to change me either. Us," she corrected with a smile. "But I've been talking with Marsha about a plan for the ranch."

"I'm all ears," Travis said, and Addie linked her arm through his leading him back up toward the house.

"Well, what would you think about us moving into your home to live. Your land is adjacent to the ranch, so it's all kind of one big land, acreage, ranch thingy, right?"

"Sure," he said nodding his head while a smile played at the corners of his mouth. "And that is what we call it by the way."

Addie elbowed him playfully but continued excitedly. "Well, we were thinking, Marsha and I, about turning the Destiny Ranch into a sort of museum slash bed and breakfast. She could run it when it's all set up."

"How long have you been thinking about this?"

"It was Marsha's idea really. Right before I found out about the money, I told her I would need to sell the ranch, and she was coming up with all kinds of things I could do with it. The trouble was, there was no money to make it happen."

"And now there is."

Addie looked over at him. "Do you like it? It's not too out there, is it?"

"I have no idea if it's too out there or not, but I know that Stella would have loved the idea," Travis said, and Addie threw her arms around his neck.

"I love you, Travis Granger," she said and pulled his head down to meet hers. She leaned into him, and Travis tangled his hands in her hair. He could feel her breasts pressed against his chest, her response to his desire. He lifted his head and looked down at her crystal clear blue eyes and full lips and couldn't quite believe she was his. He had waited for so long, and now she was his.

"Travis!" Addie squealed when he lifted her over his shoulder and ran back to the house.

"Sorry, it's the fastest way I know to get there."

Eight months later, after extensive renovations courtesy of the West Texas Investment Corporation, the new Destiny Ranch Bed and Breakfast held its inaugural event: a simple wedding in front of a windmill statue.

Addie's parents and her sister's family were the first guests of the bed and breakfast. They had arrived about a week before the wedding to help with last-minute details. Her mother had been insistent that they help pay for it, but Addie assured her that it was small enough for them to handle on their own. She had not told them of Stella's fortune. In fact, Travis and Woody were still the only ones who knew.

Addie and Travis had made a trip to Connecticut in late October so he could meet her family. Her parents were extremely fond of him and seemed to be supportive of her plans, even if her mother was not thrilled with the idea of her putting down roots in Destiny, Texas.

"Addie, you know we just love it there. And the Destiny Ranch is such an inspiring place. But it's so terribly far away," her mother confided to her as they sat on her bed one evening. "We're crazy about Travis, and you too seem wonderfully happy together, but…" her voice trailed off, and tears filled her eyes.

Addie reached over and hugged her tightly. "I know," she said and continued to hold her. "Mom," she said pulling back to look her mother in the eye, "I'll come visit. We'll come."

"Promise?" her mother choked out between sobs.

"I promise," Addie said and smiled tenderly. "I love you," she told her and wrapped her arms around her again. It was her turn to comfort her mother, the woman who had played such a pivotal role in her life for so many years.

Addie stayed with her family at the ranch the night before the wedding. Travis had insisted it was bad luck for them to see each other before the big event, which she found old fashioned and completely adorable. But she was able to sneak into the house and leave a gift for him on the bed—a beautiful pair of black dress alligator boots.

The bridal party was small, and only close friends

and relatives attended. The bridesmaids wore tea-length dresses of their own choosing. Marsha, the maid of honor, was beautiful in soft pink, and Addie's sister Janet wore pale-yellow. Addie was stunning in an elegant form-fitting white satin and lace dress. The men wore classic tuxedos. Cole stood up for Travis, and Greg Brady was his groomsman.

The town's justice of the peace, Woody Dudley, performed the brief ceremony under an unblemished sky that was just beginning its transformation into a brilliant orange horizon.

Addie's father walked her down the make-shift aisle and kissed her tenderly before presenting her to Travis. The entire affair was small and intimate.

When it was done, the new Addie Granger looked up at the exquisite windmill. "I love this piece. Did you know it has my name on it?"

"Of course. Stella had this designed for us," said Travis peering up at it.

"What do you mean?" asked Addie.

"Look at the little girl. Your name is on her leg. Now look at the little boy. See anything familiar?"

Addie squinted closely at the turning artwork focusing on the figure of the boy. 'Travis' was inscribed on the boy's blue jeans.

"She told me she put my name on it after I was so smitten with you when you visited. Stella always said I would chase around after you, but someday I would finally catch you here at the windmill."

Addie looked at him with eyes wide, and her mouth fell open. "Stella," she said simply.

Travis turned to her and placed a finger under her chin, closing her mouth. "Mrs. Granger, I believe we have a party to go to." Although the ceremony was small, the whole town had been invited to the reception, which was being held at the country club, Cole's gift to the newlyweds.

"I believe we do," Addie said as they wrapped their arms around each other.

Her soft pink lips met his and they stood as husband and wife bonded together by their love for each other and their shared love of a mystical place and the person who started it. And Addie knew that Stella would always be watching over them.

ABOUT THE AUTHOR

Julia Scott is a school teacher in North Texas and writes teaching books and fiction in her spare time. She adores her students and claims they provide her with an endless supply of both great ideas and gray hairs (which she dutifully conceals with hair color every month). Her stories always feature teachers as main characters, and Seven Miles from Destiny is her first full-length novel. You can find information about upcoming fiction projects at juliascottbooks.com.

www.ingramcontent.com/pod-product-compliance
Lightning Source LLC
Chambersburg PA
CBHW031133260626
47153CB00021B/241